TERMINUS

A harsh scream sounded behind him, causing Maker to spin around in alarm. The first thing he noticed was that the railing a few feet away from him had given way, and a portion of it now swung out ominously over the arena. The next thing he realized was that Wayne was missing.

Glancing down, Maker saw the young Marine stretched out in a prone position on the arena floor, slowly trying to rise but obviously stunned. Not far away, the monstrous jwaedin — ten feet tall and with a scorpion-like tail — growled in anger. Its meal interrupted by Wayne's yell, the jwaedin looked around to locate the source of the commotion. Almost immediately, it spied Wayne lying helplessly on the ground. The creature howled, then dropped the tentacle it had been munching on and turned its attention to its new visitor.

Maker barely hesitated — he never did when one of his people was in trouble. Placing a hand on the top of the rail, he jumped — going up and over the barrier. A second later, he landed on the dirt floor of the arena.

Maker bent his knees on contact to help absorb some of the impact. At the same time, a deafening roar erupted from the crowd. Having two humans face off against a jwaedin was more than they had expected, and Maker could only imagine the bets — and the accompanying odds — now being made.

TERMINUS

Kid Sensation Series
Sensation: A Superhero Novel
Mutation (A Kid Sensation Novel)
Infiltration (A Kid Sensation Novel)

The Warden Series
Warden (Book 1: Wendigo Fever)
Warden (Book 2: Lure of the Lamia)
Warden (Book 3: Attack of the Aswang)

The Fringe Worlds
Terminus (Fringe Worlds #1)

Boxed Sets
The Kid Sensation Series (Books 1-3)
The Warden Series (Books 1-3)

Short Stories
Extraction: A Kid Sensation Story

TERMINUS
Fringe Worlds #1

By

Kevin Hardman

TERMINUS

Copyright © 2014 by Kevin Hardman.

Cover Design by Isikol

Edited by Faith Williams, The Atwater Group

This book is published by I&H Recherche Publishing.

ISBN: 978-1-937666-21-7

Printed in the U.S.A.

TERMINUS

ACKNOWLEDGMENTS

I would like to thank the following for their help with this book: GOD, first and foremost, because each book I get to write is a blessing; and my family, for always being there. Last, but not least, I dedicate this book in loving memory of my father, Isaac.

TERMINUS

Terminus -

    1. the Roman god of boundaries;

    2. the boundary or limit of something;

    3. the end or extremity of anything;

    4. a final point in space or time.

Chapter 1

They were waiting for him when he got home. For Master Sergeant Arrogant "Gant" Maker, Galactic Marine Corps (Ret.), it was a day he had known was coming for years. Still, it was an odd sensation — to finally be vindicated.

He had been down at the practice range, firing off a few rounds as he did every day, when a blue light suddenly flashed on his left wristband. It was an indication that there was motion inside his cabin.

In the two years that he had been on Ginsberg, he'd never once had an unexpected visitor. In fact, he hadn't had any visitors whatsoever.

It wasn't that Ginsberg was a terrible planet. It was actually rather nice, with picturesque views and a rustic charm that was difficult to put into words. It was far enough out from the Gaian Hub that a retired soldier's pension could go far, but close enough to have access to all the comforts of civilization.

Maker took his time going back to the cabin. Normally, he would have run the two miles between the practice range and his home, viewing the distance as an opportunity to get in a last bit of exercise. Instead, he decided to dawdle, walking along the wooded trail that led back at a leisurely pace. He had waited years for them; they could wait half an hour for him.

As he walked, he heard a familiar scrambling in some nearby bushes, and a moment later Erlen scurried onto the path and fell into step beside him. About the size of a large dog and looking like a cross between a salamander and a spider monkey (among other things),

TERMINUS

Erlen preferred to dash about on all fours. He could, however, rise up on his hind legs when necessary.

Erlen growled softly, a low rumbling that was easy for Maker to interpret.

"Yeah," Maker said. "We've got company. We knew they'd come eventually."

When the cabin came into view, Maker saw what he expected: a hovercraft bearing military insignia parked next to his own near the front of his home. As Maker could have predicted, Erlen ran ahead, making a beeline for the unfamiliar vehicle. When he got close, the alien made a surprisingly powerful leap, landing on the roof of the military craft. Then his tongue — a lengthy and supple blood-red appendage — flicked out as he quickly licked the vehicle.

This wasn't surprising to Maker in the least. Erlen tasted everything; it was part of his nature. And it wasn't just confined to inanimate objects, either. Erlen was just as willing to taste living things. Using his tongue, however, was just for show. Erlen's paws — in addition to housing retractable claws — also contained papillae on their pads much like those on the human tongue (although his were dry). In short, the alien creature could actually taste objects merely by touching them.

Maker took another glance at the military emblem as he came abreast of the unfamiliar craft. Now that he was closer, he could see telltale markings that denoted the vehicle's point of origin: Echelon. Maker couldn't help being slightly surprised.

Gaian Space — that region of the cosmos primarily occupied and controlled by *Homo sapiens* — consisted of several discrete regions that branched out almost spherically from a central core. The heart of this expanse was the Hub — the multitude of worlds that served as the cultural, financial, and governmental nerve center of the human race.

Next to the Hub was the middle region known as the Mezzo, worlds that were generally considered the industrial arm of humanity, the suppliers of raw materials. Outside of the Mezzo was the Rim, which was typically thought of as two sections: the Inner Rim and the Outer Rim.

Following the Rim was the Fringe, the outermost edge of the Gaian Expanse and human settlement. It was an area that had garnered a reputation for attracting the wrong elements of society — unsavory individuals and men of questionable character — because of a dearth of law enforcement in the region.

Finally, other than those sectors known to be home to other sentient species, areas beyond the Fringe (most of which were uncharted and unexplored) were known simply as the Beyond or X-Space. Few people ventured Beyond without a very compelling reason.

All of this flitted through Maker's mind as he mentally noted that his current home on Ginsberg was just inside the Inner Rim. Echelon, a planet that essentially served as a huge military base, was actually situated inside the Mezzo, but on the opposite side of the Hub. In short, his visitors had come a long way to see him.

A soft growl brought Maker back to himself as Erlen leaped from the vehicle, landing deftly beside him as he reached the steps leading up to the cabin's entrance.

Unsurprisingly, there was a Marine standing guard at the door — a big, strapping fellow maybe fifteen years Maker's junior. He wore beta-class body armor, which probably meant that he wasn't really expecting trouble but wanted to play it safe. Of course, it was difficult to say since some guys wore their Class Bs all the time, as if they were afraid of some random stranger walking up behind them and shooting them in the back.

The young Marine's nametag and rank designated him as Sergeant De Beers, and he quite likely served a double role as both bodyguard and driver for whoever was waiting inside. For a brief moment, Maker wondered if he was going to have trouble getting into his own home. The question was answered a second later when the sergeant suddenly came to attention and then stepped sharply aside.

"They're waiting for you inside, sir," De Beers said, his hand snapping up into a salute.

Maker returned the salute without thinking, the result of instinct ingrained by almost two decades in uniform. Even three years later after his last salute to anyone, the old habits died hard.

Oddly enough, the young man didn't give Erlen so much as a glance as they passed, which meant that he was either highly professional or had already been briefed about Maker's "pet." Maker presumed it was the latter. He went inside and closed the door after Erlen dashed in.

There were three of them inside. He recognized the first: General Kroner — a highly decorated, career military man whom Maker had served under when he first joined the Corps. Tall and standing ramrod straight, Kroner was the walking epitome of a Marine.

The second person was a dark-eyed woman dressed in a black, full-length bodysuit. She was about average height, with pale, blond hair that fell down to her shoulders. A badge just above her left breast identified her as a civilian aide — some sort of civil servant.

Like the general, the woman had remained standing. In her hands she held a medical module — an advanced, interactive simulator typically used to allow medical students to practice surgical procedures in three-D. At the end of surgery the student would be given a grade and informed whether his patient would die, fully recover, etc. (A scaled-down version of the simulator was also sold as a game for kids.)

The module was one of several such devices that Maker owned, and he frowned upon seeing the woman holding it. He really didn't like people handling his things without permission, but said nothing. The woman, clearly noting Maker's displeasure, placed the module back where she had originally gotten it — a nearby bookshelf — next to similar simulators for other subjects such as chemistry and physics.

Maker's final visitor was a wafer-thin man with a neatly-trimmed mustache. Outfitted in a gray business suit, the man was lounging in an easy chair, clearly having made himself at home. He exuded a self-important sense of authority and entitlement. Maker recognized the type right away — a bureaucrat.

Pompous jerk, Maker said to himself. As if to reinforce the notion, Maker noticed that the man had in his lap an odd headpiece that seemed to continually shift through the colors of the spectrum. A rainbow hat — the latest fad among the trendy and elite. Maker almost rolled his eyes.

"Gant," said the general, walking towards him and extending a hand. "How are you?"

"Fine, sir," Maker responded as they shook hands.

"I see you've still got Erlen with you," Kroner noted.

"He's been keeping me out of trouble," Maker said as Kroner bent down to stroke the alien creature's head. He was one of the few people other than Maker that Erlen allowed such liberties.

After a moment, the general stood up again. "Allow me to introduce my companions. This is Bain Browing."

The man with the mustache tossed his hat onto an end table next to the easy chair, then stood up.

"A pleasure," Browing said in an unconvincing tone as he pumped Maker's hand. He cast a skeptical glance at Erlen, who was retreating to a corner of the room. "Uh, is your, uh, pet dangerous?"

"He's not a pet," Maker announced flatly. "And yes, he's exceedingly dangerous."

Browing looked slightly nervous and appeared on the verge of making a comment, but Kroner cut him off.

"And this is Dr. Ariel Chantrey," the general said, nodding towards the woman.

"So nice to meet you," the woman stated, although Maker wasn't sure it was nice at all.

"Doctor of what?" Maker asked, dismissing with the pleasantries.

The woman cast an inquisitive glance at Kroner, who gave no indication of what he was thinking.

"Psychology, for one," she said. "But also, psychiatry, psychobiology, behavioral science and cognitive science."

Maker raised an eyebrow but said nothing.

Dr. Chantrey waved a hand towards the modules on the bookshelf. "I hope you'll forgive any discourtesy I may have displayed in–"

"Don't worry about it," Maker said, cutting her off. She was obviously curious about the simulators, but — after a moment's silence — chose to change the subject rather than pry.

"Your, uh, friend," the doctor said, nodding towards Erlen. "What type of creature is he?"

"He's Niotan," Maker replied. When a perplexed look came across the doctor's face, he added, "From Niota."

"I'm sorry," she said, shaking her head. "I've never heard of it. Where's it located?"

Maker shrugged. "Beats me."

His response caused an even deeper frown on the doctor's part, but she said nothing.

"Anyway," Maker said, addressing all three of his guests, "I'm sure you good people didn't come all the way to Ginsberg for a social call, so what can I do for you?"

There was a moment of silence, as his directness seemed to have thrown them off their game plan.

All of a sudden, General Kroner chuckled. "That's a Marine for you — straight to the point. Alright, Gant, we won't waste your time." He nodded at Browing.

"There's something we'd like you to look at," Browing said, taking his cue. "But first, can you tell us how you came to leave the Corps?"

Crossing his arms, Maker snorted derisively. "Let's not play games. We both know you've seen my file. You already know how I 'came to leave' the Corps."

"But we'd like to hear it in your own words," the woman chimed in. "So could you humor us?"

7

Maker frowned. He really wasn't in the mood to humor anyone — hadn't been for years. Still, it was evident that this was a tit-for-tat situation: they weren't going to tell him anything until he told them something. Oh well...what could it hurt? Maker took a deep breath, then started speaking.

"We were on our way back to base — my unit, that is — from a mission," Maker began. "We were well outside the Fringe, deep into the Beyond — at least a dozen jump points out."

"Wait," Dr. Chantrey interjected. "Did you say you were a dozen jump points out?"

"Yes," Maker replied.

"*Hyperspace* jump points?" she asked.

"Is there another kind associated with space travel?" Maker retorted in exasperation, answering her question with a question.

She flinched a little, and he realized he'd probably responded in a sharper tone than necessary. After all, any surprise on her part was to be expected; going twelve jump points into the Beyond was unfathomable to most people. There just wasn't a reason to penetrate that deeply into the unknown. Still, he'd found the woman's question irritating, since it seemed to imply that he didn't understand the rudiments of hyperspace travel.

In essence, entering hyperspace allowed you to traverse great distances in just a fraction of the time that it would take in "normal" space, but it was not without its perils — the greatest of which was miscalculating the point of egress. Failure to accurately calculate the proper locus for exiting meant that a ship could come out anywhere, and plenty of spacecraft had been lost over the years because of it, particularly in the early years after hyperspace travel became possible.

However, it was quickly discovered that the odds of a mishap decreased astronomically as the distance between the start point and final destination of a journey diminished: the shorter the distance, the safer the trip. Thus, jump points — specified distances that a ship could safely travel in hyperspace — were established.

A person of slightly above-average intelligence was capable of calculating one-point hyperspace jumps. Someone with extensive training and perhaps experience as a ship engineer or navigator could calculate a two-point jump (that is, a distance that encompassed two jump points). Computers and navigation systems could calculate three- and four-point jumps. Anything greater than a four-point jump was considered foolhardy and dangerous, as the numbers, formulas, and algorithms became too difficult and complex at that stage for even the most advanced AIs to produce trustworthy coordinates. In essence, because the danger and distance increased exponentially with each jump point, trips involving huge distances typically had to be broken up into multiple jumps.

Maker was ruminating on these facts when he realized that Dr. Chantrey was posing a question to him.

"What kind of mission could you have that far out?" she asked.

There was a short moment of silence as Maker looked towards General Kroner, who said, "The doctor and Mr. Browing received limited clearance about an hour ago. You can give them an overview of your mission, but try to avoid specific details."

TERMINUS

Having been given the go-ahead by the general, Maker said, "We were escorting some scientists to inspect a recently-discovered cache of military weapons."

A slight look of bewilderment crossed Browing's face. "Escort duty? For an inspection? That hardly seems like something you'd need a team of Marines for."

Maker shrugged. "I didn't make the orders; I just followed them."

"Still, it had to be pretty boring for a guy used to action," Browing insisted.

"It wasn't that bad," Maker replied. "In fact, the mission had far more pros than cons. I even got to see one of the lead scientists dismantle a nova bomb."

Dr. Chantrey's eyebrows went up in surprise. "Where exactly did this occur?"

Before Maker could respond, Kroner barked, "That's classified — beyond the clearance you were given."

That answer seemed to mollify — if not fully satisfy — Dr. Chantrey, and brought the subject of the prior mission to a close. However, the interchange that had just occurred was an indication that perhaps not all of Maker's visitors were aware of everything about him, which was information that might prove valuable later.

"Please, go on, Gant," the general said, bringing Maker back on point with respect to his narrative.

Maker nodded. "As I mentioned, we were on the return leg of our mission. We had come out of hyperspace a short time earlier, and had spent about an hour getting our bearings."

None of Maker's guest commented, but his prior statement was something that they all understood. Traveling via hyperspace jumps was a lot like trying to

10

walk along a straight line for ten miles while blindfolded: if you tried to go the entire distance unable to see anything, you were likely to find yourself way off the mark at the end of your journey (with little or no idea of where you were). It would be helpful if, every so often, you could uncover your eyes and take a look around in order to get oriented. That, in essence, is what dropping out of hyperspace allowed for; it was an opportunity to recalibrate your position and plot the next jump.

"We were probably a minute away from going back into hyperspace when we picked up a distress signal — one that our instruments identified as human in origin," Maker said. "I was in charge, so it was my decision whether to ignore it or investigate."

"I thought you Marines were taught to respond to distress calls," Browing said. "Not brush them aside like bothersome houseflies."

"My mission parameters gave me discretion," Maker replied, "and I would have been well within the confines of my mandate if I'd turned a deaf ear to that beacon."

"But you didn't, did you?" Dr. Chantrey noted, her eyes narrowing as she studied Maker. "You made the call to respond. Why?"

Maker gave her an appraising stare. "Ma'am, there are worlds within the Mezzo that you wouldn't want to be stuck on. The indigenous wildlife, carnivorous flora and fauna, unstable weather conditions…that and more make a lot of planets within the *civilized* regions of human space somewhat inhospitable. But that's nothing compared to what's in the Beyond. Believe me, that's the last place you want to be stranded, and I'm speaking from experience."

TERMINUS

Maker's eyes involuntarily darted to Erlen, then back again. Dr. Chantrey noted it, recalling that the man's psych profile revealed an unhealthy and illogical emotional attachment to the beast. According to the stories she'd heard, he had illegally smuggled it aboard a ship and back to his home base several years prior to departing the service. From the records she'd come across, the animal had never passed the necessary health and regulatory inspections — no one even knew exactly what it was or how to classify it — but Maker had somehow been allowed to keep it.

"As far as the distress signal goes," Maker continued, "we were their last and only hope. That far into the Beyond, there was no other help coming. It was us or nothing. So I made the decision to investigate."

"And what did you find?" Browing asked.

Maker frowned slightly before responding, not caring for the interruption — especially when they already knew what had happened. "We followed the signal for a few hours, which is when we came across a large ship. It appeared derelict, adrift. The outer hull bore signs of significant damage — including a couple of crater-sized holes — and there was a lot of debris floating around it.

"We tried hailing them but didn't get a response. Given the condition of the ship, however, it wouldn't have surprised anyone if their comm system was down, or if they were directing all power and other resources towards sending the distress signal. We also weren't picking up any life signs, but the readings weren't conclusive. Someone could have sealed themselves into a chamber or bulkhead that our scanners couldn't penetrate. Bearing all that in mind, I decided to take a contingent of Marines with me, via shuttle, to investigate.

12

"As it happened, the bay doors were open on the derelict, so we were able to land the shuttle inside. There were seven of us, fully decked out in our Class A uniforms."

"Did you think you were heading into danger?" Dr. Chantrey asked. Her question meant that she obviously knew something about military engagement. Marines typically only wore their Class As — the full, head-to-toe metallic body armor — when they were expecting trouble.

Maker threw up his hands in agitation. "We were boarding a derelict ship stranded in the Beyond. We didn't know what to expect, but we were going to be prepared."

"So what happened next?" Browing asked.

Maker took a deep breath; this was the part of the story he hated. "I led my men through the ship, tracking the source of the distress signal. With the artificial gravity off and all kinds of rubbish floating around, it was slow going, but we made decent progress thanks to our magnetic boots. We also had mag wands that fired magnetic lines, which we used to pull ourselves through certain areas. We'd been at it for about ten minutes when we found ourselves about to enter the sick bay."

"Sick bay?" Dr. Chantrey asked quizzically. "Wouldn't you normally expect the distress signal to originate from the bridge?"

"Not necessarily," Kroner interjected. "In some of the more advanced vessels, the sick bay can actually serve as a separate, self-contained habitat — say, in the case of quarantine. As such, it would have its own individual distress beacon."

As Dr. Chantrey seemed to absorb this, Maker continued his narrative. "We found the airlock between sick bay and the rest of the ship sealed. Moreover, it seemed to be running on some sort of reserve power unit, which meant—"

"That somebody might be alive in there," Browing said, cutting him off.

"Yes," Maker agreed. "I'd left two Marines with the shuttle and I left two on the ship side of the airlock as guards. The rest of us went in. When we entered…"

And Maker closed his eyes for a second at the memory. "Inside, the gravity, pressure, and atmosphere all read as normal. But it was immediately evident that something nasty had happened in there. Every available bed had a body on it. Not just on it, though, but strapped down. Immobilized. And they were all open."

Browing frowned. "What do you mean, 'open'?"

"I mean every one of them had been dissected, splayed open like frogs in biology class," Maker almost shouted. "It was as if someone had taken them apart like cuckoo clocks to see what made them tick. There was even a head in a jar!"

Aside from the general, his guests seemed uncomfortable with Maker's description of events. After a moment, Dr. Chantrey seemed to find her resolve.

"Please go on," she said.

Maker's brow creased as a stern look came across his face. "We made a quick search for survivors. Big surprise — there weren't any. But I couldn't shake the feeling that there was something we were missing. That's when I noticed it."

There was a short silence, and then Browing impatiently blurted, "Noticed what?"

"The head," Maker said. "It was looking at me. Its eyes were following me."

"The head?" Browing repeated, somewhat confused. "You mean the head that you said was in a jar?"

"Yeah," Maker said, "but I should probably explain. It wasn't a head sitting in an empty jar; it was immersed in some kind of clear, viscous fluid. It appeared to be female, although it was completely bald, and there were electrodes attached at its temples and at various places on its scalp.

"Initially I had assumed it was just a remnant — a body part left over from the mad dissection I mentioned before. But once I saw the eyes tracking me, I noticed that the mouth was also moving."

"Wait," Browing said incredulously. "Are you saying that a decapitated head was talking to you?"

"No," Maker admitted. "But it was trying to."

"And what makes you say that?" Dr. Chantrey asked.

Maker shrugged. "When I first saw the lips moving, I didn't pay much attention. I just chalked it up to the electrodes maybe sending a current through the skull and making the facial nerves react — the way a jolt of electricity can make a dead body move. But when I leaned in close and paid attention, I could make out what it was trying to tell me."

"Which was…?" Dr. Chantrey inquired.

"Two words," Maker replied. "'Run. Trap.'"

"What did you do then?" Browing asked.

"I was taken aback," Maker admitted, "to say the least. I immediately gave the Marines with me the hand signals indicating that enemy combatants were near. I then got on the comm and told the two I'd left outside the airlock that there was nothing to see in the sick bay — no survivors. I instructed them — along with the Marines in the sick bay with me — to head back to the shuttle, Tango Bravo, and that I would follow."

Browing frowned. "Tango Bravo?"

"It's code," the general said. "It basically means that the enemy is close, so be ready to engage."

"Exactly," Maker said with a nod. "So everyone else took off, while I tried to find some way to take the head with us."

"Take it with you?" Browing muttered. "Why?"

"Because it was alive in some way, so it didn't seem right to just leave it there," Maker said. "Plus, it might be able to tell us what had happened on the ship. Finally, if what it had said was true, it had just helped us."

"And was it true?" Dr. Chantrey asked.

"Yes," Maker said. "After a few moments, I figured out that the electrodes attached to the head were connected to some sort of power pack that was magnetically bolted to the floor. In short, it didn't appear to be portable, but I spent some time screwing with the sick bay's controls just in case there was something I could do. Then I headed off after the others. Either I was moving fast or they were moving slow, because I caught up to them pretty quickly. We'd covered maybe half the distance back to the shuttle when it happened."

"The attack," Browing said matter-of-factly.

Maker nodded in response, noting that Browing's statement removed any doubt that his guests had read his file. "We had come to the end of a narrow passageway that led to a large, open area — some kind of cargo space

— with a number of catwalks along the walls. That's where they were hiding."

Maker paused, remembering — the scene vividly coming back to him as if it had happened yesterday. His audience waited patiently, and after a moment, he continued.

"They must have had some kind of cloaking technology in their armor," Maker said, "because we never had a clue that they were there when we first passed through that area on our way to the sick bay. It was the same story on the way back."

"So you still weren't picking up any life signs," Browing stated flatly.

"No," Maker replied. "But the whole area — lots of open space with very little cover — just seemed like the perfect place for an ambush, so we holed up in the passageway for a few minutes, even though we weren't getting any readings."

"But surely your sensors were detecting movement," Browing insisted.

"There was no gravity!" Maker almost screamed. "There was all kinds of crap floating around in there! Any movement we picked up the first time we were in there was probably categorized by all of us as debris. So I'm sorry we didn't initially make the decision to verify that everything moving around us was trash."

Dr. Chantrey gave him a piercing stare. "What did you do?"

Maker made a vague gesture. "What could I do? The most direct path back to the shuttle was through that cargo hold. We could try to find another route, but there was no guarantee that we'd be successful, and whoever had set this trap for us would probably be lying in wait no matter which way we went. Plus, at the moment, there was a good chance that they didn't know we'd been given a warning — that we knew they were there. So I ordered us forward."

"Forward?" Dr. Chantrey muttered, almost incredulously. "Into what you knew was a trap?"

Maker shrugged. "I put myself into our enemies' shoes. I figured that they wouldn't fire until we were at our most vulnerable, which meant the center of the room. So we moved together as a unit through the cargo area. Just before we reached the center, I gave the word and we broke away, moving in five different directions and firing at the same time."

"Firing at what?" Browing asked. "You just said you weren't picking up any signs that anyone was there."

"We assumed that, if nothing else, they had the high ground — the catwalks," Maker said. "So before we moved out into the center of the cargo hold, we each picked a spot where we figured the enemy was most likely to be. When we split away from one another, we each fired at our respective target spots. At the same time, they began firing at us from what seemed like every direction."

"And when you say 'they'...?" Kroner asked, leaving the question open-ended.

Maker frowned in thought. "They were alien — insectoid, but not a species I recognized, wearing full-plated armor. And there were dozens of them."

"But you said earlier you thought they were cloaked," Browing said. "If so, how could you see them?"

"As I understand it, cloaking and stealth technology eat up a lot of power," Maker said. "Based on that, my best guess is that they had to become visible after a certain amount of time, because at that juncture we could see them."

"What exactly did they look like?" Dr. Chantrey asked.

"Bodily, I'd say they resembled ants," Maker said. "A thorax, an abdomen, and six limbs, although they were bipedal. Based on the construction of the armor, the head had compound eyes, antennae, a proboscis, and inward-facing pinchers."

"How did you get away?" Dr. Chantrey asked.

"The Marines with me were well-trained — the best. We each nailed enemy combatants on the catwalks, although it wasn't clear how much damage we'd done. After that, we were firing almost non-stop, because they seemed to be coming from everywhere.

"One of the other Marines, Tandy, shouted a warning, then she tossed up a flash grenade. It blinded the aliens, bought us a few precious seconds, but after that it was a running firefight all the way back to the landing bay. By the time we got there, only two of us were left, me and Bennett, who was in bad shape — I'd practically been carrying him the last few minutes. One of the guys I'd left with the shuttle, Cho, opened the airlock door and started to come out. A second later, his body jerked like he was convulsing.

"It took me a second to realize what was happening, but it was one of the aliens. The damn thing had been lying flat on top of the shuttle, just above the door, probably just waiting for someone to come out. It had stabbed Cho with some kind of weird blade at the back of the neck" — Maker tapped the back of his own nape for emphasis — "right where his helmet attached to the rest of the armor, which is one of the major weak points. Then it stood up, jerking the blade free while at the same time causing Cho's body to move out of the shuttle's airlock, where it began floating."

"Wait," Dr. Chantrey said. "How was it able to just stand in zero-g?"

"The shuttle's artificial gravity," the general said. "It extends a little beyond the vessel's exterior."

Maker nodded in agreement, and then continued. "Before I could properly react, there was laser fire coming at me, originating from the last corridor that Bennett and I had taken to the landing bay. I glanced in that direction and saw a group of the aliens moving towards us, firing. I took my last flash grenade and tossed it down the corridor. It was almost a fatal error."

"And why was that?" asked Browing.

"Because when I turned back towards the shuttle, the alien who had been above the door had thrown his weapon at me," Maker replied. "While the insectoids coming down the corridor had distracted me, the one on top of the shuttle had tried to seize an opportunity and flung what I now saw wasn't just a blade but more like a lance.

"As the flash went off behind us, I instinctively tried shoving Bennett to the side while leaping away myself. The result was that my feet lost contact with the floor and I found myself adrift. Even worse, the lance hit my shoulder. It didn't penetrate my armor, but the blow sent me spinning, albeit slowly.

"Feeling like a sitting duck, I looked around for the alien. He was still on top of the shuttle, holding an appendage up to his face. I realized what had happened then. He'd been looking towards the blast when the flash grenade went off. He wouldn't be as blinded as his buddies in the passageway, but I definitely had a few seconds. I drew my sidearm and fired. The alien went down."

"You killed him?" Browing asked.

Maker shrugged. "I didn't know at the time. I was spinning, so it wasn't the best shot I ever took. Still, I was sure I'd hit him, although I had no clue whether he was out of commission. I drew my mag wand and fired a line at the shuttle. That helped arrest my momentum and allowed me to control my movement again. At that point, Powell, the other Marine I'd left at the shuttle, opened the airlock, wanting to know what the hell was going on.

"I told him that Cho was dead and that he needed to get Bennett inside and strapped down, then be ready for take-off. While he went about following my instructions, I got myself within the shuttle's gravity, then began climbing up to its roof.

"The insectoid was up there, laid out. There was a scorch mark on the side of his helmet, so I'd definitely hit him, but there was no way to tell how badly he was injured — if at all — although he seemed to be unconscious. That's when I noticed that his armor seemed different than that of his fellows. Whereas theirs just seemed to be purely functional, his seemed to have…decorations."

Browing's eyebrows shot up in curiosity. "What do you mean?"

Maker rubbed his chin in thought for a second before answering. "There was some kind of skull grafted on to the top of his helmet — some animal I've never seen before. And embedded in what I guess you'd call the breastplate, just below and encircling the neck, was a ring of other skulls. Some of them I recognized as belonging to sentient species, and at least one of them was human. But worst of all..."

Maker paused, still disgusted by the memory.

"Worst of all, what?" Dr. Chantrey asked after a few seconds, obviously impatient.

"Worst of all," Maker went on, "the skulls — they looked *gnawed* on."

He took a moment to let that sink in with his visitors. Even though the multitude of spacefaring races were of different species, they generally respected and treated one another with a certain amount of civility. It took an obscene, almost incomprehensible, level of barbarism to actually feed on another sentient life form. Basically, these alien insects were monsters.

"I didn't have time to really dwell on that fact, though," Maker said a few moments later, "because I noticed an odd device on the shuttle's roof next to the alien. It was a metallic oval about a foot in length, with a digital display that was flashing some eerie symbols. I'd never seen anything like it before, but all of my instincts screamed 'bomb.' I picked it up and flung it aside."

"You picked up something you thought was an alien bomb?" the doctor asked in surprise. "Weren't you afraid it might go off?"

Maker looked at her as though she'd just asked the most foolish question he'd ever heard. "Doctor, have you ever seen an explosion in space?"

"Only on vids and holograms," she said. "Not in person."

"Well, I have," Maker said matter-of-factly. "And trust me, you don't want to. The explosion itself isn't so bad; there's no atmosphere, so you don't have the same kind of blast wave you'd get on the surface of a planet. It dissipates pretty quickly. It's usually the shrapnel you have to worry about. There's no air resistance to slow it down, no gravity to pull it down to earth. Theoretically, it will go on forever — at that same initial high rate of speed — until it hits something. And you don't want to be that something. That's why we used our flash grenades, which only produce a blinding light, rather than the real thing.

"Knowing what an explosion could do, there was no way those bugs were going to set off the bomb in the zero-g environment of that derelict. More than likely, they were planning to remote detonate it once we got back to our own ship — assuming any of us made it."

"So what happened after you tossed the bomb away?" Browing asked.

"Apparently I let myself get too distracted," Maker said. "A second later, the alien next to me was up on his feet and I was fighting for my life.

"My immediate reaction was to go for my sidearm, but the thing was fast, faster than I would have imagined. It gripped the wrist of my gun hand before I could reach my weapon, then caught my fist when I swung at him with the hand that was still free.

"It was bigger than me — maybe seven feet in height — and heavier. Moreover, the way it was jointed made it difficult to use my martial arts training to break its hold. Fortunately, the armor kind of evened things out, but it's difficult to fight hand-to-hand when your opponent actually has six limbs. Even worse, it was using its free arms — the middle set — to try to pummel me. It wasn't totally ineffective, but it was going to take a long time to punch through my armor, if that was its intent."

Maker chuckled softly at the memory, then sobered almost immediately as he remembered what happened next. "Then I felt a weird vibration. I risked a glance and noticed that my opponent was holding one of its free hands out to the side, like it was about to catch a ball or something. That hand was the source of the vibration. Suddenly, I noticed movement with my peripheral vision, and when I looked I saw the thing's lance flying towards us. Somehow, it was calling that weird blade to it.

"Still grappling with the alien, I suddenly jumped up and kicked it in the face. Its head snapped back, but then it slammed me down on the roof of the shuttle. A moment later, it stood over me with the lance in its hand.

"It was about to run me through when the derelict suddenly began shaking like a leaf in a whirlwind. The movement jostled the shuttle, naturally, catching the insectoid off-guard."

"What was it?" Browing asked. "The shaking, that is."

"The sick bay disengaging from the derelict," Maker answered. "Like the general said earlier, it could exist as its own self-contained habitat. Even more, it could actually separate from the ship. Therefore, before I'd left the sick bay, I'd killed the distress signal and then punched in the code for it to detach in ten minutes."

"But in that case," Browing said, rubbing his chin in thought, "why even fight your way back to the shuttle? If you knew there was a trap waiting for you, why not just stay in the sick bay and initiate the separation protocol?"

"No weaponry," Maker said. "The shuttle at least had some mid-caliber cannons, but the sick bay had no offensive weaponry. It would have been a turkey shoot if our attackers had their own ship somewhere in the area, and I'd had to assume that they did."

"So why bother disengaging it if you weren't going to use it?" Dr. Chantrey asked.

"Two reasons," Maker replied. "One, I was still trying to save the head, since it might be able to tell us more about what had happened. And two, I thought it might serve as a distraction for the rest of us, assuming we made it back to the shuttle.

"In the end, it worked out great. I don't think our attackers realized that the sick bay could break away, because the one I was fighting jerked his head left and right, as if confused about what was happening. I used the opportunity to swipe one of his legs with my own. The shaking already had him off-balance, so when I tripped him, he fell over onto his back.

"His arms and legs started wriggling madly. He wasn't stuck, but just like a lot of Old Earth insects, he had trouble getting up from a recumbent position. As I got to my feet, he stopped struggling long enough to swing at me with the lance, but from the way he was laying, he couldn't get power or accuracy. I gripped it by the shaft, then yanked it away from him.

"Remembering Cho, I sliced down at him with the blade — not knowing where any weak spot was, just trying to do some damage. He twisted wildly, and the blade ended up connecting with one of the middle arms, severing it almost where it joined his body. If I thought his limbs were wriggling crazily before I was wrong, because now he was like an insane octopus.

"Before I could strike again, there was movement in the corridor that I had tossed the flash grenade into before. The bugs in there were recovering. I flung the lance in that direction, not knowing if it was going to hit anything, then I turned and gave the one on top of the shuttle with me a good solid kick in the side.

"I didn't hold anything back, and with the armor augmenting the force of my punt, he went flying. A second or so later, he was outside the shuttle's gravity and started to float.

"Satisfied, I scrambled into the shuttle. Powell was still strapping Bennett in, so I jumped into the pilot's seat and took us out of there, not even bothering to take my helmet off. Surprisingly, our ship was still there, waiting."

Browing lifted an eyebrow. "And that was surprising because…?"

"The entire time we'd been fighting our way back to the derelict's landing bay, I had been in contact with our ship, the *Orpheus Moon*. She was helmed by Captain Wendren, a good man. I had ordered him to take off as soon as the attack started, but he hadn't."

"Wait a minute," Dr. Chantrey said. "You were a master sergeant — a non-commissioned officer. Since when does a NCO give a captain orders?"

"I can answer that," General Kroner interjected. "The captain was in charge of the ship, but Gant was in command of the mission. As his assignment took priority, Gant had the authority to direct Captain Wendren's actions."

"As I was saying," Maker continued, "Captain Wendren disregarded my order to leave. Even more, he kept the ship's shields down so that our shuttle could make it back. And we almost did.

"We were closing in on the landing bay when this vessel just appeared out of nowhere. It was an alien construct — again, something foreign to my experience

— but there was no doubt that it was a warship. Cannons, turrets, missile tubes…after enough campaigns, you learn to recognize weapons, no matter how exotic the design. And the barrel swinging towards us was another dead giveaway.

"A second later we got hit by…something. Whatever they nailed us with, it wasn't like laser or plasma fire, shearing through metal like a giant overheated scalpel. Instead, it was like a fist punching through a paper bag; one second we were fine, and the next, the rear portion of the shuttle — where Bennett had been — was pretty much ripped away. As for Powell, he hadn't strapped in. Even worse, he'd taken his helmet off. He was sucked out into the void, screaming.

"We were already on our final approach when the shuttle got hit. Afterwards, I fought like the devil just to crash the thing. As it was, the shuttle scraped along one wall, gouging the metal of the hull but, thankfully, not piercing it. Then it skidded along the bay floor, sparks flying like fireworks, before banging into another shuttle and coming to a halt.

"I unstrapped myself and raced out of the shuttle through the torn-open rear. Klaxons were sounding all over, and the bay doors were already in the process of closing. I dashed through the airlock and into the ship proper as fast as the doors would open, heading straight for the bridge. All the while, the ship was shaking like it was dead center in an earthquake, and I knew that we were getting battered by whatever weapon they had used on the shuttle.

"When I got to the bridge, Wendren was just giving the order to go to hyperspace. We jumped. At that point, we all felt relief. Whoever — whatever — it was that had attacked us, we'd left them behind now.

"We had about a second to pat ourselves on the backs, because a few moments after we appeared, the ship started getting battered again. It was the alien vessel; it had popped up next to us. They had followed us through hyperspace.

"It took us a moment to collectively get over our shock. Outside of convoys with synced navigation systems, ships don't usually jump with each other like that.

"Captain Wendren recovered pretty quickly. He ordered another jump, and a second later we were gone. When we reappeared in normal space, it was another short reprieve. The alien ship had followed us again and continued its relentless attack.

"We had been firing on them, but our weapons weren't particularly effective. They had targeted our big guns — the cannons — when they first appeared, so we'd lost those early on. Basically, our offensive capabilities were limited, so we jumped a third time. Needless to say, they came out of hyperspace right next to us again.

"At this point, our ship was practically a wreck. The aliens had punched holes through us like we were wet tissue. And then, they hit us with some kind of bioshock weapon. It was like a lightning bolt passed through the ship. It didn't really appear to affect systems, only people — or rather, living organisms. We probably lost ninety percent of the crew right then and there. Those that didn't die immediately were pretty much incapacitated…limbs scorched, skin fried to a crisp. They weren't going to live long."

"How did you get through unscathed?" Dr. Chantrey asked.

"Again, I was still in my armor," Maker replied. "Their weapon scrambled my suits systems a little, but didn't really cause any damage. But I was probably the only person on the ship still of sound body at that point, unless you count Erlen, who didn't seem to have been affected." He nodded towards the alien, which was resting in a corner of the room.

"Wait," Browing interjected. "Your pet was with you? On a classified mission?"

Maker gave him a direct, almost furious stare. "I told you before, he's not a pet. And yes, he was with us. Where I go, he goes."

Browing appeared to be on the verge of saying something else, but the general cut him off. "I don't think Browing meant anything by his question. Please finish telling us the rest of your story."

Still glaring at Browing, Maker went on. "Wendren and the bridge crew were all either dead or completely out of commission at that point, like everyone else on the ship. The aliens stopped firing; I think they assumed that we had all succumbed, in one fashion or another. It didn't take a genius to figure out that they were going to be boarding us shortly. I checked the navigation systems and power levels. We had enough juice for maybe one more jump, but it wasn't going to do any good if they just followed us. I decided to take a gamble that would hopefully be too rich for their blood."

Maker paused for a second. Even though they were surely aware of what happened next, this is where his story got *really* crazy.

"No need for the dramatic pause," Browing said after a moment, clearly impatient. "What did you do?"

Maker sighed. "I overrode the navigation system...altered the protocols, annulled the safeties, everything. Then I plotted a nine-point jump and sent the ship into hyperspace."

Chapter 2

Compared to interviewers in the past, they'd actually let him tell much of his story without interruption, reserving many of their questions until he'd finished — something for which Maker found himself grateful. It wasn't that it was difficult for him to talk about what happened; he just preferred to tell the tale as quickly and succinctly as possible. When questions came in the middle of his narrative, it felt as though he was never going to get through. Now that he was finished, however, the questions started rolling out in machine-gun fashion.

"When you first encountered the derelict ship," Browing started to say, "couldn't you have simply noted the ship's position? Couldn't you have returned to base and then sent help back?"

"We didn't know what the emergency was. Being adrift, they might not be in the same spot when help arrived. Hell, another ship might not have even gotten close enough to pick up the signal — assuming it was still broadcasting at that point."

"I'm more interested in the nine-point jump," Dr. Chantrey stated. "How did that end?"

"The ship practically disintegrated upon re-entry into normal space," Maker said. "We exited well within the Hub, apparently causing a slight bit of panic since we came out of nowhere."

Panic was putting it mildly. Early on, one of the first uses conceived of for hyperspace travel was military applications. Got a world that's giving you trouble? Then just pop out of hyperspace, drop a dozen planetbusters in their direction, then zip away. With that in mind, laws

31

restricting hyperspace travel got passed pretty quickly. As a result, the only hyperspace travel allowed inside the Hub was via jump gates — giant ovals in space that essentially acted like humongous slingshots, flinging ships through H-space to their destinations. (In fact, the gates were indispensable modes of travel for many alien ships, which were required to have their jump drives completely disengaged when passing anywhere through Gaian Space more centric than the Inner Rim.)

As an added precaution, the ship navigation systems that controlled jump drives were manufactured with a built-in kill switch, an automatic regulator that operated on the basis of proximity. In other words, a jump drive simply wouldn't work anywhere within the Hub (nor within some regions of the Mezzo). In fact, the auto-regulator wouldn't allow a ship to drop out of hyperspace any closer than two jump-points from the Hub.

Theoretically, it was possible to override the kill switch, but it was synced with navigation in such a way that any attempt to pervert the system was supposed to scramble the astro-coordinates. Simply put, if a ship made such a jump, there was no telling where it would exit hyperspace.

Bearing all that in mind, the sudden appearance of Maker's ship had caused something along the lines of hysteria. In making his jump, he hadn't just done the impossible; he'd done the inconceivable.

"Some time after re-entry, I lost consciousness," Maker continued. "I came to in an ambulatory vessel. A couple of medics were trying to make sure I was okay, but Erlen wouldn't let them come near me. I felt fine, so I basically discharged myself from their care."

"And then?" Browing asked.

"I was essentially placed under house arrest," Maker stated flatly. "Held in solitary confinement until someone of appropriate rank and authority could arrive to debrief me." He glanced at the general, who said nothing.

"About a day later," Maker said, "I gave my report to a panel of three general officers. Then I spent the next six months telling the same story over and over again to an endless barrage of people — specialists in various fields."

"Specialists?" Dr. Chantrey asked.

"Military officers, doctors, scientists..." Maker said, trailing off. "The military wanted to know about the aliens and weapons we allegedly encountered. Doctors wanted to know how the hyperspace journey had affected me mentally and physically. And, of course, everybody — especially the scientists — wanted to know how I pulled off the jump."

"I wouldn't mind knowing that myself," Browing said. "You mentally plotted and successfully executed a nine-point jump in under five minutes. You want to explain how you managed that?"

"I had a powerful incentive," Maker answered, "called 'wanting to live.'"

Browing snorted in disdain, clearly dissatisfied with Maker's response. Erlen, plodding over to stand next to Maker, let out a low, rumbling growl.

"No," Maker said, seemingly in reply to the Niotan's snarls. "Not just yet."

A look of surprise crossed Browing's face, and his gaze shot from Maker to Erlen, then back again. "Did it speak?" he asked. "What did it say?"

Maker seemed to consider for a moment before responding. "He wants to know if he should kill you."

As if in confirmation, Erlen suddenly spat on Browing's hat. The spittle, acting like some advanced corrosive, began eating up the cap like acid.

"My spectrum-tam!" Browing screamed, reaching for the hat. Somehow, showing incredible responses and reflexes, Maker got there and placed an iron grip around the man's wrist before contact could be made.

"I wouldn't advise it," Maker said. "Unless you've got a wild desire to lose some fingers."

Browing angrily shook him off, and then gave him a look of utter fury. "Do you know what those cost?!" he shouted, pointing at the remnants of his hat.

"Probably less than a new hand," Maker said, smiling.

Browing looked like he was on the verge of taking a swing at Maker, something that would have been completely ill-advised given the latter's military and martial training.

"So," Dr. Chantrey said, clearly trying to defuse the situation. "What happened next, Sergeant?"

Maker took a step back, putting some space between himself and Browing, just in case the man decided to do something stupid.

"About six months after the incident, the military issued its official report," Maker said. "Their conclusion was that somewhere during our mission, the ship's hyperspace shields began malfunctioning. The result was that it exposed the entire crew to something…exotic."

Dr. Chantrey nodded in understanding. Hyperspace as a region was generally acknowledged to be unknown in a great many respects. It contained — among other things — obscure forces, unidentified radiation, and strange forms of matter. A ship's shields normally guarded against any of these; failure of those shields, however... She'd heard horrific stories of what that could lead to.

"In essence, the report stated that the failure of the shields allowed significant damage to occur to the vessel while we were in hyperspace, which ultimately led to the deaths of the majority of the crew," Maker continued. "With respect to me, the official statement was that whatever penetrated our ship caused me to become mentally unstable — imagine we were under attack. Thus, while under this delusion, I bypassed the navigation system and made my infamous jump. In the end, they couldn't pinpoint exactly why or how I did what I did, but I couldn't be trusted any longer. It also didn't help that word somehow leaked out about what I'd done, so people started calling me little nicknames. 'Maniac' Maker, 'Madman' Maker...stuff like that. I was placed on leave for another six months, then forced to take early retirement for 'medical reasons.'"

"So they didn't believe you," Dr. Chantrey noted. "Why not?"

Maker shrugged. "They said the ship's remnants were imbued with a strange radiation, among other things, but they didn't find the kind of damage that would have been consistent with any known weapons."

"Well, could they have retraced your steps?" Browing asked, apparently over the loss of his headgear. "Maybe sent a warship back to see if they could find the alien ship you mentioned?"

Maker shook his head in the negative. "Once I overrode the navigation system and disabled the kill-switch, the coordinates scrambled. So, while the nav system could confirm that we'd made a nine-point jump, it couldn't provide any specific info on exactly where we'd come from."

Browing frowned. "If it muddled the coordinates, how'd you manage to get even close to Gaian Space — let alone the Hub?"

Maker gave an unconcerned shrug. "The program that scrambles the coordinates doesn't do so completely at random. At least part of it is based on an algorithm."

"So, you figured out the formulaic portion of it," Dr. Chantrey concluded, "allowing you to control at least a portion of the jump."

"That's the theory," Maker said, nodding in agreement. "But I wasn't able to reproduce the same outcome in a simulator, no matter how often I tried; the ship always ended up in an unknown region of space. Ultimately, they concluded that whatever had caused my mental instability must have also increased my natural acumen, albeit only temporarily — similar to the way a lot of geniuses are also crazy."

Dr. Chantrey gave a sympathetic nod. "I can only imagine the kind of nightmares you must have about all this. Losing your men…"

"Doctor," Maker said almost contemptuously, "I appreciate the attempt at psychoanalysis, but I sleep just fine. My men were Marines; we knew that any of us could buy it at any time, on any mission, for any reason. And we all made our peace with that a long time before this happened. And now that I've done my song-and-dance, why don't you tell me why you're really here."

There was silence for a moment as Browing sent an inquisitive glance towards Kroner, who nodded.

Browing then pulled a holodisk from his pocket. He held it face-up in his palm, and a second later, a three-dimensional holographic image appeared in the air above the disk.

The hologram depicted the head on an insectile alien, encased in armor. On top of its helmet was what appeared to be the bony cranium of some wild, horned animal.

Maker drew in a harsh breath. It was *him*.

Skullcap.

Chapter 3

Of course, "Skullcap" wasn't the thing's name — just the moniker Maker had assigned to him. (Assuming it was a "he." It might not even have a gender, let alone an individual name.) It was the one he'd fought on the derelict ship. As if in confirmation, he could see the ring of skulls around its neck.

Maker let out a ragged breath. "When was this taken?" he practically demanded. "Where?"

"One of the Fringe worlds," the general said. "Terminus. About ten days ago."

The image above the holodisk changed, expanded. Projecting upwards until it was over everyone's head, it now showed a star chart, with worlds and suns depicted as tiny spheres. At the outer edges of the chart, a tiny dot — presumably Terminus — began to pulse brighter than its fellows.

"Fringe?" Maker said with contempt. "That world's deep in the Beyond!"

"It may appear that way on a map," Browing agreed. "But those in authority have seen fit to declare it a Fringe world and therefore the property of the human race."

Maker frowned, his distaste for what he was hearing keenly evident on his face. Claiming a world in this fashion typically meant that anything between it and the current edge of human-occupied space was also being annexed. It was pure politics, something he cared little for — because in many instances it often led to military skirmishes, if not outright war (especially if such a planet already had an indigenous population) — and his

38

companions were quick to pick up on his antipathy on this subject.

"Look," Dr. Chantrey said after a moment, "I don't need to tell you that humanity, as a species, is in perpetual growth mode. We have ever more people, needing ever more space, and requiring ever more resources. We have to keep pushing outward, keep expanding, or civilization — as we know it — will collapse. That means staking a claim to planets and territory farther and farther away from the Hub, which itself keeps expanding."

"It's always been this way," Kroner added. "You know that. There are places in Gaian Space that were considered Beyond five hundred years ago. We planted our flag on them, absorbed them into the fold, and kept moving on. This is nothing new."

"Fine. I get it," Maker said in exasperation. "Colonialism is alive and well, and also good for you. Be sure to get your recommended daily allowance."

Browing softly cleared his throat. "If we could get back on topic for a second?"

"By all means," the general said, plainly ready to change the subject.

The holograph changed again, this time blowing up the rotating image of what was apparently the planet Terminus. It was an Earth-like world in appearance — blue-green, with swirling clouds in the atmosphere and maybe a fifty-fifty split between landmass and water on its surface.

"As I mentioned," Browing said, "humanity has claimed Terminus as being part of the Fringe. However, despite our belief that it's a part of Gaian Space, it is at present a bandied world."

TERMINUS

Maker gave a short nod to show that he understood. A bandied world was one which, for various reasons, more than one sentient species was laying claim to. One race might claim it for religious reasons; another, for its natural resources; a third, because of some perceived strategic advantage; and so on. Such a planet, being in the middle of an interstellar tug-of-war, might find itself home to a multitude of species. Apparently Terminus was such a world.

"How did you get the holo-pic of the insectoid?" Maker asked.

"It's a bit of a long story," Kroner said. The general had been noticeably silent during most of Maker's earlier narrative — probably because he'd heard it dozens of times before. In fact, he'd been one of the general officers who initially debriefed Maker. Now, however, it was clearly his turn to do the talking.

"About a month ago," Kroner went on, "one of our Marine scout ships disappeared while on a routine mission. When we sent a team to investigate at the scout ship's last known coordinates, they found evidence of a battle and a strange form of radiation — but not our missing scout ship or her crew. When our scientists tried to identify the radiation, only a single matching reference came back."

"Let me guess," Maker said. "The ship I made my infamous jump in."

"Yes," Kroner said, nodding. "At that point, we hit a dead end in our search, until a few weeks ago when that same radiation was detected in outer space just above Terminus. The radiation trail led down into the planet's atmosphere, where we lost it.

"Since the only connection we had to this situation was your file, Gant, we pulled it up and went through it in exquisite detail. One of the things in there was a holographic rendition of the aliens that attacked you — a likeness that had been cobbled together based on your description."

"I remember," Maker said, recollecting the many hours spent with hologram artists who attempted to squeeze every minute detail about the appearance of the attackers out of him.

"We distributed that image to our people and allies on Terminus," Kroner continued. "We hit pay dirt, as I said, about ten days ago, when someone captured that image of the Vacra that you saw earlier."

"Vacra?" Maker asked quizzically.

"Yes," Kroner said. "That appears to be what they call themselves."

"So what are they doing there?" Maker asked. "On Terminus?"

"We can only speculate at this point, but we do have a theory," Kroner replied. "We believe the Vacra locked horns with our scout ship. They won the battle, but didn't escape entirely unscathed. They were able to make the jump to hyperspace, but their ship was damaged so they had to head someplace to make repairs…Terminus."

Maker's brow creased in thought. "That's a lot of conjecture based on nothing more than a radiation trail."

"Well, we've got a little more than that," Browing confided. "They've actually been dealing with local merchants, trying to obtain certain goods, which is how we got the holo-pic. One of our non-human allies took it."

41

"What are they trying to buy?" Maker asked.

A cocksure grin found its way onto Browning's face as he responded. "Shield generators, fusion coil, fortified alloy…"

The list went on, but it was clear that much of what the Vacra had been seeking was material used in the construction of spacefaring vessels…or the repair of them.

"Alright," Maker said when Browning finally finished reciting the Vacra's shopping list. "I suppose this is all leading up as to why you're here. If you're just looking for confirmation, you got it. They're the ones that attacked us four years ago."

Maker spent a moment thinking about how much time it had been, although he knew it almost down to the second: kicked out of the service a year after the incident, then bumming around the Gaian Expanse for another year before finally settling on Ginsburg for the past two. Altogether four years. Four long years for it to finally become clear that the encounter he'd reported hadn't been some figment of his imagination.

It felt good to finally be vindicated. Maker looked expectantly at his visitors, suddenly wondering if his corroboration was all they had come for. He didn't have to wait long to find out.

"We want more than confirmation," General Kroner said after a few seconds. "We want you to go after them."

Chapter 4

Maker didn't immediately respond to the general's statement, prompting Kroner to repeat himself.

"I heard you the first time," Maker said. "I'm just not sure what you're asking. Are you saying that you want me as some kind of civilian advisor to a military campaign, or maybe as—"

"We want you to lead a recon mission to locate the Vacra on Terminus," Kroner said, interrupting him.

"Recon??!!" Maker shouted incredulously. "These things have attacked and destroyed at least three of our ships! You need to be organizing a *strike*!"

"We'll cross that bridge if we come to it," the general said. "For now, we need to find out more about them. They clearly have weapons and technology that we don't understand. A show of force probably isn't the wisest course of action. As you yourself said, Gant, they've destroyed three of our ships. We need to know what we're up against before we start picking a fight."

Maker spent a few moments brooding on what he'd just heard. He hated to admit it, but the general's position actually made sense. An attack really didn't seem prudent when they had no idea what they were facing.

"We understand how you feel," Dr. Chantrey suddenly chimed in, apparently interpreting Maker's silence as opposition. "However, charging in with almost no intel would be complete folly. We need you to do this our way."

"Assuming I agree with you," Maker said, "I can't recall the last time a civilian led any kind of military action on the front lines like you're suggesting."

"We'll reinstate you," Browing said. "Full time and credit for the past few years. You'll be a full-fledged Marine again, with uninterrupted service as far as your record goes."

Maker laughed derisively. "I spent fifteen years getting my butt shot off for the Marines, and at the end of the day they gave me the bum's rush. Why would I be eager to sign up for that again?"

"Because you're a patriot," the doctor said, "and a Marine at heart. Service is in your blood, and right now that service is needed."

"Stop it," Maker told the doctor, still smiling. "Just stop it."

"Stop what?" Dr. Chantrey asked, seemingly surprised.

"Stop trying to psychoanalyze me," Maker replied. "Quit trying to push my buttons."

The doctor shook her head. "I'm not—"

"Sure you are," Maker said. "But back to the subject at hand. I'm not wild about the idea of being the military's scapegoat again if things go sideways."

"What if we sweeten the pot a little?" Kroner asked.

Maker's eyes narrowed. "I'm listening," he said.

"Before your last mission," the general said, "you applied to the officer's program and were accepted. Of course, all of that got put on hold after you came back. And then you…left the service."

Maker nodded, almost dumbly. So much had happened in the aftermath of his return from that last mission that he had practically forgotten about this last thing, that he had applied to become an officer.

"What are you saying?" Maker asked.

44

"I'm saying that we'll go ahead and push the paperwork through," the general stated. "You won't just be coming back to the Marines, but you'll be coming back an officer. Something you always wanted."

Maker blinked, the general's offer clearly catching him by surprise.

"One question before I decide," Maker said. "Why me?"

"Frankly speaking," Browing said, "you're the only human being who's ever seen these things — the Vacra."

"Wrong," Maker declared, shaking his head. "I'm just the only one who's ever seen them and lived to tell about it."

"Be that as it may," Dr. Chantrey said, "you've got the most experience with them, which — along with your military training, knowledge, and skill — makes you the most qualified to lead this mission."

Maker frowned, seeming to mull things over. "Alright, let's say I accept," he said after a moment. "I'll need a team—"

"Already taken care of," Browing interjected. He pulled a p-comp from a pocket and extended the palm-sized computer to Maker. "If you take a look at the profiles on the screen there, you'll see that we've assembled a select task force to—"

"No thanks," Maker said, cutting Browing off as he returned the man's p-comp, having spent no more than a moment glancing at the information on its monitor. "If I'm going to do this, there are some conditions you have to meet, the first one being that Erlen comes with me."

"Done," Kroner declared with a nod.

Of course, that one was pretty easy and expected. Even before he got railroaded out of the Marines, anyone acquainted with him knew that he didn't go anywhere without the Niotan. However, he felt the need to make it clear that Erlen was part of the deal.

"Next," Maker said, "I pick my own team."

"Agreed," Kroner stated.

"Now wait just a minute," Browing said, clearly not happy. "This is a high-level mission requiring people who—"

"It's fine," the general said, cutting Browing off with a wave of his hand. He turned his attention back to Maker. "What else?"

Maker took a deep breath. "I want eclipse authority," he announced.

The room went silent. Maker's visitors exchanged telling, knowing glances. His last request was a big one; eclipse authority meant that he would have the privilege and prerogative to exceed his mission parameters whenever and however he liked. It was a literal license to do whatever he wanted, no matter how unlawful, unethical, or unscrupulous. It was usually granted to only the most trusted of individuals on the most important of missions. In fact, only three people were ever alleged to have received it since *Homo sapiens* began their expansion across the stars.

After a few moments of uncomfortable silence, Browing opened his mouth to say something, but Dr. Chantrey spoke up first.

"I'm sorry," she said, shaking her head, "but we can't do that. No one here has the power to grant you eclipse authority, or even promise that we'll get it for you.

We can try, but frankly speaking, it's not likely to happen."

"I see," Maker said, not looking particularly happy with her statement.

"However," the doctor continued, "you shouldn't be looking at this in terms of what you can't do, but see it as an opportunity for what you can."

"Which is…?" Maker asked.

"To catch the one that got away," she replied, the corners of her mouth turning up into a smile. At that point she had him hooked, and she knew it.

"Alright," Maker said. "I'm in." As he said the words, an odd sense of relief that he hadn't expected flooded through him.

"Outstanding," said the general, shaking his hand.

"Oh, there is one more thing," Maker said. "I get to use *this*."

He pressed a button on his wristband, and a nearby panel of wall slid up into the roof with a mechanical whirr, revealing a hidden, coffin-sized cubbyhole. Intrigued, Maker's visitors walked over to the alcove for a better look at its contents: a suit of battle armor.

Browing frowned as he looked at the outfit. "This is illegal, you know. It's a violation and a felony for civilians to possess Marine armor."

"This isn't Marine armor," Maker countered. "It's mine. I built it from scratch."

"But probably from Marine specs," Browing insisted, "since it's the best battle gear out there."

"It's the best *mass-produced* gear out there," Maker corrected. "But you can custom-build armor that's a whole lot better, and I did. I even put my own sigil on it."

He slapped his hand on the left pectoral of the armor, where a small image of Erlen was engraved in the metal. Kroner laughed when he realized what it was.

"Using your own armor shouldn't be an issue," the general said with a smile, clapping Maker on the shoulder.

"If the general approves, I have no objection," Browing added. "Glad to have you aboard. And if you've got an idea of who you want on your team, just tell us and we'll start making it happen."

"For the most part, I don't know who I want just yet," Maker said. "That being the case, I'm going to need complete access to the military personnel database."

Browing looked stunned. "Complete access? To the *entire* database?"

"Yes," Maker responded. "How else am I going to screen for the people I'll need? I need to check not only their skill sets, but their entire backgrounds. That means I need full access."

"So, you don't even have names at this point?" Browing asked.

"Well, I can give you *one* name," Maker said. "Chief Master Sergeant Hector Adames."

Browing pulled out his p-comp, and then rapidly moved his fingers across its screen, sorting information. A moment later he stopped, then stared at the screen, eyes flitting back and forth as he read what was on the monitor. A second later he let out a harsh laugh.

"You've got to be kidding," Browing said, looking up. "The man's a criminal, from a family of criminals."

"Hector left his wayward ways behind and severed his family ties when he joined the Corps," Maker said defensively.

"Actually," Browing retorted, again looking at the screen, "it looks like joining the Marines was just a cover to continue his illicit activities. Let's see…accused of using his position as quartermaster to smuggle goods…implicated in the sale of restricted weaponry to civilians…" Browing looked up. "About the only reason he's not spending the rest of his life in a military prison is lack of evidence."

"So he's either innocent, smart, or both," Maker concluded. "And not many dummies make it to Chief."

"And neither did your friend," Browing said. "He's been demoted twice, so Chief isn't on his résumé at the moment."

Maker shrugged, taking it in stride. "Still, I want him on my team."

"We'll make it happen," the general said, obviously ready to leave before Browing found a way to queer the deal. "We'll get you access to the database. Be ready to move out in three days."

He shook Maker's hand again, said his goodbyes, and then headed to the door. Growling, Erlen raced over and gently raked a paw across Kroner's shin.

"Of course I didn't forget you," the general said, bending down to scratch Erlen's head.

Next, Browing stiffly shook Maker's hand before swiftly heading to the door, sidestepping General Kroner, who was still petting Erlen.

"Well," Dr. Chantrey said, extending her hand, "it's been a pleasure."

Maker shook the proffered hand. "Before you go," he said. "Two questions."

The doctor seemed intrigued. "Go ahead."

TERMINUS

"First of all, I know you and Browing must have read my file before coming here, so why ask all those questions like you didn't know my story, my background?"

For a second, Maker didn't think she was going to answer. Then when it appeared that she *was* going to reply, her eyes twitched in a way that made her seem sly, shifty even, and he knew that he wasn't going to get a truthful response. But at that moment, something happened; her demeanor changed and a kind of resolve seemed to settle within her.

"This is why," she said, and suddenly there was a thin metallic rod in her palm. It must have been some form of prestidigitation, because Maker would have sworn that her hand was empty a moment earlier. He looked at the rod, noting that it was about six inches in length and maybe half the width of his middle finger. At one end of it were a number of tiny lights and diodes that randomly gave off soft flashes of light.

"What's that?" he asked.

"It's a cerebral scanner, although a small-scale variant," she said. "The full-sized version is typically used to try to detect mental activity in the cerebrum of patients who've suffered traumatic brain injury."

"And this one?"

"Our queries were meant to be triggers. I used the scanner to examine your brain activity whenever we asked something that was likely to get an emotional response from you. In short, it fed information back to my databand as to whether or not you were mentally stable."

"And?"

"You passed," she said with a knowing smile. "Now, what's your second question?"

"What's Browing's deal?" Maker asked. "I mean, why is he here? I know why you and the general are here. Kroner's here as a senior and respected officer so I'll listen to what he has to say. You're here to evaluate me and overcome any resistance I have to jumping at the carrot you guys are dangling. But what's Browing's role?"

Dr. Chantrey gave him an appraising glance, as if seeing him for the first time.

"The general said you were smart, but you're more astute than I gave you credit for," she said.

"Thanks," Maker said. "But I only use my brain every other day, so just come back tomorrow if you're disappointed."

A hurt look came across her face. "Sorry, I didn't mean to offend."

Maker sighed. "It's okay. I guess I'm just a little on edge given everything that's happened. Now, about Browing?"

"That's easy enough. He's the government liaison on Terminus. He represents humanity's interest there, so he insisted on having involvement in selecting the person to deal with the Vacra."

"*He's* representing our interest?" Maker asked, surprised. "It's a wonder we still have a claim on the place."

****

The back of General Kroner's staff car was spacious, if not luxurious. The rear compartment held seats for four — two that were back-to-back with the driver and front passenger seats, and two across from those that were forward-facing. Browing sat in the rear-facing seat behind the driver, while Dr. Chantrey sat directly across from him. The general sat in the seat next to the doctor.

Browing waited until they were pulling away from Maker's cabin, then checked to make sure that the soundproof glass that separated the front and rear compartments was in place. Satisfied that the driver couldn't hear them, he then turned to Dr. Chantrey almost angrily.

"Why did you tell him that we couldn't get him eclipse authority?" he asked. "You should have just told him 'yes.' You could have ruined everything."

The doctor didn't even deign to look at him when she responded, preferring to stare out the window at the passing scenery. "That demand was a ruse. He didn't care about having eclipse authority, and he already knew we couldn't get it for him. He just wanted to see what we'd say."

Browing was visibly confused. "Why?"

"Because, if we lied about that it would probably mean that we were lying about other things," the general said, weighing in. "Then all three of us would have come off as idiots instead of just one of us."

Browing gave the general a hard stare. "You don't like me very much, do you?"

"Son, I don't even know you well enough to dislike you," Kroner said. "What I definitely don't like, though, is helping you recruit Marines for missions under false pretenses, no matter how well-connected your family is. However, I was ordered to come here and enlist Gant's services on your behalf, so that's what I did. But it doesn't mean I have to be happy about it."

"That's fine by me — as long as you do what you're told," Browing said, earning him a glare from

Kroner. He turned his attention back to Dr. Chantrey. "What about his story regarding the derelict and his crazy hyperspace jump?"

"Very convincing," the doctor replied. "But he's definitely lying about what happened."

Chapter 5

Maker walked off the transport shuttle, struggling to keep his emotions in check. Decked out in his service dress — dark trousers, dark three-button jacket, and service cap — he was just one of hundreds of people in uniform disembarking here on Stinger III. However, while most of his fellow shuttle passengers were returning to duty and the humdrum of their everyday routine, this was his first time setting foot on a military planet in years.

He stepped off the exit ramp and just stood there, looking around almost in wonder. High above him, a squadron of fighters zipped by, flying in unbelievably tight formation. Just outside of the shuttle landing site, a convoy of military hovercraft with a heavily armed escort went streaking through the traffic lanes, obviously hauling something of high importance. Roughly ten yards away, an argument between two other uniformed servicemen suddenly escalated into full-scale fisticuffs. Maker smiled. *Damn but it felt good to be a Marine again!*

People flowed around him like water around a rock in a stream, giving him odd looks as he stood there like a petrified tree. Of course, the wide berth they gave him might also have had something to do with Erlen, who waited patiently while Maker seem to adjust to his new environs.

The trip itself had been fairly uneventful. As promised, there had been a military craft, the *Manley*, waiting for him at the Ginsburg spaceport three days after his visitors had departed. The captain of the ship, a sour-faced man named Wilmer Han, had administered the oath of office to Maker, swearing him in as an officer of the Marine Corps. In addition, a special a courier had hand-delivered a datachip to him that provided not only secure access to the military's personnel database, but also Maker's itinerary and initial orders. The military vessel later dumped him off at a commercial spaceport, where he'd taken civilian transportation for the rest of his trek.

All in all, the entire journey took about a week: two days aboard the *Manley*, then another five aboard the civilian ship. (As broad as Gaian Space was, there was little direct interstellar transportation anywhere. Counting in layovers and such — the *Manley* itself had had to make two additional stops before Maker left the ship — even hyperspace travel could only get you so far, so fast.)

He had used much of his time on the *Manley* reviewing personnel records. Before he left, he thought he had his team picked out. Thus, before getting off at the commercial spaceport, Maker had used the military vessel's secure comm to send General Kroner his selections. He also added that he wanted them on Stinger III when he arrived. (That was probably pushing things, but he might as well see what he could get.)

After a few moments — and several not-so-subtle bumps from other exiting shuttle passengers — Maker started moving again. Under normal circumstances, the presence of a "pet" like Erlen would have required that they go through Customs. Fortunately, Maker had long ago (and at great expense) gotten the necessary paperwork to allow the Niotan to have unrestricted travel — including in the passenger compartment of transport ships. All of the requisite information and permits were now encrypted and encoded in the dog tags that Erlen wore, which were quite similar to tags that Maker himself carried. That being the case, they were able to head straight for the exit gate.

TERMINUS

Once outside, Maker had planned to take one of the numerous forms of public transportation — train, bus, etc. — to his duty post. Thus, he was more than a little surprised to find a car and driver waiting for him.

Oddly enough, Maker initially walked past the young Marine holding the sign with "Lt. Maker" on it, his mind automatically processing the scene and dismissing it in terms of being related to him. It was with something of a start that he realized a moment later that *he* was in fact Lt. Maker. (Being an officer was going to take more getting used to than simply being a Marine again.)

Doubling back, he approached the fellow holding the sign, who looked almost too young to be in the service.

"Excuse me," Maker said, "but I'm Lieutenant Maker."

"Lt. Arrogant Maker?" the young man asked.

"Yes," Maker confirmed.

"Then I'm your ride," the young Marine intoned, smiling. "Right this way."

Maker followed the fellow — whom he presumed to be his driver — to a parking area reserved for high-ranking individuals. His guide led him to a general staff car and opened the door.

"Since when do el-tees rate this kind of treatment?" Maker asked.

The driver shrugged. "Don't know. I was dropping an admiral from the Space Navy off when I got the order to hang around for you. I'm assuming that someone got worried that you might get lost."

Maker and Erlen got into the car; the driver went to close the door and then hesitated.

TERMINUS

"Uh…" The young Marine seemed at a loss for words. "Any luggage, sir?"

"It's being sent ahead," Maker said.

"Excellent," the driver said, seemingly relieved. He closed the door, and then went around to the driver's side and got in. A few seconds later, they were on their way.

****

The entire planet of Stinger III actually served as a military installation. The planet's various continents served as command centers, which were themselves broken down into regions. The regions were further divided into zones. Finally, within each zone, were numerous military bases.

The base Maker was reporting to was located in a tropical area near Stinger III's equator. It was a short drive away from the shuttle landing site, but long enough for Maker to get the driver's story. He was young, as Maker had thought, and new to the Corps. He'd only enlisted six months ago, and since completing basic training his only job had been serving as a driver. However, on a recent pick-up he had forgotten to get a general's luggage, the result being that the general in question had given the young man a verbal mauling that had only been slightly less vicious in nature than a physical attack (which explained the young man's earlier nervousness about Maker's luggage).

The car dropped him off at the Visiting Officer's Quarters. It was there that Maker received the first real indication that his reputation had preceded him when he reported for his room assignment.

The VOQ lobby closely resembled that of a hotel. There was a waiting area (comprised of upholstered chairs and sofas scattered about the room), a small gift shop along one wall, and a bar/lounge in a far corner.

Maker took all of this in with a glance, and then — spotting the check-in desk almost directly across from him — made a beeline for it. En route, they passed a robotic maid sweeping the floor.

The robot's optical sensors, glowing with a soft blue light, swept across Maker but then flared up when they came to Erlen.

Maker recognized that the robot was scanning the Niotan. *Good luck with that*, he thought. He had yet to encounter a machine or technology that could truly examine Erlen. Not even x-rays could penetrate his dense hide. Still, not knowing what the robot might be programmed to do — especially if it found the Niotan to be a threat — he halted.

"Unidentified life form," the robot announced to no one in particular several moments later. "Race: unknown. Species: unknown. Planet of origin: unknown. Life form is unclassifiable."

The robot appeared to engage in a few more seconds of processing but said nothing else. Then its optical sensors returned to their normal shade and it went back to work. Maker continued towards the check-in desk.

The receptionist on duty, a perky young blonde, gave him a warm, welcoming smile as he strode up, Erlen padding along beside him.

"Welcome," she said. "How can I help you?"

"I think I'm supposed to have a reservation," he answered. "Last name's Maker."

"I'm happy to check on that. Please place your palm on the pad," she said, indicating a rectangular device with a transparent face that sat atop the check-in desk.

Maker did as requested. There was a brief flash of light as his palm, fingerprints, and biometrics were scanned for identification purposes.

The receptionist glanced at a computer screen facing her as it brought up Maker's identifying information, then did a double-take. She stared at him in slack-jawed surprise, but — to her credit — she quickly recovered.

"Just a second, sir," she said as her fingers began tapping on the screen. "I'm just coding the room to your biological identifiers…."

Maker simply nodded. She had clearly recognized his name, but apparently her professionalism and training overcame her surprise at being face-to-face with someone so infamous. That was better than most were able to accomplish. On the *Manley*, for instance, any sojourn outside his cabin made him the subject of numerous sidelong glances and harsh whispering.

"There you are — all set," the receptionist said a moment later. She then gave Maker his room number and precise details on how to get there. Maker listened attentively before heading towards the building's elevators.

Suddenly seeming to take note of Erlen, the receptionist called out to Maker's retreating form.

"Excuse me, sir," she said, causing Maker to turn around. "I'm sorry, but we have a strict policy about animals on the premises. All pets have to be kept at the base kennels."

"Thanks," Maker said. "If I get any pets, I'll know where to take them."

He turned and resumed walking towards the elevators. A few minutes later, he was in his room.

Chapter 6

Maker's quarters were nice, but nothing out of the ordinary. It was basically a one-bedroom suite with a kitchenette, a bathroom, a living room, and a small closet.

As anticipated, the rest of his luggage had already arrived and was sitting in the living room. Although ample in size, it really didn't comprise very much. The bulk of the items consisted of a large, heavy-duty trunk with a high-tech lock that housed his body armor. Other than that, there was a piece of locked, hard shell luggage that actually served as a weapons case, and a large garment bag containing what was essentially the rest of Maker's wardrobe.

Maker removed his service coat, tossing it and his cap onto a nearby recliner. Erlen yawned, then hopped onto the living room sofa and curled up. Maker, giving the Niotan a look of disgust, grabbed the weapons case.

"No, no," he said sarcastically, staring at Erlen. "I've got this. You take a break."

Erlen let out a playful growl but didn't even bother opening his eyes as Maker went into the bedroom. Once there, he shoved the weapons case into a corner on the floor of the closet and was just starting to put away his clothes when a soft chime sounded, indicating that someone was at his door.

Maker exited the bedroom and headed towards the door, noting as he passed through the living room that Erlen had come silently to attention and was now wide awake.

Affixed to the wall next to the door was a large, flat monitor that was currently dark. Maker tapped the screen once and it immediately came to life, showing him the face of his visitor.

It was a man, dark-haired but with a military buzz cut. He also had shaggy black eyebrows, an olive complexion, and brown eyes.

"Little pig, little pig, let me in," the man uttered in a singsong voice.

"Open," Maker said, grinning.

There was an audible click as the door unlocked before sliding into a recessed portion of the wall. Maker's visitor, dressed in military fatigues, took three stiff strides into the room. He turned to face Maker as the door slid shut again, and then gave a snappy salute.

"Master Sergeant Hector Adames reporting for duty, sir," the man announced in a stentorian voice.

Maker returned the salute. "At ease," he said.

He and Adames locked eyes, staring, as if each were sizing the other up. Almost simultaneously, they both let out a hearty laugh, and then hugged briefly, clapping each other on the shoulder.

"Gant Maker, an officer?" Adames said, feigning incredulity. "Did they have an extra set of lieutenant bars left over that they didn't know what to do with?"

"What about you, you scamp?" Maker retorted. "The brass hasn't managed to kick you out of the Corps yet?"

"Not for lack of trying," Adames said, only half joking. He suddenly noticed Erlen. "I see you've still got your pet monster. Funny, I would have thought that thing had killed and eaten you by now."

Adames reached into his pocket and pulled out what looked like a small red ball. He tossed it in Erlen's direction; the Niotan caught it in his mouth in mid-air, and then began to gnaw eagerly on it.

"I see Erlen still has a fondness for rock candy," Adames said. "Now tell me, how in blazes did you get reinstated in the Corps — and as an officer no less?"

Maker told him the story, which took almost no time at all.

"Hey, you know that I never doubted you," Adames assured him when he'd finished, "so I'm glad you were finally proven right. Still, I don't understand my role in all this."

"I need an acquisitions specialist."

"I see," Adames said, frowning in thought. Maker obviously wanted him to get something — or some *things* — that couldn't be obtained through normal channels. "And what exactly are you looking to acquire?"

Rather than respond, Maker handed his p-comp to Adames, who stared at the device's screen. He then flicked a finger across the machine's monitor, scrolling down what was obviously an inventory list.

Adames' eyebrows went up and he let out a long, low whistle as he scanned the items noted. "I'll say this for you, Gant: you dream big. More than half this stuff is verboten."

"So you can't get it?"

"Don't be stupid. Of course I can get it. It may take a little time—"

"You've got three days," Maker stated matter-of-factly. "That's when we move out."

"In that case, I'd better get started," Adames said, returning the p-comp.

Maker tried handing the device back. "You can keep this — in case you need to refer to the list again."

"No need," Adames said, tapping his temple with a forefinger. "Besides, for a guy in my line of work, a list like that is practically a trail of breadcrumbs if the wrong people start asking questions."

"Got it," Maker acknowledged with a nod. "Now, about our team — did you get their files?"

"Yeah, but I haven't had a chance to look at them. I do know that everyone's here, though. The last one arrived yesterday."

"Well, try to review them before tomorrow. We're briefing them in the morning."

"Sounds like we're going to be moving fast on this thing. Like I said, I should get started."

"Excellent," Maker said. "I'll sleep better tonight knowing you're on the job — although first I really need to get something to eat."

The two men shook hands again and exchanged pleasantries, clearly happy to be working together. Adames headed for the door with Maker seeing him out, but paused unexpectedly before exiting. He turned back towards Maker, looking particularly serious.

"Look, Gant," he said. "The word is out that you're here. I've only been planet-side for two days, and I've already been hearing all kinds of chatter."

"Like what?" Maker asked.

"There are a lot of individuals out there who still think you killed a ship full of people, including a bunch of good Marines. People who think you should have been charged, gone to prison...or worse. I know that you can handle yourself, but you may want to be extra careful."

"I will, thanks," Maker said, but Adames really didn't sense a lot of sincerity in his friend's words. Still, he simply nodded and left.

TERMINUS

After Adames departed, Maker spent a few seconds thinking about what the man had said. It had only been a couple of years since the incident that had ruined his prior career, but still, it *had* been years. And, while Maker couldn't escape being infamous, he had never been charged with any kind of crime. Surely that meant something.

He would soon learn that he was completely wrong in that regard.

Chapter 7

Maker went back to unpacking his clothes after Adames left. Knowing that he'd only be on Stinger III a short time, he left most of his apparel in their respective bags. Satisfied that he had enough attire hanging in the closet to last a few days (but not so much that it would take him more than a few minutes to pack), he went back into the living room.

"Dinner," he announced to Erlen, who was stretched out lazily on the sofa again. The Niotan raised his head a few inches as if thinking it over, then waved a dismissive paw at Maker as he plopped his head back down again.

"Fine," Maker said, heading towards the door. "I'll bring you something back."

Maker stepped out, and then headed down to the VOQ lobby. There he found the same perky receptionist still on duty. He waited patiently while she helped a Space Navy commander, then stepped forward.

"Excuse me, but can you tell me how to get to the N— I mean, the Officer's Mess from here?" he asked. He had almost said "NCO Mess" but caught himself in time.

"There's a complimentary bus that comes by the front door every fifteen minutes," she said. "In addition to the mess, which is located in the Officer's Club, it also goes by a couple of other facilities, like the base gym…"

Maker politely let her rattle on for a few seconds, naming various places that he could get to on the bus if he were so inclined. When she paused to take a breath, he thanked her and headed out of the main door of the lobby to wait. Not long thereafter the bus pulled up, and a short time later Maker found himself stepping off the vehicle in front of the O Club.

The club consisted of a large, two-story building painted a drab gray. Close to the door were a number of parking spots reserved for generals, admirals, and the like — a few of which were occupied.

Maker stared at the door for a moment. This was as close as he could ever remember getting to the Officer's Club of any base he had ever been on. It hadn't occurred to him before how odd it would feel to be on this side of the fence, to not just be an officer but being committed to their institutions and traditions.

Oh well, too late for second thoughts now...

And with that he walked up to the door and went inside.

The interior of the club was a minor disappointment. Of course, he hadn't expected to find water fountains dispensing champagne, paintings by Old Earth masters on the walls, or any of the other drivel they tell you when you're new to the Corps about how special the O Club is. But what he hadn't expected to see when he walked down the various hallways were things he was already well-acquainted with: familiar busts of famous war heroes, framed copies of well-known military documents, etc.

In short, in terms of aesthetics, the O Club wasn't particularly different than any NCO Club that he'd been to. Apparently the only thing exceptionally appealing about the O Club was its exclusivity, and now that he was — nominally — a member, it wasn't that impressive.

Maker let out a dissatisfied, almost disgusted sigh. A moment later, he stopped a passing captain and asked where the mess hall was located. Five minutes later, he was sitting down at a table with a plate full of food and a glass of water.

The dining area was spacious, with cafeteria-style seating. While not completely packed, there were enough diners present that Maker actually had to share his table with other people — a party of three other lieutenants seated at the opposite end of the table.

Against one of the walls, Maker noticed three tables that constituted more traditional dining room furniture — not the picnic-table crap that he and his fellows were currently seated at. In fact, those tables (and the heavy, cushioned chairs that went with them) were positively ornate, and each was emblazoned with a star on top.

It didn't take a genius to figure out that the area he was looking at was reserved for general officers. In fact, there were a half-dozen of them presently sitting at one of those tables now — including a Navy rear admiral who was staring at Maker with a particular degree of intensity.

Maker tried to ignore the man and focused on his food. His meal consisted of some kind of indigenous fowl, a local strain of wild rice that was as long as his finger and had to be cut with a knife, and a couple of rolls.

After a few minutes, Maker picked up movement out of the corner of his eye. The admiral he'd noticed before was beckoning a young officer over — a Navy lieutenant. The young man bent down and the admiral began whispering vehemently in his ear. Suddenly, the lieutenant's head snapped in Maker's direction; at the same time, his fist curled up into a white-knuckled ball. This in no way looked like a positive development.

TERMINUS

The lieutenant — a tall, well-muscled fellow — gave Maker an angry look as he returned to his seat. Once there, he began speaking in an urgent manner with the other officers seated with him, occasionally pointing in Maker's direction.

Maker knew what was coming next; it was something he had started experiencing shortly before he was run out of the service. The whispering began spreading across the room like a plague of locusts, always accompanied by a glance or a nod in his direction. Eventually, it reached the young officers seated at the other end of Maker's table. One of them gave him a dumbfounded look, but at the urging of his companions picked up what was left of his dinner and moved to another table.

All the while, Maker kept eating, acting as if nothing was wrong. If this was the worst that they did, he could handle it. If they were planning to take things a step further...

As if reading Maker's mind, the lieutenant who the admiral had spoken to suddenly stood up. Accompanied by three companions, he approached Maker's table with a stride that said he meant business. When they got close, Maker glanced at the lieutenant's nametag: it read "Kepler."

Kepler and one of his cronies — a big, burly fellow who looked like he wrestled bears in his spare time — sat down on the bench across from Maker. Their other two friends sat down on either side of him (even though the one near the end really didn't have enough room, and must have had half of his posterior hanging off the bench seating). The room essentially went silent; Maker, knife and fork in hand, kept eating.

"You're Arrogant Maker," Kepler said. It wasn't a question.

"Every day," Maker retorted.

"*Madman* Maker," Kepler said. "*Maniac* Maker."

Maker didn't reply; he simply cut another piece of fowl and ate it.

"You know, some of us had friends serving on the *Orpheus Moon*," Kepler went on.

"What a coincidence," Maker said. "So did I."

"Well, one was Admiral Greeley's son." Kepler nodded in the direction of the admiral, who looked like he wanted to shove a grenade down Maker's throat. "My cousin."

Maker took a moment to reflect. He remembered Lieutenant Greeley. He'd been a little green, but with some seasoning he had been likely to become a fine officer.

Maker spared another glance for the admiral, who still looked as though he believed Maker would make excellent lawn fertilizer. A general officer was a powerful foe to have working against you. For the first time, it occurred to Maker that a number of people on Captain Wendren's ship had come from families with long military traditions and were related to high-ranking officers. In fact, Wendren himself had come from a politically well-connected family.

Maker frowned slightly. How many enemies had he made that day when the *Orpheus Moon* took its fateful jump? How many people had called in favors to see that he got the boot? And now that he was back, how many would be gunning for him again?

All of this flitted through his mind over the course of a few seconds. Maker decided to see if there was a diplomatic way to end things.

"Look," he began, "what happened aboard the *Orpheus Moon* was tragic, but wasn't my doing. I'm sorry for how things turned out, but it wa—"

Kepler pounded the table with his fist hard enough to rattle Maker's plate, the sound seemingly magnified by the hushed tone pervading the room.

"Nobody cares how sorry you are!" Kepler hissed. "The fact of the matter is you're somehow alive when everyone else is dead, and it's your fault!"

Maker gripped the knife and fork in his hands so tightly that it was a wonder that he didn't hurt himself.

"Alright," he said flatly, sizing up his opponents and trying to imagine how this scuffle was going to unfold. "Let's do this."

His tone and willingness to fight seemed to catch them off-guard, but Kepler recovered soon enough. Maker could see the man's muscles tensing underneath his shirt as he prepared to go into action.

An unexpected cough, clearly intended to get their attention, sounded from the general officers' table. Kepler and his friends all turned in that direction — towards Admiral Greeley. Maker warily cast a glance in that direction and caught the admiral fiercely shake his head. Kepler clearly got the message: *Not here.*

Kepler stood up, and his friends followed his lead.

"You got lucky this time," he angrily told Maker. "But you can bet that we'll see you before you leave."

With that, they exited the mess hall. The threat of an imminent fight now gone, Maker focused on trying to finish his dinner; afterwards, he hung around the O Club for an extra half hour — just in case his new friends were waiting on him outside — during which time he was able to talk the kitchen staff into giving him a bag in which to carry some food back for Erlen.

He made it back to his room without encountering any more vengeful individuals. He found a plate in the kitchenette and dumped the food he'd brought back onto it, then set the entire thing on the floor for Erlen.

Satisfied that he'd done enough for one day, Maker took a quick shower and then flung himself into bed. He was sound asleep within minutes.

TERMINUS

Chapter 8

Maker awoke bright and early the next morning. Back on Ginsberg, he'd maintained a strict policy of exercising daily. However, the week of space travel he'd recently experienced had seriously disrupted his routine — something he intended to remedy asap.

He tossed on his old PT uniform — a t-shirt from his old unit and a pair of exercise shorts. A few moments later he exited the room, leaving Erlen sleeping on the couch. Normally, Erlen would have come with him, but apparently Maker wasn't the only person whose regular habits had been thrown out of whack.

He went downstairs and out through the lobby. By his estimates, the closest base gym was about five miles away — far enough to get in a good run. Maker started jogging.

Thirty minutes later he arrived at the gym, sweaty and out of breath, but feeling good. He went inside and spent a few minutes locating a water fountain to slake his thirst and resting on a bench before going into the weight room.

Maker spent about thirty minutes pumping iron, focusing primarily on his back and legs. (With respect to weights, his exercise regimen called for working out different body parts every other day. Thus, he would focus on chest and arms on the morrow, followed by legs and back again the day after that.) As at the mess hall the previous evening, he couldn't help but notice the stares and whispers that seemed to be focused on him in the weight room. Still, he did a good job of staying focused on the task at hand and managed to get through his reps and sets without incident. When he finished, he headed for the locker room.

Once there, he found an empty clothes-cleaner, then stripped down and tossed everything inside. He set the cleaner for ten minutes and pushed the start button, and then headed for the showers. By the time he finished up, his clothes should be clean and dry.

The showers were typical of gyms everywhere: just a long line of about a dozen retractable showerheads set in the wall. About half of them were in use at the moment, but Maker saw one open near the back wall and headed for it.

Once there, he took a moment to glance at the control pad for his showerhead. It was essentially a touchscreen set in the wall at about chest height. Maker set the water temperature at eighty-five degrees and hit the start button. The showerhead's sensor, detecting someone in front of it, activated the jets and a second later hot water came cascading out.

Maker put his head under the shower, allowing the warm water to flow soothingly over him for a minute — starting at his head, then down his neck, torso, and legs until it reached his feet. Turning back to the control pad, he increased the water pressure. Next, he gripped the showerhead and pulled; attached to a retractable hose, it came away easily from its notch in the wall.

Maker reached over his shoulder and aimed the shower at his back. With the increased pressure, the water was like a much-needed massage — kneading his muscles and joints, relieving tension he didn't realize he'd had.

After a few minutes of allowing the forceful water to work the stress out of his body, he placed the showerhead back in its notch. He then punched additional codes into the control pad, this time pulling up a list of cleaners — specifically soaps and shampoos. Frankly speaking, the shower could manufacture thousands of them, so that a person could wash up with almost anything they desired once the proper code was entered.

Rather than be smothered by nigh-infinite options, Maker chose — as he always did — a standard soap that had been a personal favorite since he first joined the Marines. It was great for getting yourself really clean, and had a refreshing, but not overpowering, fragrance that gently lingered after its use.

After making his selection, Maker put his hand into a small recessed area just below the control pad. A dispensing nozzle squirted soft, scented soap into his hand. Maker lathered up.

He had scrubbed himself twice and was in the process of washing his hair — had his head under the shower, in fact — when he heard three things that struck him as odd. First, the one or two random conversations between other people in the showers (and which Maker had been tuning out) all seemed to end abruptly at the same time, as if someone had hit a mute button on all the speakers.

Next, all of the other showers turned off almost simultaneously, like water had unexpectedly stopped flowing through the pipes.

Finally, there came the cadence of numerous feet suddenly in motion. It wasn't in unison, the way one would expect of, say, a squad of soldiers marching in formation. Instead, this was the random patter that might accompany people who were trying to get out of the path of a runaway car.

TERMINUS

Individually, the three things might have meant nothing, but taken altogether, they set off Maker's personal alarm bells. He quickly ran a hand across his face, wiping down from his forehead to his chin. Looking towards the entrance of the showers, he saw several men — who had presumably been showering just moments before, since they were still naked and wet — beating a hasty retreat from the area. And he also saw the reason why: standing just inside the showers were Kepler and his three friends from dinner the day before.

Chapter 9

Kepler and his cronies were fully clothed, wearing fatigues. This obviously wasn't an accidental meeting; this particular encounter was intentional. They probably thought that ganging up on him while he was in the shower, nude, gave them a psychological advantage. Even if it didn't, they still had him outnumbered and had more or less caught him unprepared.

Maker took a moment to size up his opponents. Aside from Kepler, there was the big one that Maker had mentally tagged as Bear, who looked like he lived for ripping arms out of sockets. The last two looked a little nervous, less sure of themselves. Maker recognized the type: born followers — guys who went along with any idea that the group had, no matter how asinine or idiotic. In his head, Maker named them Tagalong 1 and Tagalong 2.

In brief, it was four-on-one. Needless to say, Maker wasn't particularly wild about the odds; he needed a plan, and fast.

He reached up and gently pushed the showerhead to the side, turning it so that it faced the direction of the other four men as much as possible. Its sensor, recognizing that there was no longer anyone directly in front of it, stopped the flow of water.

Still keeping Kepler's group in sight, Maker began punching codes into the shower control pad.

"You boys are going to find it a little tricky to get clean while still dressed," he said.

Maker put his hand beneath the soap dispenser; a second later, his hand full of liquid soap, he began to lather up.

"Don't worry about us," Kepler said with a wicked sneer. "We're not worried about getting a little water on our clothes. Blood, on the other hand? That can be a little tricky to get out."

Maker reached for more soap. "Well, let's hope nothing happens that's likely to get blood on your uniform." He continued covering himself as much as possible in suds from his neck to his ankles, still keeping an eye on his adversaries.

"Now that I think about it," Kepler said, rubbing his chin as if in thought, "it's really not that big a deal — as long as it isn't *our* blood."

He stared at Maker furiously, clearly telegraphing his intent. "Get him!" he screamed.

All four rushed at Maker, who by this time had lathered himself up enough to have a nice sheet of foam coating his body. He reacted immediately to their charge by reaching for the showerhead and pulling it down, pointing it so that it faced his foes.

The showerhead sensor, detecting a body in front of it, suddenly came on at full blast. It shot a powerful stream of scalding hot water directly into the scowling mug of Tagalong 1, who went down screaming and clutching at his face.

Maker smiled to himself. When he had worked the shower controls earlier, he'd done more than tell it to give him soap; he'd also put the water temperature well into the boiling range.

Kepler tripped over his fallen friend and went down as well. Oddly enough, it probably kept him from being put out of commission, because Maker next aimed the showerhead in his direction. Being face down on the ground, however, it was his back that ended up getting doused rather than his face. His clothing gave him some protection, but not enough, as evidenced by his screams of pain.

Maker then tried to spray the two remaining attackers as well. Tagalong 2, however — showing more presence of mind than Maker would have given him credit for — had changed tactics. Immediately recognizing the threat, he had headed for the control pad, and — while Kepler and Tagalong 1 were still on the ground — slapped it with his palm. The water turned off.

Meanwhile, Bear, who had been in the rear of the charge, had agilely leaped over the two on the ground. Maker attempted to throw the showerhead at him, but almost the second he released it, the tension in the retractable hose pulled it back into its mount on the wall. (Maker did note, with more than a smidgen of satisfaction, that it smacked Tagalong 2 on the cheek as it went by, slicing it open. Tagalong 2 screeched, wincing in pain as he raised a hand to his injured jaw.)

Maker, meanwhile, found himself in the midst of a vicious hand-to-hand battle. Bear wasn't particularly quick and his technique was sloppy, but he was incredibly strong. Thus, while Maker was able to evade and block almost with ease, the blows he landed had little effect other than evoking a mild groan from his opponent.

Still, the fight almost ended prematurely when Maker, after landing a solid blow to his adversary's midsection, found that Bear had grasped his forearm before he could pull it back. However, still covered in soapy foam, Maker was able to slip out of the big man's powerful grip. When it happened a second time a few moments later, Maker caught on: Bear was deliberately leaving himself open, hoping Maker would take the bait and go for a blow that would allow Bear to get his hands on his smaller opponent.

What the larger man hadn't counted on, however, was Maker smearing himself with a particularly slick cleanser. There was no way Bear could get a firm grip on him. However, the soap would eventually dry, and then…

Suddenly Maker saw movement with his peripheral vision. It was Tagalong 2, whom Maker had almost forgotten about. He rushed in from the left side, almost tackling Maker.

As he struggled with this new opponent, pain exploded in Maker's right side like a land mine going off, and he immediately identified the source. Grappling with Tagalong 2 had left him open to Bear, who had deftly landed a punch just below Maker's ribcage. All of the air went rushing out of his body, and with it, much of his stamina. He stayed on his feet, but just barely.

Using both hands, Tagalong 2 got a firm grip on Maker's left arm; in addition, his right wrist was being held by Bear, who lifted it, thereby raising Maker's entire right arm. This was, presumably, so that the big man could land another blow in the same place on Maker's side as before, like a boxer working the same spot on an opponent.

Bear pulled back his free hand; just as he began to throw the punch, Maker let all of his weight drop. He went down, sliding towards the shower floor. There was a slight hesitation as his adversaries tried to retain their respective holds on him, but then he slipped completely out of their grasps. Even so, he didn't escape completely unharmed: Bear's swing grazed the side of his head painfully as he went down, much like the showerhead had hit Tagalong 2 in passing.

TERMINUS

The big man's meaty fist hit the wall with a sound like a sledgehammer, echoing through the showers as it smashed the tile. Bear howled, cradling his injured hand.

Still on the floor, Maker knew better than to waste an opportunity. He swung his arm as hard as he could, swiping Bear's legs out from under him. The larger man landed on his back, his head smacking against the floor like two bricks being used as cymbals.

Maker was fully in motion almost before Bear hit the ground. Ignoring the pain in his side, he drew his legs under him and lunged up at Tagalong 2, who still hadn't seemed to process what had happened. Maker hit him with an uppercut square on the chin; the man's head snapped back, and he went down.

Sensing motion next to him, Maker turned and was surprised to see Bear slowly starting to raise himself up. Maker dropped onto the man's chest, which elicited a grunt of pain and caused him to collapse back down. Straddling his opponent, Maker placed his hands on both sides of the man's head, lifted, and then smashed it back down onto the shower floor — twice.

Convinced that Bear was now unconscious, Maker let out a deep breath. He was exhausted and in pain. Still, he didn't think anything was broken and was about to rise when suddenly there was humming all around him — a weird vibration that made the very air seem to quiver. It was a sound Maker immediately recognized.

Maker threw himself to his right, rolling as fast as he could and staying as low as possible. As he went into motion, he felt the air shiver madly as something passed through the spot where he had been astride Bear just a moment earlier. He came up into a fighting stance, facing Kepler.

In all honesty, Maker had practically forgotten about the man, who had instigated this entire mess. Apparently Kepler had recovered. More to the point, he now held a vibro-blade. Oscillating at a rate almost too fast to be seen, it was a formidable weapon in the right hands. You'd have a difficult time using it against someone in Marine armor, but the weapon could slice through flesh and bone like it was ice cream.

"You..." Kepler hissed with murder plainly in his eyes. "I'm going to slice you up into so many pieces that it's going to look like you swallowed a grenade."

Kepler kept talking, a torrent of abuse and idle threats pouring from him as he moved in on his prey, occasionally taking a swipe with his weapon. On his part, Maker ignored the man's words, focusing instead on the blade and how Kepler handled it, as well as staying out of his opponent's reach.

One of the first things he noticed was that Kepler was moving slowly, stiffly. He didn't seem capable of extending as far as he should with the blade. *Of course! His back!* The scalding water had burned him to some degree, so not only was he stiff and less mobile, but he was probably in pain as well.

Unobtrusively, Maker slid his right hand slowly down his side, gathering the soapy foam in his palm. Steeling himself, he stepped forward, the move catching his adversary somewhat by surprise.

Maker flicked his right hand towards Kepler's face, and then took a skittish hop backwards as his opponent swung the blade at him and missed. He had been aiming for Kepler's eyes, but foam isn't known for its adhesive or kinetic properties. It basically flew apart as it left his hand, most of it going wide and missing Kepler altogether. Some of it went into his hair, and a bit got on his shirt.

One speck, however, came close. It didn't go in Kepler's eyes, but it did hit the bridge of his nose, spattering into tiny motes that went flying to either side. Kepler reacted instinctively, automatically closing his eyes. It wasn't perfect, but it was the opening Maker had been looking for. He moved in.

Kepler swung the vibro-blade wildly as he reached up to rub his eyes with his free hand. Maker avoided the weapon with ease, then gripped the wrist holding it. He brought his knee up and viciously slammed the wrist against it. Kepler screamed, releasing the blade.

Without a hand on the hilt, the vibrations ceased; the blade hit the ground like an ordinary knife. Maker kicked it to the other end of the shower, well out of reach. Releasing the wrist he still held, Maker kicked the back of Kepler's legs, sending the man down to his knees. Kepler attempted to turn and Maker chopped him on the back of the neck with the edge of his palm. Kepler fell face forward and didn't move.

Maker looked around warily; all four of his opponents were still out. (Actually, Tagalong 1 was moaning and shaking all over — clearly in pain but apparently conscious. However, one look at his face — which was red, swollen, blistered, and peeling — and there was little concern that he was likely to present a problem.)

Maker headed towards the shower exit, stopping to pick up the vibro-blade. Now that he could examine it without fear of the business end finding its way inside

83

him, he was very impressed. It was a late-model version, high-end, too. (It probably cost a month's salary.) Well-made, well-balanced, constructed of the finest material — an excellent blade all the way around. And not only was it a new model, it was a new knife (as in recently purchased). In fact, Maker wouldn't have been surprised to find out that Kepler had gone out and bought this knife just for him.

The power-switch on the blade's guard was still in the "On" position. However, as it was designed only to operate when being held, the only way it would become live again would be if it were turned off and then back on again, or…

Holding it in his palm, he gave the hilt a firm squeeze. Almost immediately, it began vibrating, as it had done for Kepler just moments earlier. Maker smiled, then switched the blade off. Glancing back, he saw that Kepler had rolled over and was staring at him.

"Thanks for the knife," Maker said over his shoulder as he left. "If you get any more new toys you want me to have, you know where to find me."

Chapter 10

Taking the bus from the gym to the VOQ, Maker made it back to his room without incident. His one pit stop consisted of popping into the gift shop to purchase some meal bars for himself and Erlen, since he hadn't really given any thought to breakfast.

He ate two of the bars on the way up to the room. Once inside, he tossed two of them to Erlen, who had been patiently staring at the door when he came in.

"There you go," Maker said. "A full meal, including all the necessary vitamins and nutrients, in one tiny package."

The bars were still wrapped, but he knew that the Niotan would have fun getting the covering off. With his companion eating, Maker went into the bedroom and began to change clothes.

He grimaced slightly as he pulled off his PT shirt, grunting softly in pain. He looked at the spot where Bear had hit him. The area was red and angry, but the skin wasn't broken, thankfully.

A mewling from the door caught his attention, and he looked up to find Erlen there.

"I'm fine," Maker said as the Niotan padded over to him. "I said I'm fine. I'll be good as new by the end of the day."

Erlen ignored him, instead rearing up and inspecting the injury like a doctor. A second later, he pressed his muzzle to the area.

"Hey!" Maker shouted. "Either your nose is cold and wet or you just licked me!"

Erlen, seemingly deaf to anything being said to him, stalked back into the living room and, from the sound of it, began working on the bar wrapping again.

Maker looked at his injury once more, touching it gingerly. A moment later, he went back to getting dressed.

****

Adames was sitting at a table, looking at his p-comp, when Maker came in, Erlen right beside him. He was far less than happy with what he'd been viewing and it showed on his face.

"Your first day on the job as an el-tee and you show up late," he said, suddenly smiling and coming to his feet. "I'd say you're getting the hang of being an officer just fine."

"Well, if officers actually did any work, NCOs would be out of a job," Maker replied with a grin. "Now, I saw that look on your face when I came in. What's the problem? My requisition list?"

"I told you that's fine," Adames said dismissively. "I've got that under control."

"Then what — the facilities?"

Maker glanced around. They'd been given the use of some deserted buildings in a little-used training area on the base. They were in the main structure now, which housed about a dozen rooms, most of which had previously been used as offices. In fact, the room they were in now was part of the former commander's suite, with a couple of well-used desks and chairs.

"No," Adames said, shaking his head. "It's fairly run-down — nobody's probably been out here in a decade — but considering we'll only be here for a few days, it should be fine."

"Well, there's only one thing left," Maker said, taking a seat at one of the desks. "You don't like my roster."

"Bingo." Adames went back to looking at his p-comp, scanning the information. "Look, Gant, if I'm being honest, I just don't know what you're thinking. I was so thrown off by the first few that I didn't even finish reading all of them. I mean, we can have any crew we want according to you, and you pick *these* guys?"

"Well, tell me what's wrong with them."

"What's wrong with them? Well, for starters, one of them sounds like a total psycho, another one seems completely unstable — and that's on a good day. And this guy..." Adames stared at the screen in almost disbelief. "It says that he's an Augman. What the hell's an Augmented Man doing in the military?"

"You'll have to ask him."

"You bet I will," Adames said matter-of-factly. He tapped the p-comp monitor and the screen went dark. He looked at Maker. "Well, they're all supposed to be in the briefing room at the other end of the building. How do you want to play it?"

"I don't know," Maker said, drumming his fingers. "Let's just try it the way we always wished officers did it with us."

"What, straight?" Adames asked, a little surprised. Then he shrugged. "Couldn't hurt. How long?"

"Give me five or ten minutes."

"Sounds fine," Adames said. He turned and left the room.

TERMINUS

Once in the hallway, Adames quickly walked the thirty yards to the other end of the building where the briefing room was located. En route, he thought about the briefing Maker was going to give to their new recruits in just a few minutes.

Commanders often selected a theme when addressing the troops on a new mission. Some might appeal to your patriotism. Others might try to make you feel special for being selected. Still more might lay claim to your sense of loyalty by telling you that your fellow soldiers were counting on you. Playing it "straight," however, meant being honest and direct, with little embellishment.

Adames was still thinking about that when he found himself nearing the entrance to the briefing room. The door slid open automatically as he approached, and he stepped in.

The room was about ten by twenty feet in size, with most of the space occupied by a huge conference room table. There were four people inside — two men and two women. Adames frowned in distaste; there should have been five of them. Top of the morning on Day 1, and somebody was already AWOL.

Three of the room's occupants, the two women and one of the men, were seated at the table. They all came to their feet as Adames entered.

"Carry on," Adames said, and the three sat back down. Looking them over quickly, he saw that the first woman was a petite sergeant who had her brown hair done up in a ponytail. She had a slightly pinched nose and high cheeks that, in combination, would probably have been quite appealing. However, Adams couldn't tell because the most prominent feature on her face was a pair of goggles comprised of a tinted circular lens set in a metal frame over each eye.

The man seated next to her was an imposing figure. Noting his stature when the man had stood, Adames pegged him at well over seven feet in height. He wore military fatigues, like everyone else in the room, but they appeared stretched to the limit by the man's incredibly muscular body.

This, then, was the Augman. Like everyone else in his genetically-engineered strain, his face was a horror: mad, bushy eyebrows; round, bulging eyes; a nose like an overripe banana; and a mouth full of razor-sharp teeth that looked like they'd be better-suited for a jaguar. Upon closer inspection, Adames noticed that the man wore a caduceus symbol on his uniform shirt, prompting a recollection that the Augman was actually a medical doctor.

Sitting on the other side of the table, across from the first two, was the second woman. She had incredibly pale skin, with onyx nails and ebony eyes. Her hair, cropped closely on the sides but long and flowing in the middle, was as dark as a starless night. All in all, the remarkable contrast in her countenance — between light and dark, black and white — gave her an almost exotic appearance. She would probably have been considered beautiful, were it not for a perpetual scowl that seemed frozen on her face.

The second man was a slim, boyish-looking fellow of average height and looks. He was already on his feet when Adames entered, so intent on looking through a trash can at the back of the room that he almost missed the fact that someone had come in.

"What are you doing?" Adames asked him. "Looking for something to eat?"

"No, Sergeant," the man replied, apparently struggling not to grin.

Adames gave him a harsh stare before finally saying, "Take your seat."

The man headed to the conference table, plainly intent on taking a seat next to the pale woman. An intense glare from her froze him in his tracks. He almost seemed to wilt under her gaze. A second later, he seemed to change his mind with respect to the seat he preferred, instead choosing to move down one spot, leaving an empty chair between them.

"Sound off," Adames commanded a moment later.

"E-4 Edison Wayne," said the young man who had been looking in the trash can. "Engineering."

As Adames had suspected, the fellow was young. Based on his rank, E-4, he'd only been in the service a few years.

There was a time in the distant past when ranks below that of sergeant actually had names — things like airman, corporal, and such, depending of the branch of military service you were in. However, when human beings finally decided to stop squabbling among themselves and show one face to the universe as they ventured farther into space, they had merged their various fighting forces.

That said, some military traditions (including the rank structure) went back thousands of years, and no service was willing to readily give that up. Thus, it was decided that enlisted members would only be ranked by letter and number until promoted to sergeant (E-5). It wasn't a perfect system, but it beat trying to incorporate a hundred different names for the same position.

"Sergeant Isis Bronwyn Diviana," said the woman with the exotic countenance, cutting off Adames' thoughts. "Intel."

Everyone looked at her, expecting more detail. "Intel" was a catchall phrase that was used to encompass a number of disciplines, both open and clandestine. It covered everything from analysis to spying to assassination.

After a few seconds, it became clear that Diviana was not going to offer any more information about her expertise. That being the case, the woman in the goggles spoke next. "Staff Sergeant Luna Loyola," she announced.

"Hold on," Adames ordered before Loyola could state her specialty. "Take that eyewear off. I want to see who I'm talking to."

Adames couldn't read her expression, but the woman's demeanor seemed to change. She suddenly seemed to be unsure of herself in some way, nervous. However, the feeling apparently passed, because the next second she reached up, grabbed her goggles, and lifted them up so they rested on her forehead. There was a harsh intake of breath from Diviana, who was sitting across from her; Wayne, also on the other side of the table, looked as though he was about to lose his lunch.

Loyola turned her face directly towards Adames, whose jaw almost fell open. Sitting where her eyes should have been were two dark, sunken cavities. It was as if her eyeballs had simply dissolved.

The sockets were not totally empty, however. In each was a circular piece of reflective material — some weird amalgam of metal and glass — that seemed to be held in place by almost invisible bits of metal thread that connected to the holes where her eyes should have been.

"Holy *caca*!" Adames screamed, practically in shock. "What the hell happened to your eyes?!"

"Premature detonation of a shaped charge," the woman replied. "It destroyed a good chunk of my face, not just my eyes. They were able to reconstruct almost everything, although a large portion of my skull is metal — as well as some other hardware — and a lot of the skin on my face was grown and grafted."

"But...your eyes," Wayne said, still looking sick but no longer on the verge of heaving his guts out. "Why didn't you get new ones?"

It was the Augman who answered, his voice a deep baritone. "In a very small percentage of the population," he said, "new organs are occasionally rejected by the host body — even when grown from cultures of the host's tissue."

"And I was lucky enough to be in that small pool of lottery winners," Loyola said.

"So, you're blind?" Adames asked.

Loyola pulled her goggles back down over her eyes. "Yes and no," she answered. "I can't see the way you do, but the synthetic alloy in my sockets acts as a kind of artificial oculus."

"How does it work?" Wayne asked.

Again, it was the Augman who answered the question. "In simple terms, it reads electromagnetic waves — like light. When those waves strike an object, a number of things can happen. They can be absorbed, reflected, what have you."

"My oculi observe what happens to the waves," Loyola said, "and a computer chip in here" — she tapped the side of her head with a forefinger — "interprets that data and sends an image to my brain."

"So it's like a visual version of radar or sonar," Wayne concluded.

"In essence," Loyola agreed.

"Alright, now that we've satisfied everyone's morbid curiosity about your eyes, why don't you tell us your specialty?" Adames asked.

"Precision weapons and tactics," Loyola replied. "Primarily long-range marksmanship combined with apatetic dissimulation."

Adames frowned, letting her words roll around in his head, and then his eyes bulged as realization hit.

"You're a sniper?" he asked incredulously.

"I prefer the term markswoman," Loyola said somewhat mischievously, causing the Augmented Man to briefly give a barely-noticeable grin.

"Okay, what's your story?" Adames asked him.

All eyes turned towards the Augman, who shifted uncomfortably in his seat under the attention.

"I'm an experienced physician, newly commissioned as a warrant officer," he said. "My name is Batch Four-Seven-Two-Five Locus Deoxyribonucleic…"

Adames' eyes almost glazed over as the Augmented Man spouted what sounded like a continuous stream of scientific jargon for about thirty seconds.

"Wait a second," Adames said when the Augman finally finished speaking. "That's your name?"

"Yes," the Augman replied. "Even though Augmented Men are officially citizens and genetically classified as human beings, we are — for cognominal purposes — required by law to be identified by our autochthonous ancestor and the original genetic material from which he was created."

"What?" Adames asked, his brow creasing as he attempted to process what he'd just heard.

"His name tells you which of the original Augmen he's descended from," Loyola said. "It identifies the batch of genetic stock used, the DNA sequence that was targeted, the molecular recombination—"

"Alright, alright," Adames said, cutting her off. He shifted his gaze back to the Augman, noting for the first time that the fellow didn't have a nametag. "So what do they call you?"

The Augman looked unsure of himself for a moment. He cleared his throat, and then replied, "Batch Four-Seven-Two-Five Lo—"

"Stop," Adames said, raising a hand palm-outward. No wonder the guy didn't have a nametag; with a moniker like that, it would cover the entire front of his uniform.

"I'm not going to rip my tongue to shreds trying to say your name every time I want to talk to you," Adames continued. "You're getting a call sign."

Adames frowned in concentration for a moment, trying to think of something appropriate. The problem with Augmen was that their nature was completely contrary to their intended purpose. With almost superhuman strength and incredible stamina, they were created to be super-soldiers, bred for battle. Moreover, their faces were intentionally made to be monstrous so as to terrify the enemy.

Unfortunately, despite their physical gifts and basically being born to kill, there was one problem with these genetically-engineered warriors that no one could have predicted: Augmen refused to fight. They rejected combat and war in all forms, on all levels. Some flaw in their DNA coding made them all pacifists. Furthermore, it didn't matter what kind of environment that they were raised or nurtured in — whether warm and loving or harsh and brutal, the end result was the same: no Augmented Man would embrace physical violence — not even to save his own life.

All of which was a shame, Adames thought, as he looked at the Augman seated in front of him. Just that face alone was completely intimidating...

And just like that, it hit him. "From now on," Adames said with a smile, "your call sign is 'Fierce.' You're Fierce Augman from this day forward."

"Fierce," clearly not taken with his new moniker, started to sulk and was on the verge of making his displeasure known when one of his new squad mates spoke up.

"Hey, that's not fair," Wayne said. "If he gets a call sign, I want one, too."

Adames rolled his eyes in exasperation. "Look, our medic gets a call sign because I'm not going to spend all day saying his name every time I want his attention," he said. "Moving on, does anyone know where your missing squad member is?"

There was silence as the four people sitting at the table exchanged glances, almost daring one another to speak.

"Still in the barracks," Wayne said after a moment. "He mentioned something about unearned deference — that he needed the situation resolved before he reported for duty."

95

"We'll deal with him later," Adames said, suddenly feeling vexed. "For now, listen up. I'm Master Sergeant Hector Adames. You've all been selected as part of a special squad being led by Lieutenant Arrogant Maker. He is your new commanding officer, but make no mistake. For all intents and purposes, I'm in charge of you clowns for the foreseeable future, and that includes keeping you alive. The el-tee will be in here shortly to brief you on the—"

Adames stopped in mid-sentence as the door to the briefing room slid open and Maker stepped in, accompanied by Erlen.

Adames snapped to attention. "Room, ten-hut!" he bellowed.

The four people at the table all jumped up, coming to attention.

"As you were," Maker said, coming over to stand next to Adames, who went from standing at attention to parade rest, with his hands behind his back. The four Marines at the table all sat back down.

"For those of you who don't know me, I'm Lieutenant Arrogant Maker," he said. He pointed to the Niotan. "This is Erlen. He's not a pet, so if you value your health don't treat him like one.

"Now, some of you may have heard of me, or heard me referred to as Madman Maker or Maniac Maker. You may have also been privy to certain stories about me. Whatever you heard, you are free to assume that it's true. I don't care what people say about me. I don't care what tales you've heard about me. I don't care what you think you know about me. All I care about is the mission, and if you make that your priority, you and I will get along just fine.

"As to what that mission is, we are ostensibly being dispatched to one of the Fringe Worlds. There's a hostile force there of unknown size that we're being asked to locate. Everything about the assignment is explained in greater detail in the official briefing, which has already been securely downloaded to your p-comps. Any questions?"

Silence reigned for a moment. Marines always had questions after a mission briefing; the issue was whether anyone would be bold enough to actually ask them.

It was Diviana who finally spoke up. "Just one: why us?"

Maker seemed to reflect on the question for a moment before responding.

"All of you have had problems adjusting to life in the service," he said, "despite, on average, being in the military for several years. Whether it be gross insubordination, almost killing members of your own units, or some other reason, you've shown an inability to fit in. That said, you've got skills — all of you — and if anyone can find a way to make use of those talents, it's the Marines. Trust me on this, I'm a prime example.

"As I said, some of you may have heard my story. If you haven't, you will, so I won't bother telling it. But the long and short of it is that I've had my own issues adjusting, so you're in good company. Moreover, with me, you get a clean slate. Nobody's past follows them here. But make no mistake: you're Marines, and I'll expect you to act like it. I can't promise you fame. I can't promise you fortune. I can't even promise you that you'll survive the first few minutes of this mission. But what I can and will promise is that I will always be in your corner, and I will always be looking out for you to the best of my ability."

With that, Maker turned and left the room, Erlen dogging his heels. Adames called the room to attention as he left, then went to at ease as the door slid shut.

"Alright, you all heard the el-tee," Adames said. "You've got the mission briefing on your p-comps. It will purge itself from your computer systems in three hours. I would suggest you use that time — and this room — to get extremely intimate with the details of our task and your roles in it."

Satisfied that everyone knew what they had to do, Adames promptly departed.

Chapter 11

Silence reigned in the briefing room for about two minutes after Adames' exit, with all four of those at the table studiously looking over the information on their p-comps.

"So what happens if we finish the briefing before the three hours is up?" Wayne suddenly asked of no one in particular.

At first it seemed that his question would go unanswered, but then — without looking up from her p-comp — Diviana responded. "Since this is the only time you'll have access to the mission specifics, I'd suggest you use any extra time to review them twice."

"And if we still finish early?" Wayne asked, before meekly adding, "I'm typically a quick study."

"Have at it a third time," Diviana said.

"And if there's still time on the clock?"

Diviana irritably jerked her head in his direction, giving Wayne an unusual look — a weird mixture of exasperation and incredulity.

"Sorry," Wayne said, withering under her glare. "I was just trying to be sociable."

Diviana let out a sigh of frustration.

"Maybe he's right," Loyola chimed in. "If we're going to be working together, maybe we should break the ice." She pushed her p-comp slightly away from her on the tabletop, then turned in Wayne's direction. "Where are you from?"

"Frugulon III," Wayne answered, as if it were the most popular destination in the universe.

Loyola made an odd gesture — shrugging her shoulders while turning her palms outward and slightly tilting her head — which seemed to convey both the sentiment of that's-all-you-can-say-about-it? as well as never-heard-of-it.

"It's a high utility outpost," Wayne went on. "We have long-term contractual arrangements with various partners that allow us access to merchandise and commodities that others have mis-appraised in terms of fiscal worth."

Both Loyola and the newly-named Fierce frowned, obviously trying to find meaning behind Wayne's words. Diviana, on the other hand, chuckled in derision.

"It's a trash world," Diviana declared. "Other planets pay you to dump their rubbish on your doorstep, which you then dig through to try to find things worth salvaging. You're nothing but galactic garbage men."

"No," Wayne said defensively. "We're a planet that has developed the ability to extract value from things that most people overlook."

"At least now we understand why you were looking in the trash bin when Sergeant Adames came in," Fierce said. "How'd you end up here?"

"That's easy enough," Wayne said. "Some of the most salvageable items we ever found on my homeworld were military cast-offs — things the Marines, Navy, and such had gotten rid of for some reason. I figured that enlisting was a great way to find out about the process employed when the services decide to scrap a product — and maybe develop some contacts, so that when I got out I'd have a pipeline and first dibs on anything the military discarded."

"No," Fierce said, shaking his head. "I mean, how'd you end up *here*, with us? The lieutenant said that everybody here has had issues, trouble fitting in. What landed you here?"

Wayne seemed to reflect for a moment, then took a deep breath and began speaking. "There was a guy in my prior unit with sticky fingers. He developed a nasty habit of taking things that didn't belong to him. Not just personal things, like snacks and medicine, but also things you needed to do your job — tools and such.

"I'm very good at improvising, building something out of nothing. Where I come from, we all are. I rigged my footlocker with an aerosol-jet that I built from things lying around the barracks. It sprayed a chemical agent into the thief's face the next time he tried to steal from me and he almost died as a result."

"So, you're the one the el-tee mentioned who almost killed a member of his own unit," Loyola noted.

"Hey, if I'd wanted him dead, he'd *be* dead," Wayne said defensively. He rubbed his eyes with his thumb and middle finger before going on. "The spray only contained some chemical irritants — just something to make his skin itch like crazy, maybe give him a coughing fit if any got into his mouth. He ended up having an extreme allergic reaction it. Among other things, his lungs seized up and his throat constricted."

"But you said he survived, right?" Fierce asked.

"Ultimately, he spent about two weeks in the hospital," Wayne answered. "Because it wasn't intentional, my superiors were willing to overlook the incident, as long as I promised never to jury-rig anything else."

"What did you say?" Loyola asked.

"What could I say?" Wayne responded. "Tinkering with crap is part of who I am. What they wanted was the same as asking me to cut off my arm or give myself a lobotomy. I refused, so I got a letter of reprimand in my file and was removed from all duties. Until now."

There was silence for a moment, and then Loyola spoke up. "Well, I'm more than happy to keep things rolling, although it's not hard to guess how I got here. A soldier with no eyes who insists on firing a weapon — I turned down the offer of a desk job — is bound to have problems being accepted."

"And you?" Wayne said, looking at Fierce. "What lands you in this sideshow?"

"I would think it was obvious," the Augmented Man said. "I'm a soldier who refuses to fight or kill."

"It certainly ranks way up there as an odd career choice," Wayne said. "I'd take your guidance counselor off the Christmas list if I were you."

That got a chuckle out of Loyola and a short-lived smile from Fierce. All eyes then swiveled towards Diviana, who didn't seem particularly eager to open up.

"Alright," she finally said after a pregnant pause. "My story is pretty straightforward. I was part of a special unit. On our last mission, everybody died except me."

Diviana spoke with a sense of finality, as if there were nothing more to say on the subject. Wayne, however, didn't seem to be satisfied.

"That can't be all," he said skeptically. "That's not enough to earn you a place with this crew."

Diviana scowled, clearly not comfortable saying more than she already had.

"It's okay," Loyola said empathetically, in a woman-to-woman tone. "We're going to be trusting our lives to one another in the field. Surely that merits a little faith in here."

Diviana merely stared at her for a moment, and then let out a ragged sigh. "My shields collapsed in the middle of the mission."

"Your shields?" Loyola repeated. "You mean like on some kind of armor?"

"No," Diviana said, shaking her head. She then tapped her temple with a forefinger. "My *mental* shields. I usually keep a strong buffer between my mind and those of other people, but on that occasion it failed."

It took a moment for her words to sink in with her companions, then Wayne almost jumped out of his seat.

"Wait a minute," he said, eyes bulging. "Are you saying you're psychic? That you can read minds?"

"You don't have to be a mind reader to know what you're thinking every time you look at her," Loyola said.

Wayne began to visibly turn red. "That's not..." he sputtered. "No...I mean, I'd never..."

Loyola laughed. "Take it easy, tiger. I was just joking."

Wayne appeared somewhat relieved, although he still looked a bit flushed.

"No, I'm not really psychic," Diviana said, getting the conversation back on track. "I don't read minds. However, I *can* sense thoughts."

"What do you mean?" Fierce asked.

"I don't know what they're thinking, but I can detect the presence of other people by their thoughts," Diviana said. "It's a lot like hearing someone speak outside a room that you're in. You can't see the person, and their speech is muffled so that it's just sounds rather than distinct words you can pick out. However, you know there's someone out there, and even if they move you have an idea of where they are, as long as they keep talking."

"So basically, no one can sneak up on you," Wayne said.

"That's one effect," Diviana agreed. "It helped during the first phase of my career in Intel, which basically consisted of data gathering and compilation — usually in a person-to-person format."

"Espionage?" Fierce asked. "You were a spy?"

Diviana shrugged. "More or less. But — when my superiors found out what I could do — I was transferred to a different unit. At that juncture, my talents became a critical part of my new job — to keep others from sneaking up on us out in the field."

"You said it was *part* of your job," Loyola noted. "What was the other part?"

Diviana looked down, preferring to stare at the table rather than meet anyone's eyes, as if ashamed of what she was about to say. "In addition to my own personal buffer, I also have the ability to project mental shields around other people — their minds, rather. That was the other part of my job. And because of my particular skill set, I was part of a unit that took on 'special' assignments that involved a high level of interaction with opposing forces.

"We were highly successful for the most part. I could pinpoint the location of enemy combatants, giving us a tremendous advantage in almost any engagement. I suppose, in the end, we started getting cocky, which in turn led to us getting sloppy — me included. On our last mission, my shields — the ones around my own mind — just seemed to snap."

"Snap?" Wayne asked. "Snap how?"

"Snap's probably the wrong word," Diviana said. "It's more like they just dissolved. One second they were there, and the next — poof. Without my shields…"

Diviana trailed off, lost in thought. After a few seconds she blinked, and then continued.

"You have to understand," she said. "I don't just sense thoughts; I feel them. It's like walking through a crowd and continuously getting bumped by other people — sometimes lightly, sometimes forcefully. Without my shields, eventually I get knocked down, mentally trampled.

"When my shields vanished, it was a shock, almost like losing a limb. But what came over the next few minutes was worse. The rest of my unit was killed…and I felt every one of their deaths."

There was silence for a moment, and then Loyola, her brow furrowed, asked, "Felt them how?"

Diviana seemed to reflect for a moment before responding. "When I shield another person mentally, it's not so much that I put a protective coating around them, but more like I take them into the shelter of my own mind. Being that close, I sense a lot of things that the person does, even though I don't know what they're thinking. So, on that last mission, when the others in my unit started dying…"

"You felt it," Fierce finished, a moment after she trailed off.

Diviana nodded, eyes watery and looking almost forlorn. "My squad basically walked into a trap. I survived, but experiencing their deaths — *feeling* them intimately — unhinged me, so to speak. I spent most of my time after that crying, with barely enough energy to move, constantly trying to forget.

"It took me a long time to become functional again, emotionally stable. It was at that point that I realized what had affected my shields — another psychic. From that moment forward, I focused solely on one thing: making them pay. To be honest, it was the thought of going after them that really gave me the strength to pull myself back together. But by that time, I had been a shambling wreck for so long that I wasn't considered fit for field work — or anything else for that matter. It just seemed like a matter of time before the military shuffled me out the door."

"Then fate intervened, and you found yourself here," Fierce said. "With a clean slate and a new mission."

"So it would seem," Diviana said.

"Speaking of our mission," Wayne said, leaning in conspiratorially, "isn't anyone going to address the elephant in the room?"

His three companions looked at one another, exchanging silent glances, then back at him.

"Oh, come on!" Wayne cried. "Lieutenant Maker! *Madman* Maker!"

"What about him?" Fierce asked. "I'm genuinely in the dark, as I've never cared for military matters or kept abreast of them."

"They say he killed his entire squad on his last mission," Wayne said. "But not just that — the entire crew of the ship transporting him also died. They say he went crazy, did something during their last jump that basically wiped out every other living thing on their vessel. And that weird pet of his? Word throughout the

Corps is that he smuggled it back illegally from a quarantined world a few years back. You can probably pick up something contagious just from being around that thing."

Fierce chuckled at that, an almost frightening series of grunt-like noises. "I can almost assure you that isn't the case. I'm a doctor and familiar enough with infectious disease protocols to know that the lieutenant's 'pet' as you called it, wouldn't be here, on a vital military installation, if it posed any kind of biological threat. And, if it were contagious in some way, I'm sure we'd know by now since — as you said — he brought it back years ago."

"Be that as it may," Wayne said, "aren't you the least bit worried about serving under a commander whose last squad was completely wiped out?"

"Being a sole survivor," Diviana said, "as I can attest, is not evidence that you did anything wrong or lack leadership qualities."

"But still," Wayne insisted, "you've got to be concerned on some level."

There was silence for a moment, and then Loyola, apparently weary of the conversation, voiced her opinion.

"Let me enlighten you about something," she said to Wayne. "That man you're disparaging happens to be one of the most decorated Marines in the service. He's led more men on more missions and had more successes than you've ever dreamed of. Even more, prior to his last mission, he had a stellar reputation and a well-documented habit of bringing back his men both alive and intact.

"In short, you'd do better to listen and learn all you can from Arrogant Maker, because what he has to impart may one day save your life. And, if nothing else, you'll live out the rest of your days as a legend — one of the few Marines to have served under the infamous Madman Maker. As for me, I'm just thankful for the chance to be a real Marine again."

Chapter 12

"Somebody has a fan," Adames said with a smile, turning away from the holographic image of Loyola, who had just delivered an impassioned speech on behalf of Maker.

They were back in the offices they had occupied earlier, with Erlen dozing in a corner and Maker himself sitting once more behind a desk. He waved off Adames' comment, and then muted the volume on the display, although he kept the image showcased.

"Well, what do you think?" Maker asked. Ordinarily, they wouldn't have been spying — for lack of a better term — on their new recruits. Under normal circumstances, they would have tried to develop an understanding of their new unit organically, developing relationships with and an understanding of each individual in stages. However, they were pressed for time and needed to get an immediate idea of who these people were outside of what was in their files, as well as how they would get along.

Adames rubbed his chin in thought. "Well, let's take a tally. We have a blind sharpshooter, a genetically engineered killing machine who refuses to fight, a mentally unstable psychic, and a dumpster-diving engineer who rigs booby-traps in his spare time. I'd say we hit the jackpot — and that's before we even get to the fifth guy, who was a no-show."

"Yes, you mentioned that," Maker said, drumming his fingers on the desk. "He's still in the barracks?"

"That's what his new best buds say."

"Well, we'll deal with him shortly. As to these guys, let's get them outfitted with gear. We're off-planet in a few days."

"Yeah, it'll be like the Spaceship of Misfit Toys with this crew. And the Augman" — Adames pointed to the holographic image of the briefing room, where Fierce was now speaking — "is a mystery I'll never be able to get my arms around. I mean, what's he doing here?"

"I thought you were going to ask him."

"I was, but I got distracted and then you showed up. But I promise you, it will be the first question I pose the next time I see him."

Maker smiled. "So, you still haven't figured it out yet."

Adames looked confused. "Figured what out?"

"Well, Augmen in general aren't just conscientious objectors. They rally for peace on all fronts."

"Yeah, everybody knows that. They usually enter professions that promote universal harmony or some other crap like that — becoming doctors, goodwill ambassadors, tree huggers, etcetera."

"Exactly. They typically become dedicated to a cause or a service — for example, medicine or the environment. But the object of their devotion doesn't have to be an abstract concept. It can also be a person."

"A person?" Adames repeated, somewhat surprised. Then it came to him. "Loyola?"

"Exactly. Our Augman was the doctor who treated her injuries. He was also instrumental in developing the technique and apparatus to let her see again. He left his practice and entered the military on condition that he be allowed to serve with her."

"So he's here because he's committed to her." Adames scratched his temple. "Do you think he's in love with her?"

Maker shrugged. "Possibly. But would that be so strange? The law recognizes Augmen as human beings, despite their petri dish origins. They don't typically marry non-Augmen, but it's not unheard of. And at the moment, we have no idea of the depths of their relationship. We just know that where she goes, he goes."

Adames shook his head in disbelief. "This entire setup gets weirder by the second. Tell me again why, in the name of all that's holy, you would pick this particular crew when you could have a squad of decorated Marines under your command?"

Maker pondered the question for a moment before responding. "Because they're like me — people that the military was ready to wash its hands of, but who still have something to contribute."

"So," Adames said, "this is about second chances."

"Not just that. I didn't simply want another group of skilled, qualified soldiers. I wanted a unit that felt the need to be more than just competent, that had a reason to go above and beyond. I wanted people with a grudge, people with a chip on their shoulders. People with a burning desire to succeed at whatever they were tasked with. People who had something to prove."

"I see," Adames said, nodding. "Does that include me?"

Maker laughed. "Ask me again after we finish this mission."

Maker got up and headed towards the door.

"Where are you going?" Adames asked.

TERMINUS

"We're still short a man," Maker said. "I'm going to find out what's going on with our missing Marine."

Chapter 13

Maker didn't have any trouble finding his wayward Marine. The man was sitting cross-legged in the middle of the barracks when Maker entered, eyes closed, apparently meditating.

He was dressed in a sleeveless t-shirt and shorts. He had close-cropped blond hair and average, although not homely, features.

"Cano Snick," Maker almost shouted, saying the man's name as he closed the distance between them.

Snick's eyes, so blue as to be almost violet, snapped open at the mention of his name. He came to his feet almost immediately, his body seeming to gracefully unfold rather than rise as he stood up. Maker noted that he was slightly shorter than average, but well-muscled without being bulky.

"You were AWOL this morning, Marine," Maker continued, stopping a few feet from the man. "Care to explain why?"

Snick inclined his head slightly towards Maker before answering. "You are, I presume, the new commander?"

"*Your* new commanding officer, yes. And you still haven't answered my question."

"I assumed it would be better for us to interact here, rather than in front of the others."

"The others? You mean the other members of our unit?"

"Yes. They might have found it necessary to interfere with our interchange."

"Interchange?" Maker was confused.

113

"In my previous unit, the other soldiers saw fit to interfere with the interchange between me and the captain in charge."

"You mean they pulled you off your commanding officer after you jumped him."

Snick shook his head in a disapproving manner. "That is a far from accurate description. I challenged him, and the outcome was favorable to me."

"According to your file, you tried to kill him."

"Again, that is a mischaracterization."

"Regardless, it's what got you sidelined from any other duty until I came along and put you on my team. I'm trying to give you a fresh start, and your first official act is to be insubordinate."

"That was not my intent. However, I have reached the point where I can no longer take orders from questionable leadership."

Maker shook his head. "I'm not sure I follow you."

"Then I shall endeavor to explain," Snick said. "On my homeworld, we pride ourselves on our martial skills. Mastering hand-to-hand combat is considered an essential element of manhood. In fact, the most capable among us in the martial arts are those who become our leaders — first in our families, then our communities, and then our cities and so on."

Maker nodded in understanding. Humanity was a greatly fractured society and contained a lot of fringe elements. Compared to some other things Maker had experienced, electing leaders based on their martial arts skills seemed rather tame.

"In many instances, advancing requires that you challenge someone for their position," Snick continued.

"You mean fight them," Maker intuited.

"Yes. It is how we prove our worth."

"So what happens to the poor slob who's terrible at martial arts and never wins a fight?"

"It seldom happens that anyone goes a lifetime without at least one victory, but it has been known to happen. Such an individual would ordinarily live a life of great shame. The expectation is that they would go off-world, to some place where their stigma would be more bearable."

"Is that what happened to you? You joined the military to escape the alleged disgrace of some loss?"

A look of incredible fury passed across Snick's face, and his fist curled into tight balls so forcefully that Maker almost expected to see them bleed. But a second later the feeling obviously passed, as Snick's features returned to normal.

"That is not an unwarranted assumption, but it is incorrect," Snick said. "My father was a local leader — what you might call a mayor — with responsibility for a small city. Although young, I had risen up through the ranks, but to go any higher, I would have had to challenge him."

"What, fight your own father?!" Maker asked incredulously. "That's crazy!"

"Not on my planet. In fact, it's rather common, although fathers will often abdicate rather than fight their own children. Still, I didn't want to do it — especially since, in my family, no one ever steps down willingly. But if I didn't even issue the challenge…"

Snick let the sentence linger, but Maker picked up on his meaning. "If you didn't at least try, you'd be ashamed and disgraced."

Snick nodded. "So I joined the Marines. Enlisting kept me from having to fight my father, while at the same time allowing me to sidestep any humiliation in that I was becoming a soldier to improve my martial skills. That was something the people on my planet could understand."

"So how does that lead to you fighting your commanding officer?"

"I did not have a full understanding of how men become officers and leaders in the military. It is based less on skill and experience and centered more on training — having attended the proper classes and such. It amazes me that one can be appointed an officer with no practical background in terms of combat or battle."

"It does sound a little counterintuitive when you put it that way."

"On my world, only those whose mettle has been tested are deemed fit to lead. Those who are suspect are challenged. The end result is that you typically are only subordinate to someone who is a better combatant than you."

"I think I've got a fair understanding now of what led to the 'interchange' between you and your last commander."

"Then you also understand why I was not present earlier today when my new unit was ordered to assemble."

"Yes. You'll only follow a commander who can best you in combat. Someone who's proved himself your superior."

Snick smiled and inclined his head towards Maker. "So you really do understand." He reached down towards his waist, crossing his arms. He gripped the t-shirt, then pulled it up over his head.

"If that's the way it has to be," Maker said with a sigh. A moment later, he had stripped down to the waist as well. He slid into a fighting stance, facing Snick.

"Let's dance," Maker said.

Chapter 14

"What the hell happened to you?" Adames asked, staring at Maker's puffy right eye and swollen lips. He had just come back into their office suite to find Maker flipping through a file on his p-comp and looking like he'd just been mugged.

"If you think I look bad, you should see the other guy," Maker answered.

"Well, I hope you took something for the swelling. We can't have the guy in charge looking like he's been in a drunken brawl."

"I did. You'll be looking at my normal mug in almost no time. By the way, I had a talk with our missing soldier, Cano Snick."

"Oh?" Adames raised an eyebrow.

"Let's just say he won't be AWOL at any point in the future."

Adames looked at him slightly askance, feeling that there was more that Maker wasn't saying, but merely nodded before changing the subject. "Anyway, our team's all geared up, and the off-menu items you ordered will be here and loaded onto the ship by the time we're ready to leave. Truth be told, though, I'd prefer to have more time to get our squad functioning together. We will be far from being a well-oiled machine when we reach Terminus."

"I know," Maker agreed. "But time is a luxury we don't have. I'm betting the Vacra will only be there long enough to make repairs. Our allies, who they've ordered equipment from, can only stall for so long. It's already been a month. It'll be a miracle if they aren't suspicious already."

"Well, the place *is* situated in the Beyond. It's not like ordering takeout from a place right next door."

"True, but I don't want to give them a reason to get their guard up."

Adames went silent for a moment. "Gant, these things that we're going after," he said solemnly, "from everything you've said, they're some vicious little buggers. Do we really know what we're getting into?"

"No, not in the least," Maker said, shaking his head. "But when has that ever stopped a Marine from doing his job?"

TERMINUS

Chapter 15

The next few days passed without incident for the most part. Leaving any issues related to their new squad in Adames' hands, Maker devoted most of his time to studying Terminus — its geography, terrain, etc. — in preparation for their mission. Thus, it wasn't until he was actually entering the ship that would carry them to the Fringe, the *Mantis Wing*, that he realized with a shock that he'd have more to contend with on this tour of duty than just the mission.

The *Mantis* itself was an aging but well-maintained Navy vessel. It had impressive speed but also formidable firepower, making it both an offensive and a defensive weapon.

Upon boarding, Maker — with Erlen at his side, as always — was introduced (as a courtesy), to the ship's officers. Starting with the captain, a hardened lifer named Ward Henry (better known as "Warhorse"), he shook their hands one by one, going next to the first mate, and so on.

Of course, the ship's officers hadn't assembled for Maker's benefit — not with him being a lowly lieutenant. They had turned out for Browing, who was returning to Terminus on the same ship and whose political position (or connections) apparently afforded him some standing. Maker, officially listed as a member of Browing's retinue, recognized that he was simply being given a minor bit of deference as a part of the politico's entourage.

Anyway, it was there, near the end of the line of officers Maker was glad-handing like he was trying to get elected for something, that he came across someone he'd practically put out of his mind: Mr. Shank-you-in-the-shower himself, Lieutenant Kepler.

Maker hid his surprise well, shaking Kepler's hand is if running into him were a pleasure. Inwardly, however, he cursed his bad luck. What were the odds that he'd end up on a ship with a guy who wanted him dead? Oh well, maybe they could each just do their jobs and stay out of each other's way for the time it took to reach Terminus.

Unfortunately, that was not to be, as Maker discovered a short time later.

He was in his cabin with Erlen, just getting settled in, when the purser arrived with his luggage. Ordinarily, as this was to be a short trip, he could have allowed it to remain in the cargo bay. However, as he would be putting it into service at just about the moment they reached their destination, he felt better having it close at hand. Upon its delivery, he noted something missing almost immediately: his weapons case.

"I'm afraid it's been confiscated," the purser said in response to Maker's query.

"I don't understand," Maker said, frowning. "My entire squad is cleared to carry weapons while en route."

"Still, it's being held," the purser noted, checking her p-comp.

"On whose authority?"

"Lieutenant Kepler," the purser answered, suddenly nervous as Erlen, who had previously been occupied touching his tongue to one of the walls, let out an irritated growl.

"We'll see about that," Maker said angrily, heading towards the door. It wasn't until he'd actually exited his room, with Erlen and the purser at his heels, that he realized that he really didn't know where he was going. Inadvertently, the purser provided the answer.

"—tain Henry," she said.

"What?" Maker said, turning to face the purser with a scowl as he grasped the fact that, in his anger, he had been tuning her out.

"I said, impounding certain items falls under Lieutenant Kepler's authority," she replied. "Only the captain can override him."

"Fine, let's go see the captain," Maker said.

****

At the moment, Captain Henry was not a particularly happy man. Their voyage had barely gotten underway and he was already having to deal with obstinate passengers. Thus he found himself in his meeting room rather than on the bridge, which would have been his preference.

In the room with him were four other people. Most important among them was Browing, the Gaian representative (among other things) for Terminus. Next was Lieutenant Kepler, one of his officers. There was also a Marine lieutenant — Maker. Henry knew something of him by reputation, but had long ago developed a habit of judging people based on what he'd seen of their nature, not what he'd heard. Finally, there was a woman, Dr. Chantrey; Henry had no idea what her role was or why she was present.

The meeting room itself was a spacious interior cabin that had essentially been converted into a lounge with a plush sofa, several easy chairs and even a dart board. Maker found himself entertaining a vision of the place late at night and filled with cigar smoke, as Captain

Henry and a bunch of cronies sat around playing poker with stogies hanging out of their mouths. At present, however, the good captain was seated in one of the easy chairs, scowling. Dr. Chantrey and Browing were seated as well. Maker, on the other hand, was standing — as was Kepler — but in a relaxed manner since the captain had already announced, "At ease."

"Okay," Henry said. "Somebody tell me what the hell this is all about."

"Permission to speak freely, sir?" Maker asked. Henry nodded. "We've been authorized to carry our sidearms in transit. Lieutenant Kepler has confiscated my weapon without justification."

"The weapon's been modified," Kepler said defensively, not waiting to be given permission to speak. "It's outside standard tolerances and has been enhanced to fire an irregular weapons load."

"Irregular?" Henry repeated, slightly confused.

"Illegal, sir," Kepler said. "It can still fire regulation projectiles, but it can also handle things like neuro-pellets, rocket rounds, shiver shots — all of which are banned forms of ammunition."

A dark cloud passed over Henry's face, and for a moment his lips worked involuntarily, and then he stated with finality, "Dismissed, Lieutenant Kepler."

Kepler looked bewildered for a moment, then snapped to attention, saluted, and left the room.

"Listen," the captain said, glaring at Browing, "I don't give a damn what your mission parameters are, or what kind of authority you think you have. I won't allow contraband weapons on my ship."

"Actually, sir, the weapon itself isn't illegal — even with the current modifications," Maker interjected before Browing could reply. "It's only prohibited to utilize certain forms of ammunition with it. That being the case, I've traveled regularly with it and never encountered an issue prior to this. Moreover, I think you'll find no form of banned ammunition amongst our cargo."

"Not *declared* amongst your cargo, you mean," Henry retorted. "It wouldn't be the first time someone tried to smuggle something aboard my ship, so maybe it's a good thing Kepler caught this."

"Then, in the interest of full disclosure, I have to confess something," Maker said. Captain Henry's eyes narrowed, and both Browing and Dr. Chantrey leaned forward in their seats.

Maker took a deep breath before continuing. "I'm afraid that Lieutenant Kepler and I have had several run-ins over the past few days — once in the officer's mess on base, and again at the gym. I don't know how long he's served with you, Captain, or the level of thoroughness he normally exhibits, but I think his confiscation of my weapon may be more the result of personal animosity rather than professional competence."

Captain Henry reflected on this for a moment before responding. "Kepler's actually new to my command, a last-minute transfer. I wasn't wild about swapping out a seasoned officer for someone unknown, but the transfer came directly from on high. In essence, I don't know much about him."

Maker suddenly realized that Kepler's presence on the *Mantis* was no coincidence. The man had gotten an eleventh-hour assignment to his current post (probably courtesy of his uncle, the admiral). They were obviously very serious about this grudge against Maker and determined to see it through to the bitter end.

"Well, I'm sure he'll confirm that we had an…altercation," Maker said.

"I'll speak with Kepler, and if this is more of a vendetta on his part, I'll see that you get your weapon back," Henry said. "However, none of my crew know anything about your mission. I've deliberately kept them in the dark so as to provide them with some measure of deniability if things go haywire."

Maker understood now why Kepler had been dismissed; the captain hadn't wanted him privy to any discussions about their operation to locate the Vacra.

"In the meantime," Captain Henry continued, coming to his feet, "bearing in mind the potential of your weapons, I'd be grateful if you'd refrain from committing any war crimes until you were off my ship."

"You can rest assured that war crimes are the last thing you have to worry about," Browing said, finally getting a word in.

The captain gave him a hard look, and then turned to Maker, who came to attention and raised his hand in salute. Henry returned the salute, then left the room. The minute the door closed him, Browing turned furiously to Maker.

"What the hell??" he almost screamed. "The doors have barely closed and you find a way to start screwing up."

"Calm down," Dr. Chantrey said. Frankly speaking, Maker had been surprised when she walked into the room with Browing, as he didn't realize that she'd be accompanying them. "Let's at least give him a chance to explain."

"Calm down?!" Browing shouted. "We've barely set out, and he's already making enemies and planning to commit high crimes?"

"I didn't *make* any enemies; they were already in existence," Maker retorted. "Apparently there have been people waiting in the wings for years, ready to sacrifice their firstborn in order to get a shot at me." He then gave them an overview of his encounters with Kepler.

"Okay, it's possible that this guy is out to get you," Dr. Chantrey conceded. "But modifying your weapon? You have to admit that it looks bad."

"Not to mention the fact that utilizing any of the outlawed ammunition that Kepler mentioned on the Vacra would be a violation of the Rigilos Convention," Browing added angrily.

"Oh?" Maker said quizzically, raising an eyebrow. "Did these things sign some treaty that I missed? If so, then by all means, I will comply. But if not, then they can't expect to be the beneficiary of an agreement or convention they aren't party to. They certainly didn't extend us any courtesies when they blasted three of our ships to bits."

Maker stormed out of the room without giving the doctor or Browing a chance to comment further.

Chapter 16

The rest of the trip — which only took a few days — was notably unremarkable. True to his word, Captain Henry had Maker's sidearm returned to him, for which the latter was grateful. And, although he saw Kepler in passing on one or two occasions, their paths never really crossed again. (Maker chalked this up to Henry maybe having a chat with his young lieutenant about letting his emotions affect the performance of job duties.)

He also saw Dr. Chantrey several times. Apparently, she was going to be utilized as a behavioral scientist when it came time to parley with the Vacra.

"Encounters with at least two military vessels have resulted in unexpected casualties," she'd said when Maker asked her about it. "Hopefully, my training will help us avoid any type of skirmish should we locate them."

Maker found that to be unlikely, but kept his thoughts to himself. He'd only had a brief encounter with them, but in his estimation the Vacra were a violent and vicious species. That being the case, he intended to be fully prepared. Part of that preparation meant having a conversation with a particular member of his unit: Edison Wayne.

Maker's squad spent much of the transit time in a secure ready room that had been made available for their use. In addition to strategy and tactics, they devoted considerable resources to studying a holographic representation of Terminus, learning about its topography, atmosphere, and the like.

It was on their next-to-last day aboard the *Mantis* that Maker finally approached Wayne, catching him in his cabin shortly before their regular briefing time. Upon being invited inside, Maker wasted no time explaining what he wanted. Using his p-comp, he brought up a holographic image of a small personnel transport vessel.

"This is a dropship," Maker explained. "It's what we're being allowed to use planet-side while we conduct our mission."

Wayne nodded, staring at the three-dimensional image as it slowly rotated, showing him all angles of the ship in question. It was far from the latest model and had clearly seen much better days, but appeared as though it would hold together well enough for their purposes.

"She appears to be in decent shape," Wayne commented. "At least capable of the type of recon we'll be doing."

"You don't have to mince words with me," Maker said. "You won't hurt my feelings; it's not *my* ship. It's a piece of crap."

Wayne gave a slight shrug of acknowledgment. "As you say, sir."

"I actually wanted something a little more formidable, but that jerk Browing says this is all he can spare."

Actually, Browing had made it clear that — after the issue with the modified gun — he had concerns about Maker's judgment. That being the case, he was wary of letting Maker use a ship with imposing weaponry.

"The long and short of it," Maker continued, "is that I think the potential for danger on this mission is being underestimated. That being the case, I feel we need to boost the firepower and defensive armament on this craft. Is that something you think you could do?"

The question caught Wayne a little by surprise. He had been spending some of his free time sorting through items being sent to the ship's disposal bin, and his first thought upon seeing Maker at his door was that someone had reported him. Relief flooded through him, and the corners of his mouth turned up into a smile.

"Of course," Wayne said. "Shouldn't be a problem to come up with some design modifications along the lines of what you want."

"Good," Maker said. "Get with Adames. He's already started making some changes, but this kind of thing really isn't his bailiwick. I know you're busy, so just give him the specs when you're done and he can do the work."

"Yes, sir."

Maker gave him a slight nod, but then continued staring at Wayne in an odd manner, as if trying to figure something out.

Wayne grew slightly uncomfortable under the scrutiny. "Is there something else, sir?"

The question seemed to snap Maker out of his reverie. He frowned slightly, and then — mind made up — brought up another image on his p-comp, only this time he kept it on the computer's screen rather than projecting it holographically. He held the computer out so that Wayne could see the display.

"Do you know what this device is?" Maker asked.

Wayne went bug-eyed and let out a low whistle. "Yes, sir," he answered after a moment.

Maker didn't say anything, merely stared at him. Wayne continued ogling at the screen, eyes darting around the picture displayed, but eventually he felt the weight of Maker's gaze.

Wayne seemed to painfully tear his eyes away from the screen to glance at Maker. "Was there something else, sir?"

Maker said nothing, but his eyes cut to the screen briefly, and then returned to Wayne. The younger man looked baffled for a moment, then his eyebrows shot up and his mouth fell open.

"You can't mean...I mean, you don't want..." Wayne shook his head in disbelief. *He can't possibly want...*

Wayne took a moment to compose himself. "I'm sorry, sir. There's no way I can build that. Not only is it illegal—"

"It's okay," Maker said, clapping him on the shoulder before removing the image from his p-comp. "I wouldn't want you to do anything you're uncomfortable with. But, if not the device itself, could you construct an activation key if you had the schematics?"

"You mean a trigger," Wayne answered, almost nervously. "No sir. I don't think I'd be comfortable with that either."

"Understood," Maker said, nodding. "I'll see you in the ready room."

Maker thanked Wayne for his time and left.

****

The last day on the *Mantis* was merely more of the same for Maker's group, with further review of the mission. One difference from their previous time in the ready room, however, came via a self-invitation from Browing to give them a personal overview of the geo-political situation on the planet.

It annoyed Maker to have his team and time hijacked in this manner. But, much to Maker's surprise, Browing — who was accompanied by Dr. Chantrey — did a more-than-adequate job, starting with a discussion of the different factions vying for power.

"There are more than twenty different species all laying claim to Terminus," Browing said to Maker's squad, who sat around a large conference table. A large, three-dimensional image of Terminus slowly rotated above the center of the table. "Each has a liaison assigned to represent its interest. I, for instance, am here on behalf of the human race."

"Twenty?" Adames repeated. "That seems like a lot of races to be sparing over a hunk of dirt in the middle of nowhere."

"At one time there were over fifty," Browing countered. "Over time, some negotiated away their stakes, others gave up their claims, and so on. Eventually, we expect to whittle the claimants down to one — humanity."

"So what you're really doing here is negotiating," Diviana said. "You're seeing what it will take to make your alien contemporaries give up their claim."

Browing smiled. "We're seeing what it will take to make them *peaceably* give up their claims. Where these types of conflicts were once decided with arms and troops, they are now determined via diplomacy. Which is one reason why we don't want any of you shooting up the place and creating an interstellar incident."

"What's the rest of the population like?" Maker asked.

"There are no sentient lifeforms among the indigenous plants and animals," Dr. Chantrey said. "Still, there are thousands of species from various parts of the galaxy on Terminus at any point in time."

"Many of whom," Browing added, "are the typical scum you expect to find this far out. Outlaws, bandits, and the like."

"You don't do anything about them?" Wayne asked in surprise.

"My mandate is first and foremost to secure this planet for the human race," Browing said. "After we own the place, then we'll focus on fumigating."

"But what about local law enforcement?" Wayne asked.

Browing sighed. "There's a composite group of uniformed officers made up of the races seeking control here. However, their jurisdiction is extremely limited. It's basically confined to the ten square miles that comprise what's known as the Diplomat District — the areas that you and I would deem 'civilized.' It's where I, and all of my counterparts representing other races, live and work."

Maker snorted. "Funny how the only cops on the planet choose to work solely in the region occupied by bluebloods."

"As I said," Browing continued, unperturbed, "they're a small force. Having them do much more than police one district is too difficult. With the sheer scope of criminal activity in a place like this, they'd be overwhelmed."

"What about things like murder?" Fierce asked. "Surely they investigate those?"

"Only if it's an open-and-shut case," Browing said. "For instance, if there were witnesses — and witnesses who'd be willing to testify, I might add, which there never are. Other than that, they just record the act, as well as collect evidence and statements. In short, our officers try, but they simply lack the manpower and resources to be truly effective."

"So it's basically a Wild West show," Wayne concluded. "A lawless frontier."

"Welcome to the Fringe, tenderfoot," Adames said, clapping Wayne — who was sitting next to him — on the shoulder.

"It's not entirely anarchic," Dr. Chantrey added. "Once you get this far out from the Hub, there's a sort of rough justice that becomes the standard — a stand-in for the rule of law."

"Rough justice?" Wayne repeated. "What does that even mean?"

"It means that most people here handle their own disputes, without resorting to the law," Maker said. "If you cheat someone, they're going to come after you. If you kill someone, don't be surprised if his family or friends come looking for revenge."

"But not everyone out here is a crook," Dr. Chantrey said. "Many are honest people looking for a fresh start."

"Along with criminals looking for fresh victims," Diviana said. "Speaking of which, we'll be the new meat — faces they've never seen before. Won't people be suspicious when we start snooping around?"

Browing shook his head in the negative. "Our arrival at Terminus is timed to coincide with that of a large passenger ship. As Dr. Chantrey said, people are constantly coming to the Fringe to seek their fortune, start over, etcetera. There will be a huge influx of individuals headed down to the surface, so you will be among thousands of new faces popping up all over the planet."

"Sounds good," Adames said. "Any idea on where we should start conducting our recon?"

"Based on physical descriptions and images provided," Dr. Chantrey said, "our scientists — entomologists, really — believe that the Vacra will be most comfortable in a dry, arid region."

"Bearing in mind the location of the merchant they're dealing with and the range of the average planetary vehicle," Browing said, "we believe you can narrow the scope of your recon efforts to this area."

As Browing spoke, a yellow, amoeba-shaped region on the Terminus image became magnified.

"You call that narrow?" Adames asked. "That's got to be a million square miles of desert."

"More like two," Loyola interjected.

"Then I'd say you've got your work cut out for you," Browing remarked unsympathetically, earning him a glare from Maker.

"Why do we have to go after them at all?" Snick asked, speaking for the first time since Browing's briefing began. "If they made purchases from our allies, can't we simply wait in the vicinity until they come to retrieve their merchandise?"

"Unfortunately, our confederates are far from being the only vendors on the planet," Dr. Chantrey said. "We have reason to believe the Vacra have agreed to buy what they need from others as well, and will do business with whoever obtains the goods first."

"In other words, parking ourselves outside someone's storefront isn't necessarily the best plan," Adames said.

"So we comb the desert until we find them," Loyola remarked. "Or until our allies tell us they've made contact."

"In essence, yes," Browing said. "Any further questions?"

There were a few seconds of silence, and then Maker spoke up. "Just one," he said. "If this whole planet is full of lowlifes like you said, how do we know that we can trust our so-called allies?"

"We don't," Dr. Chantrey said, without missing a beat.

Chapter 17

Maker's squad was essentially packed up, with all their gear on the dropship, when Diviana approached him with her idea.

"No way," Maker said, frowning in distaste when she finished speaking. "It's completely out of the question."

"Think about it," Diviana said. "We're suffering from an almost complete lack of intel. We're going to need to know more if we want to pull this thing off with any hope of success."

They were standing just inside the doorway of the dropship, which was magnetically clamped to the floor of the bay. Maker, who would be piloting, had been making a final inspection when Diviana had come in. Outside their vessel, the landing bay was the site of frenzied activity as various ships — including Browing's personal yacht — prepared to depart for the surface.

"Maybe that's true," Maker said, "but what you're suggesting is an unnecessary risk."

"What's an unnecessary risk?" Adames asked, appearing from the cockpit area.

"Diviana here wants to go off on her own," Maker replied. "She thinks our cover story sucks and wants to deviate from the plan."

Adames nodded, soaking this in. The current game plan called for them to pretend to be a group of scientists — oceanologists, xenologists, etc. — trying to answer numerous questions about Terminus: whether the planet had ever been home to intelligent life, whether the desert had once actually been an ocean, and so on. It wasn't the greatest ruse, but one that would be easy enough to pull off considering the short notice they were given for the entire mission.

"It's not a plan," Diviana countered. "It's a pretext — a fabrication to keep anyone from giving us a good hard look. In the meantime, we're supposed to stumble around two million miles of desert and hope we get lucky? That won't work. We need quality info in order to come up with anything close to a plan."

"And she thinks she can get it for us," Maker said. "By going solo."

Adames gave her an appraising glance. "Can you?"

"Of course!" Diviana said dismissively. "It's what I was trained to do. Why put me on the team if you didn't plan to let me do my job?"

"Because I have a different job for you!" Maker grumbled irritably.

His statement seemed to take both Adames and Diviana by surprise, but he didn't give them a chance to respond.

"You know what? I don't care," Maker said harshly. "Go on — get yourself killed if that's what you want."

His tone was grim, but Diviana barely seemed to notice. Instead, she seemed to be fighting a smile. "You mean it?" she asked almost gleefully. "I can go?"

"Be my guest," Maker said. "And one other thing...I think I *am* going to give you a call sign. From now on, for all coded communications, you're Athena."

Diviana blinked. "Athena?" she repeated somewhat timidly.

"She's an ancient goddess of wisdom and courage," Adames said. "She sprang fully grown, as well

137

as clothed and armored, from the head of her father, Zeus, the king of the gods."

"I know who Athena is," Diviana retorted sharply. "She's also the goddess of warfare and strategy." She turned her attention back to Maker. "So, is branding me 'Athena' your way of saying there's some merit to my plan?"

"No," Maker answered. "I'm calling you that because — much as your namesake did to Zeus — you're giving me a headache. Now get out of here before I change my mind."

Diviana once again fought to keep a grin off her face, then saluted and left.

"She's right, you know," Adames commented. "Without more info, we're going to be stumbling around in the dark here. If she's experienced in gathering intel, letting her do it is the right decision. You know that, Gant."

Maker was unconvinced. "Maybe, but knowing it won't make me feel any better if she has to make the trip back home in a casket."

"I'm sure it won't come to that," Adames said. "Anyway, I'm pretty much done with those, uh, *upgrades* you wanted, although some of the stuff Wayne drew up will have to wait until we're on the surface. I've got to be honest, though, Gant. I trust you with my life, man, but what are we doing here? I mean, some of these integrations and configurations you've had me do are things I've never seen before. I don't even know what all this crap is supposed to do, and it makes me nervous, to put it mildly."

"Good," said Maker, who had spent a great deal of his own time making modifications to their ship with the materials Adames had obtained. "I'd be worried if it didn't."

****

The trip down to the planet in the dropship was mostly without incident. As Browing had said, a large passenger ship, the *Celestial Crown*, had arrived at Terminus roughly around the same time as the *Mantis*. With the surface seeing a steady stream of weary travelers via the *Crown*'s three shuttles, as well as cargo vessels and freight transports, it was very easy for one more ship to head planet-side without drawing a lot of attention.

Diviana, of course, wasn't with them, having made other arrangements for getting down to Terminus. When questioned about her absence by others in the squad, Maker had merely replied that she'd been given a last-minute, sidebar mission.

"We expect to hear from her at regular intervals, though," he'd lied as they were making final preparations to depart the *Mantis*. In truth, all he'd been able to wring from Diviana with respect to future communications was that she'd contact them when she knew something.

As they descended to the planet, the subject of Diviana came up again — this time in a half-sensible argument from Wayne about how their absent teammate had been given a call sign (meaning that two members of the unit now had them) — and he still deserved one. Maker let Adames handle the reply and instead focused on piloting the dropship and focusing on what lay ahead.

Browing had provided them with official papers to prove up their claim of being a scientific expedition (should anyone care to ask). As Diviana had noted, it wasn't a great cover, but it would provide a plausible reason for their presence, as well as explain why they were zipping all over the place, sticking their noses in every corner of the desert.

It took about an hour to reach the area they had settled on as base camp — a region of desert far enough out that no one was likely to stumble across them accidentally, but close enough to the outpost where the Vacra had been seen that they could reach it within a reasonable time. The dropship itself served as their command center; in addition, they set up several atmospheric tents to serve as storage, a mobile hospital, and other functions.

They had set down late in the morning, and the rest of the day got swallowed setting everything up. The atmosphere wasn't one-hundred-percent compatible with human life — you could breathe it, but after a while toxins would start building up in your system — so they wore noseplugs. (There were also drugs you could take that would serve the same purpose, but they were known to have nasty side effects.) The only person who didn't require help with breathing was Fierce, whose genetic modifications included an advanced respiratory system — and Erlen, who stayed in the dropship while the others worked.

When everything was done, Maker called for a halt and the entire group gathered together for a celebratory drink of water. Everyone was dripping with sweat except the Augman, who would probably be just as comfortable standing in a blast furnace. They were sitting around a foldaway table under a large frame tent, which was one of the few open-air structures they had set up. It was then that Maker noticed that Loyola was missing. In fact, he quickly realized he hadn't seen her in hours.

"She took off a while back," Fierce replied when Maker put the question to the group. "Said she needed to do some recon."

"And no one thought to tell me?" Maker grumbled angrily. "We can't just have people taking off whenever they like!"

"According to our briefing, it's what she's supposed to do," Fierce responded. "Scout out the area we establish as our base and confirm the previous report that it's clear."

"Yeah," Maker said, "but it would be a nice gesture if she let her commanding officer know *when* she was doing it — or wait for the order!" His hand automatically went up towards his ear, intending to tap the comm unit he was wearing and activate it. At the last second he stopped, then looked at Wayne, who was also responsible for communications.

"We're good," Wayne said, practically reading his mind. "All communications are secure. But, uh…"

Maker arched an eyebrow as Wayne trailed off. "But what, Marine?"

"You need to refer to her as 'Scope,' sir," Wayne said sheepishly.

"We already have coded designations for this assignment," Maker said, not quite understanding. "We've got Baker, Doughboy—"

"I know," Wayne said. "But on the way down here in the dropship, the rest of us decided we'd rather have our own individual call signs. You were busy piloting, so you probably didn't notice."

"Call signs," Maker intoned, almost mockingly.

"Yeah," Wayne replied enthusiastically. "Loyola is going to be Scope. I'm going to be Tinker. And Snick is going to be Buddha."

"Unbelievable," Maker muttered, almost to himself. He tapped the comm piece in his ear, bringing it online. "Scope, this is the Baker," he said distinctively. "Come in."

The response from Loyola was nigh-immediate. "This is Scope, sir."

"Scope, please convey your locus."

"I'm about three hundred yards south of your location," came the reply.

Maker moved away from the table and looked in the direction indicated; he saw no sign of Loyola, only wave after wave of windswept desert dunes. Even after employing a pair of field glasses, he couldn't pinpoint her location.

"Scope, please repeat," Maker said. "Did you say three hundred yards south of our location?"

"Affirmative."

"I can't get a make on your position," Maker said, scanning as far as the horizon. He glanced back at the others with him; the fact that they were all staring south indicated that they were listening in via their own comms, but none of them seemed to have eyes on Loyola either.

"Again, I can't get a make on your position," Maker repeated

"Isn't that the point?" Loyola's voice heckled through the comm. There was a sound of snickering behind him, but Maker ignored it.

"Her camouflage is excellent," Snick said softly.

"If her marksmanship is as good," Adames commented over the airwaves, "we might just have ourselves a winner."

"Would you like a demonstration?" Loyola asked. "Take a look at the pole at the southeast corner of the tent you're standing under."

The five men looked at the tent pole indicated. It was white, roughly eight feet tall, and about a quarter-inch in diameter. A moment later, a beam of laser light sheared the pole about one foot from where it joined the tent. The tent itself leaned precipitously to one side, but did not fall. It was, without question, a world-class shot.

Before anyone could comment, another beam came along and took another foot off the remaining length of pole still sticking out of the sand. Three more shots followed in rapid succession, each cutting another foot off the tent pole. Wayne let out a long, low whistle that conveyed the sentiment of everyone present: Loyola's marksmanship wasn't just impressive. It was on a scale few of them had ever seen.

Maker quickly looked in the direction that the shots had come from. He still couldn't make out where Loyola was holed up.

"Permission to carry on with recon, sir?" Loyola asked.

"Permission granted," Maker said. "One more thing — you owe the Marines a new tent pole."

Chapter 18

Loyola didn't come in until after dark that first day, and she was gone again before sunup the next morning. Maker, who arose early himself to take care of some things on their ship, couldn't help but admire how seriously she took her duties, and everyone else seemingly did the same.

Fierce woke up with the dawn and started cataloging medical supplies, as well as making sure all of the surgical equipment worked. Adames decided he would spend the day puttering around the dropship, allegedly making sure that the vessel remained travel-ready in case they had to make a quick exit.

As for the rest of their band, the focus was on finding the Vacra. To that end, a number of drones were dispersed that first morning. Ostensibly, they were mapping devices, used to chart the surrounding region and pinpoint areas of interest for scientists to study. In actuality, they were, of course, trying to locate Maker's quarry (or any place they might be hiding).

Maker, Snick, and Wayne spent much of the day analyzing the data relayed back by the drones. In the end, although they got a fix on the location of some of the planet's indigenous life as well as several bands of sentient species traveling across the desert, they had no luck in locating their intended targets.

That day ended much like the previous evening, with Loyola making an appearance after sunset and being gone again by daybreak. Moreover, the actions of everyone else the following morning basically mimicked what they had done the day before: Fierce worked in the hospital tent, Adames fooled around with the ship, and the others sent out drones (albeit to survey new terrain), and scoured the images and data sent back to determine if there was anything there to help them locate their target.

As their second full day on Terminus came to a close, Maker found himself extremely frustrated. Sitting at the table under the frame tent, he groaned aloud and pushed away the computer monitor he had been staring at. Wayne, sitting across from him, looked up from his own screen in concern.

"This is hopeless," Maker announced angrily. "As fast as those drones go, as much range as they have, there's just too much desert. We might as well just stick a pin in a map."

"Easy there, el-tee," Wayne said, reaching across to protectively pull the monitor farther out of Maker's reach. "Don't take it out on the merchandise."

"The lieutenant's frustrated," said Snick, who was sitting at the far end of the table. "He's a man of action — like me. He feels the need to be more assertive."

Wayne looked at Maker for confirmation, who merely said, "That's not exactly right, although there is a little bit of truth to Snick's statement. I just feel like we should be doing more than simply staring at screens all day."

"Well, you could always take a hovercycle out and eyeball the place yourself," Wayne suggested. "You won't cover nearly as much ground or be as effective as a drone, but if it makes you feel like you're doing something, maybe it'll be therapeutic."

Maker frowned. "I don't need ther—"

Maker stopped in mid-sentence as Erlen, who had been happily taunting a small desert insect, abruptly became alert, growling menacingly. Sunlight suddenly flashed off something metallic in the corner of Maker's eye, and his peripheral vision picked up unexpected motion. He turned his head in the direction of the movement, at the same time drawing his sidearm in one seamless motion and taking aim.

"No! Don't!" screamed Wayne, flinging himself between the barrel of Maker's gun and the object that just strolled (or rather, floated) into the shade of the tent.

It was about a foot tall and made completely of shiny, gray metal. It had what appeared to be a cylindrical body, connected by a multitude of wires to a head that looked a lot like a soup can. It floated about a foot off the ground.

"Don't shoot!" Wayne continued. "It's just Jerry."

"Jerry?" Maker repeated quizzically. "Who — and *what* — the hell is Jerry, and why is he crashing what should be a private party?"

Wayne, still seemingly nervous although Maker finally put his gun away, said, "I really haven't been able to sleep since we got here. Too pumped up or something, I guess."

Maker nodded slightly in understanding. This was probably Wayne's first real mission, which meant he was quite likely just a bundle of raw nerves on the inside. Maker remembered how wound up he'd been on his first assignment, how the knot in his gut didn't untangle until after everything was over.

"That first night," Wayne went on, "when I couldn't fall asleep, I started tinkering. We had some odds and ends lying around — mostly from the drones — so I started putting them together. Next thing you know, Jerry was born."

"So why's he just wandering around my camp willy-nilly?" Maker asked.

"He's got a makeshift tracker — something I cobbled together from spare parts," Wayne replied, "so this was a bit of a test to see how long it would take for him to fi—"

"Wait a minute," Maker said, cutting Wayne off. He tapped the comm piece in his ear. "Scope, come in."

"Scope here, sir," came the response a moment later.

"Do you have eyes on the camp?"

"Affirmative."

"Did you happen to see a floating tin can wandering around haphazardly?"

"Affirmative."

"Any particular reason why you didn't blast it to bits?"

"It's Jerry, sir."

"Jerry," Maker said, squinting and rubbing his temples. "Exactly how do you know about Jerry?"

"Tinker showed him to me this morning before I left," Loyola said. "Wanted me to know that he wasn't a bogey should I see him about."

It took Maker a moment to recall that Tinker was now Wayne's call sign. He shook his head in frustration before muttering, "That's all, Scope. Carry on."

Loyola's acknowledgment of his last order barely registered with Maker as he turned his attention back to Wayne.

"I'm sorry, Lieutenant," Wayne began. "I didn't think it would be a problem."

"Don't worry about it — it's not a big deal," Maker assured him. "I think we're all just on edge here waiting for something to happen."

"Yes," Snick agreed. "At least you've found a way to entertain yourself. I've been meditating more than usual to keep myself focused, but I really wish things were a bit more exciting at the moment."

A short time later, he got his wish.

Chapter 19

It was the first real test of Maker's group, and it occurred in the wee hours of the following morning. Well before dawn, Maker found himself being awakened by a relentless tugging on his arm. It was Erlen, who had a firm-but-gentle grasp on Maker's wrist with his teeth.

"I'm awake," Maker announced, sitting up. Erlen released his wrist and Maker spent a moment rubbing the sleep from his eyes. Erlen growled softly, in a way that Maker had no problem interpreting: something was wrong.

He was inside his tent, which — although larger than average (as befitted an officer) — was actually somewhat barren. Other than the portable cot that he slept on, there were few creature comforts. Aside from a single chair, the most notable remaining item was a footlocker that doubled as a nightstand; on it were Maker's p-comp, sidearm, and comm piece, through which he could hear a tinny voice.

He put the comm piece in his ear. "Maker here," he said, dispensing with the coded designations. "Somebody talk to me."

"Tinker here, sir," Wayne's voice declared, which was expected since he was currently on watch in the dropship. "We've got inbound hostiles, two humans and a Lepido, heading in from the west on foot."

"Give me a fix on our people," Maker said.

"All accounted for, snug in their nests, awaiting your orders."

Mentally, Maker let out a sigh of relief; his people were safe in their quarters. Initially, he'd had a slight concern about only leaving one person on watch, but they

149

were a small crew and already stretched thin even before Diviana took off. They needed every member of their squad to go above and beyond, and Maker was relieved to see that they seemed capable of doing so.

"Send me a feed," he said, reaching for his p-comp. "Everyone else as well."

"Feed initiated," Wayne replied.

Maker looked at his p-comp's screen, which revealed the two humans and the reptilian Lepido that Wayne had mentioned stealthily approaching their location. Although the camp was dark, the surveillance units that had been set up for security were equipped with night vision lenses, and therefore broadcast very clear images.

The three intruders wore light body armor, but appeared well-armed. Also, despite wearing night vision goggles, they clearly failed to realize that they had triggered both the motion sensors and the cameras surreptitiously placed around the camp.

Idiots, Maker thought to himself.

From the images, it appeared that their visitors were getting close to one of the sleeping tents, of which there were four. Maker and Adames both had their own; a third tent was designated for the use of Loyola and Diviana (although only the former was currently using it). The fourth and final tent was for Wayne, Snick, and Fierce, and it was also the one which the intruders were closing in on.

Maker reflected for a moment. With Wayne standing watch in the ship, that left Fierce and Snick in the tent. Moreover, the tents themselves, although equipped with motion-activated lights, were also completely sealable in order to keep out the elements:

wind, sand, etc. In other words, the tents were light tight, and anyone approaching wouldn't be able to guess as to whether the tent's occupants were asleep or awake.

"Buddha," he said, remembering Snick's call sign, "prepare to engage."

"Roger that," Snick replied.

"Tinker," Maker said, "light 'em up."

"Showing these heathens the light, sir," Wayne said.

A moment later, a small, luminous circle appeared on the monitor of Maker's p-comp, then rapidly bloomed in size until the entire screen was whited out. However, before the image vanished, Maker saw their intruders whipping off their goggles in agitation.

"Now!" Maker shouted, before running out of his tent.

Outside, the entire camp was bathed in bright light. Maker headed directly for the area where the intruders were, but soon found himself trailing behind Erlen, who pulled away with impressive speed.

The sound of gunplay echoed from the target area, spurring Maker to try to run faster. Off to one side, he saw Adames headed in the same direction. He also saw both Fierce and Loyola exit from the women's tent, but filed it away as something to address later, if necessary.

By the time the four of them reached the area of conflict, it was all over. The two human intruders were on the ground — one stretched out unconscious, the other cradling what appeared to be a broken arm — with Snick standing over them, grinning. The Lepido lay on his stomach, mewling pitifully while trying to reach around to his back, which was crisscrossed with clawmarks. Off to the side, Erlen dragged his claws back and forth through the sand, trying to get the reptilian's green blood off them.

****

They had their three "guests" inside the dropship, sitting on the floor with their backs to a wall. They had been stripped of their armor and other gear, which Wayne was now going through. Loyola and Snick were covering the trio with their own weapons, something that the man with the broken arm — who seemed to be the leader — took great offense to. His other human companion, while conscious now, seemed dazed.

Probably a concussion, Maker thought.

The Lepido, although it hissed evilly, actually seemed terrified of Erlen, who sat directly in front of it, staring intently.

"Care to tell us what you were doing sneaking around our camp?" Maker asked, getting right to the point.

"We weren't doing any sneaking around," Broken Arm said between painful breaths. "We were just passing through when you people attacked us."

"So passing through means that you cut through the center of our camp in the middle of the night wearing body armor and NVGs while armed to the teeth," Maker said.

"Did you forget where we are?" Broken Arm asked. "This is Terminus! This is Beyond! Out here, toddlers walk around wearing armor and weapons."

"Oh, so you're saying we simply misjudged the situation and overreacted," Maker concluded.

"Exactly," Broken Arm replied, trying to convey sincerity and failing miserably.

Maker just stared at him. The man, scruffy and unshaven, was a little less than average in height when standing. He had a shifty look about him and an overall demeanor that screamed "criminal."

Maker knew this type of individual — had encountered others just like him often enough to know that he was dealing with a born thief and liar.

"Well, since this is just a misunderstanding, I suppose we should just give you back all your equipment and let you go," Maker said.

"That seems fair," Broken Arm said, nodding.

"Ha!" Adames laughed mockingly. "Do you really think we're that stupid?" Unexpectedly, his tone turned menacing. "We'll see if you're singing that same tune when I get through with you."

Adames leaned in and reached threateningly towards the broken limb of their captive. The man flinched, trying to back away but there was nowhere to go. However, before Adames even touched him, a familiar voiced boomed out, echoing resonantly within the confines of the ship.

"Don't," Fierce said emphatically, the force of his tone making Adames stop and look at him. Rather than address the master sergeant, Fierce turned instead to Maker. "Please," he said. "These people may be our enemies, but we don't have to torture them to find out what they know."

"Thanks, handsome, but I don't need your help," Broken Arm announced, seemingly finding a reservoir of courage from somewhere. "I've already told you the truth, so my story's not going to change. Do your worst. I can take anything you *pruchuzos* can dish out."

To add emphasis to the insult, he spat, leaving a glob of bloody phlegm on the floor of the ship.

"Oh, a tough guy," Maker said in disdain. "Maybe *you* won't talk, but is the same true of your companions?"

"Erlen," Maker called out, before Broken Arm could reply. "Tear the Lepido's face off."

The Lepido screamed, holding its hands up in front of its face as Erlen growled and began to move slowly towards him. It continued shrieking, but after a moment Maker realized that it was actually speaking (albeit with a thick accent) and not just wailing in abject terror.

"*Tell him! Tell him!*" The Lepido was shouting. "*You tell him or I will!*"

Broken Arm looked at the Lepido like he wanted to lobotomize it. "Fine," he said, his façade breaking down as a quick word from Maker made Erlen stop advancing on the Lepido. "We came here to rob you, just like you figured."

"So what — millions of square miles of desert and you just happened to stumble across us and decided to take advantage of the situation?" Adames asked.

"No," Broken Arm replied. "We heard that there was a crew of scientists out here doing research. A scientific expedition means supplies, tech, and so on. Things we can sell or trade — including a ship."

"So your plan was to take our equipment, ship and supplies," Adames said. "And what were you going to do with us?"

Broken Arm averted his eyes, staring at the floor. It didn't take a lot of imagination to figure out what would have happened to their squad had the intruders' raid succeeded.

"Wait a minute," Maker said before the silence grew too lengthy. "You said you 'heard' we were out here. Heard from who?"

Broken Arm was visibly relieved at the change of subject, stating, "We bought your information."

"Huh?" Maker asked, more than a little confused.

"The scope of study you filed," Broken Arm said, "indicating the region you'd be in, the type of work you'd be doing, the equipment you'd be using."

Maker fought hard to keep his face expressionless, but he was utterly perplexed. Moreover, he couldn't help exchanging an involuntary glance with Adames — something Broken Arm picked up on.

"You don't have any idea what I'm talking about, do you?" their captive asked rhetorically, and then his eyes narrowed. "You're no scientists."

"You picked a bad time to reveal your detective skills," Adames said to him, and Broken Arm's eyes widened as he realized he and his companions were in a knows-too-much position with respect to their captors.

Adames turned to Maker. "What do you want to do with them?"

Maker reflected for a moment, and then stated flatly, "Ice 'em."

TERMINUS

Chapter 20

Approximately a day-and-a-half after Erlen had first awakened him to warn of the impending attack on their camp, Maker found himself riding in a hovercart, pulling up to the loading dock at the rear of the Gaian Consulate in the Diplomat District. The cart was a little on the small side, but could hold four people. At the moment, Wayne sat in the front passenger seat next to Maker, while Erlen lay in the back. Behind them, attached to the cart, was a large cargo trailer — a metal container about twenty feet in length, five feet in width, and eight feet in height — that floated just a few feet above the ground.

The loading dock itself was nigh deserted. There were no deliveries at the moment, so all of the bay doors were closed. Next to the dock was a large set of double doors, and beside them was a small guardhouse, inside of which Maker saw a couple of people moving around.

He drove the cart towards the double doors, slowing to a halt when two armed men stepped out of the guardhouse. As they approached, one asked to see their credentials while the other held his weapon at the ready.

Maker had sent word ahead that they were coming, and apparently the knowledge had trickled down to the appropriate parties. A few moments after identifying themselves, the two guards waved them through as the doors next to the loading dock began to open.

As he maneuvered the cart inside, Maker thought for the umpteenth time how he'd have preferred to make this trip alone. There was about to be a confrontation, and it wasn't the type of thing he really wanted people under his command to see. However, once Wayne found out where he was going, the young engineer had insisted on coming along. (Wayne's excuse was that he needed to visit some shops in the District to obtain parts to upgrade their drones, but Maker suspected that was simply a pretext for finding items to enhance Jerry the Robot.)

The area beyond the doors angled downward, revealing an enormous, well-lit substructure beneath the consulate. It had the appearance of a parking garage, although — from what Maker could see — there were only a handful of vehicles in the place, and they were all parked against a far wall. (All of them, however, appeared to be expensive, high-end hovercars.) Most of the space seemed to be used for storage, as there were boxes and bins stacked all over the place.

Standing near the center of the room, directly ahead of them, was Browing. With him, as Maker could have guessed, was Dr. Chantrey. She gave Maker a faint, involuntary smile as she saw him, but quickly suppressed it.

Browing stepped slightly to the side as the cart got closer, and Maker pulled it abreast of the man, aggressively jumping out almost before the vehicle came to a halt. Erlen jumped out as well, and then ran his supple tongue along the flooring of the garage.

Dr. Chantrey winced. "Does he have to do that? It's disgusting."

"Sorry, but Erlen tastes everything," Maker said.

"Nice cart," said Browing sarcastically, drawing Maker's attention away from the doctor. "And trailer. I knew the dropship had a decent amount of space, but I didn't realize all of this could fit in there."

"Oh, it didn't," Maker replied. "The cart and the trailer fell into our possession courtesy of some bandits."

"Bandits?" Browing said, as if he couldn't quite understand what he was hearing. He turned to Dr. Chantrey, who also looked confused.

"Yes, bandits," Maker repeated. "You know, the ones you sent to kill us."

The statement seemed to catch Browing off-guard. "What?! I don't...I never...What are you talking about? I didn't send anyone to kill you."

"Well, you might as well have," Maker declared angrily. "Wasn't it you who filed a scientific scope of study identifying the region of the desert we'd be in?"

"Yes, because that's what a *real* scientific expedition would do!" Browing snapped back. "They don't just set up shop on any parcel of land they want and do whatever they please. They file paperwork, outline their plans, get a permit, and more. In case you forgot, there's a score of races all trying to get their grubby little paws on this rock — including us. Each one of them is doing whatever it takes to legitimize their claim, from bringing in settlers to establishing trading posts to performing scientific studies."

Maker shrugged. "So what?"

"The last thing we need is for someone else to make a claim on or attempt to use the region we'd designated for your base camp," Dr. Chantrey said. "It would cause all kinds of problems."

"And you don't think it's problematic for other people to know our location?"

"Not in and of itself," Browing said. "And it was easier to just do everything officially."

"He's right," Dr. Chantrey agreed before Maker could voice his dissent. "Plus, every lie needs to have a grain or two of truth or it's too easy to see through."

Maker shook his head vehemently. "How the hell are we supposed to complete a secret mission when everyone knows where we are?"

"It's only your *mission* that's secret," Dr. Chantrey replied. "Your *presence* is not."

"That's actually a flawed hypothesis, because it assumes that there would be no interest in us outside the parameters of our mission," Wayne noted, finally speaking up. "The fact that someone sold — and found a buyer for — information about our expedition proves that there is some other interest in us. From what we can tell, it's our equipment and supplies."

"But that makes no sense," Browing said. "The filing on behalf of your 'expedition' is still working its way through the system, but will be public information in a few days. Why bother buying it?"

"To get a leg up on the competition," Maker said. "To get there first, easily take out a bunch of nerdy scientists, then walk off into the sunset with a bunch of expensive tech and gear."

"Even if all that's true, isn't this a moot point?" Dr. Chantrey asked. "You say some men tried to raid your camp, Lieutenant, but since you're standing here somewhat calmly discussing the matter instead of screaming for reinforcements, it's probably safe to assume that they failed, correct?"

Maker seemed to reflect for a moment, then stated, "That's correct."

"Do you think they're going to try it again?" she asked.

Maker shook his head. "That's highly unlikely."

"Well, if the group that attacked isn't likely to come back, then I'm not sure that there's a problem," the doctor said.

"The problem is that, over an eighteen-hour period, we were actually attacked by *three* groups," Maker said.

There was a moment of silence while Dr. Chantrey and Browing digested this.

"So what are you saying?" Browing finally asked.

"What I'm saying is that the person who sold our information didn't just pass it along to one set of criminals," Maker said. "He sold it to several of them."

"Are you trying to tell us that you've actually been attacked three times in the past few days?" Dr. Chantrey asked.

"The last two days actually," Maker said. "Apparently there's an entire cottage industry that's sprung up around the concept of raiding our camp. But we're fine, thanks for asking. And, as I mentioned, we got a few nice housewarming gifts out of it." He patted the hood of the hovercart almost lovingly.

"Which reminds me," he added, "we brought a little present for you." He walked towards the rear of the cargo trailer, motioning for Browing and the doctor to follow him. Erlen followed in their wake, while Wayne began disconnecting the cargo trailer from the vehicle.

Just before he reached the back of the container, Maker stopped and turned his attention to a small keypad located at about chest height on the side panel. Browing and Dr. Chantrey, recognizing that Maker was about to enter a code of some sort (presumably to open the cargo unit), stepped around him and then stood facing the rear of the trailer, positioning themselves so that it was impossible for them to see the digits Maker pressed.

"No worries about the code." Maker chuckled as he pushed buttons on the keypad "As I said, this is an item we liberated from our attackers."

"If it belonged to the bandits, how do you know the entry code?" Dr. Chantrey asked.

"E-4 Wayne, who's with me, cracked their encryption," Maker replied. "He's a genius with all things tech."

Maker entered the last digit; there was a short beep followed by an audible click. Maker stepped around to the rear of the trailer just as the door began to open.

Like most cargo units, the back wall of the container was also the door (not to mention the only point of ingress and egress). Mounted on rollers in a sturdy track, the door automatically cycled up towards the ceiling with barely a whisper of sound, revealing the trailer's contents.

An unnatural silence took root as Browing and Dr. Chantrey got a gander at what Maker had been dragging around in the container. In fact, Browing's mouth fell open slightly, while the doctor went bug-eyed and drew in a sharp breath.

The cargo trailer was full of bodies. Some obviously human, others clearly not — but bodies all the same (and at least a dozen of them, at that). They apparently had not enjoyed a smooth ride, as they appeared to have been tossed around haphazardly.

"What...what is this?" Dr. Chantrey asked. "Who are these people?"

"These are the bandits that attacked us," Maker said. As if in confirmation, Erlen growled.

"So, why bring them here?" Browing asked. "What are we supposed to do with a bunch of dead bodies?"

"Oh, they're not dead," Maker countered. "Not all of them, anyway. They're on ice — in stasis."

Taking a good, hard look at the bodies, the doctor saw that Maker's statement was true. Each person in the trailer seemed to be covered by some thin, transparent material, which she assumed was cryo-film.

As Dr. Chantrey understood it, cryo-film was a product capable of putting various objects — including people — into a state of suspended animation. On the battlefield, it had garnered a stellar reputation for its ability to put wounded soldiers in temporary stasis until they could receive medical treatment. As a result, it was almost standard issue on any mission.

"You still haven't answered my question," Browing said to Maker, snapping the doctor out of her reverie. "What are we supposed to do with them?"

"I don't care," Maker said. "I just know that they can't stay with us."

"I don't see why not," Browing countered.

"Because we're not a jail," Maker responded. "Even with them in stasis, we don't have room to hold all these creeps. We'd be stacking them up like cordwood. Plus, we have a finite amount of cryo-film — which has to be reapplied every few days to keep a body in stasis — and I wasn't going to waste it all on these dregs. So our options were to either kill them, let them go, or this."

Browing seemed on the verge of saying something, but Dr. Chantrey cut him off. "That's fine, Lieutenant," she said. "We'll take care of it, and we'll find a way to resolve the issue of everyone knowing where you are."

"No worries on that one," Maker replied. "We took care of it. We moved."

"Moved?" Browing asked, brow furrowed. "Moved where?"

Maker gave him a cocksure look. "I'm not sure I want to tell you that. You may have to broadcast a holo-image of the area."

For a moment, Browing turned red with anger, clearly on the cusp of saying or doing something they'd all regret. Then, unexpectedly, he laughed.

"Alright, if you don't want to simply tell me," he said with a chuckle, "maybe you'd be interested in a little horse trading."

Given the sudden swing in Browing's disposition, Maker was immediately suspicious. "What do you mean?" he asked.

"The message that you were coming in today just happened to arrive at a very fortuitous time," Browing said, "because I was just getting ready to reach out to you. Care to guess why?"

The answer came to Maker almost immediately. "Our allies have been in touch," he said. "They've had contact with the Vacra."

Chapter 21

The town was called Shady Falls, but there were no falls (which was quite likely a result of being located in close proximity to the desert). However, per Browing, the rabble that constituted the local residents gave ample reason for the place to be considered shady.

Browing had, of course, provided Maker with the name of a contact, as well as a time and place to meet; in turn, Maker had supplied him with the current location of their camp, and then set out immediately for the rendezvous with their allies.

It was just getting dark when Maker, Wayne, and Erlen arrived. At present, they were driving through the town's entertainment district, which basically consisted of bars, strip clubs, gambling houses, or some combination thereof. Their destination was a gaming venue known as the Pit, where they were to meet their so-called allies who would help them locate the Vacra.

Looking at Wayne, Maker couldn't help but notice the young soldier's nervousness. He had obviously never been in combat, and his greenness showed in the way he kept glancing around, as if expecting danger to leap from every shadowy corner. It certainly didn't help that, since entering the town, they'd heard random gunfire coming from several buildings that they passed — in addition to witnessing two deadly knife fights.

In retrospect, Maker felt he probably should have seen if another meeting time could be arranged. Then maybe he would have had an opportunity to go back to camp and swap out Wayne for someone more experienced, like Adames. However, his eagerness regarding the Vacra overrode his common sense, and he'd felt the need to strike while the iron was hot. Thus, he now found himself paired with an untested Marine. Maker prayed that this meeting would be uneventful.

A short time later, they arrived at their destination — an enormous, dome-shaped edifice with the words "The Pit" emblazoned above the entrance in bright colors. Maker parked their vehicle in a nearby lot earmarked for patrons. As they got out, an odd creature that seemed to be nothing more than a six-foot tall pile of slime offered to ensure that their vehicle remained unmolested while they were inside for the paltry sum of twenty credits. Maker haggled his way down to ten, and then paid, heading for the entrance of the Pit with the odd certainty that — had he not paid — he probably would have returned to find the cart full of goo of some sort.

No one stopped them as they tried to enter, which was a new experience for Maker; typically, someone — a bouncer, owner, patron, etc. — made an issue of Erlen's presence, but not tonight. That fact turned out to be the only bright spot as they got a good look at the interior.

Judging from appearances, the Pit looked to be an all-in-one establishment. Its huge, circular interior — currently packed with customers — seemed to be divided into odd sectors. Near the wall in one area, Maker saw numerous games of chance, where most of those participating were likely to gamble away whatever money they came in with. In another section, he saw a small stage where a dancer was performing an intimate striptease that elicited a number of whistles and catcalls. There were several other areas set up where the patrons were primarily non-human, and with respect to a couple of those, Maker admittedly had no clue what was going on. (For example, the action near one group seemed to consist of equal parts bird-calling, sword-swallowing, and finger painting.)

There were also tables and booths set up throughout the place, but there were nowhere near enough seats to accommodate all those present. The patrons themselves — loud, rowdy, and uncouth (and, if Maker's nose were any judge, unwashed) — all seemed to be of the same predatory ilk as the groups that had tried to raid their camp.

Silently, as they moved through the room, Maker came to the conclusion that the place was accurately named. It was an *arm*pit, a *snake* pit, a *cess*pit…just about any other kind of pit you could think of.

A scantily-clad woman with orange skin and feathers for hair turned and stroked Maker's face seductively as he walked by.

"How about some fun?" she said. "I'll make it worth your while."

"And at what price?" Maker asked, feigning interest.

"I'm sure we can work something out," she said, running her fingers through his hair.

"Another time, perhaps," Maker replied, pulling himself away.

He was propositioned two more times as he moved through the place — by an eerily beautiful woman with all-white eyes in one instance, and then by something that looked like a hairless, winged gorilla in a dress (and quite possibly could have been male). He turned to see how Wayne was faring and saw his companion with his head bent towards a woman with

166

horns on her temples. The woman whispered feverishly in his ear before extending a forked tongue that lovingly caressed the young man's cheek. Wayne turned beet red, and then began shaking his head fiercely before moving on, much to Maker's amusement.

Despite everything else taking place around them, Maker noticed that most of the action seemed to be fixed on an area in the middle of the room, where patrons — shouting and gesticulating wildly — appeared to be gathered in a humongous circle.

As he began walking towards that area, Maker felt Wayne tap him on the shoulder. He turned around to see what the young Marine wanted, but just as Wayne started to speak, a thunderous roar went up from the crowd encircling the middle of the room.

Wayne leaned in close and Maker inclined his head to hear him better. It probably would have been easier to use their comms, but they weren't working properly; the Pit utilized some kind of dampening field that hindered certain types of electronics — primarily communications, but also things such as cloaking and stealth technology — plausibly to prevent cheating with respect to various games of chance.

"Look!" Wayne shouted, and pointed towards the stage where the stripper was performing. Maker looked in that direction, but didn't see anything particularly out of the ordinary. He turned back to Wayne and made a *so-what?* gesture, shrugging his shoulders.

"Look!" Wayne screamed. "The stripper!"

Maker chuckled, thinking that Wayne must have had a severely sheltered upbringing if the sight of a half-naked woman got him this riled up.

"Yes, it's a stripper!" Maker shouted back. "When we finish this mission we'll find a nice club and you can hang out with girls like that all night long!"

Maker started to turn back when Wayne, clearly frustrated at this point, put a hand on his shoulder and spun him around again with surprising strength.

Maker felt himself getting angry now, as Wayne shouted once again, "*Look!*"

Although tired of this game, Maker glanced at the stripper once again...and then did a double-take.

The stripper was Diviana.

Maker was so taken by surprise that for a few moments he just stood there, watching her dance. (Somewhere in the back of his mind he also noted that she was *very* good.) Clearly she'd had no trouble fitting in, and Maker made a mental note that her background in intel might be extremely valuable to them in the future. She didn't seem to have noticed them, and for a second he debated approaching her, then jettisoned the idea.

A clap on his shoulder brought Maker back to himself.

"Come on! It's just a stripper!" Wayne said, laughing. "When we finish this mission..."

Maker waved off the rest of what his companion was saying, turning his attention back towards the throng of bodies clustered around the middle of the room. Rather than push his way through the crowd, Maker decided to let Erlen go first. It proved to be a wise choice.

As the Niotan began threading his way between numerous pairs of feet, those around him suddenly started yelping, leaping to the side as if burned with a hot poker. Maker had no idea whether Erlen was nipping ankles, secreting some irritant through his skin, or doing

168

something else, but it was highly effective. Within just a few seconds, the crowd began parting of its own volition, with everyone giving Erlen (as well as Maker and Wayne, who were following close behind) a wide berth.

A few moments later they were near the interior of the crowd, and Maker saw the namesake of the building: a large, circular arena — easily seventy feet in diameter — in the middle of the room. At the floor level where Maker stood, there was a railing that enclosed the area. However, there were several openings in the railing, through which stairs descended down among numerous rows of bleachers, all of which were currently occupied.

The bleachers themselves ended at another, interior circle — this one about twenty feet in diameter and also encircled by a railing. However, where the external circle gently angled down into bleachers, the internal circle seemed to be a straight drop of about fifteen feet that ended at a dirt floor. It was this area that was the true arena, the actual pit.

In the arena were two creatures that Maker had never seen before. One looked like a furry, four-legged octopus with a wicked-looking claw at the end of each tentacle, while the other seemed like a ten-foot tall, bipedal warthog with knife-like tusks and the tail of a scorpion. Both combatants were bloody, and it was clearly evident that this was a fight to the death.

Maker frowned in distaste; he wasn't particularly a fan of this kind of entertainment, which was really just an elevated cockfight between two larger and more vicious animals. The crowd in the bleachers, however, was enthusiastically following the action in the pit, cheering madly whenever one of the creatures scored a hit or seemed to get an advantage. Most of them probably had money wagered on this fight. In fact, Maker saw numerous bets being placed as the fight went on.

He scanned the horde of bodies around them, intensely looking for their contact. Browing had shown him an image of who they were looking for, and after a few moments Maker spotted him: an odd little creature who looked like a five-foot tall hummingbird, with wriggly worms all over its body instead of feathers, each of which ended in a bulbous eye. It was of a race known as the Panoptes, and it was sitting on the front row directly in front of the arena — a ringside seat.

Maker and his companions headed towards their contact. As they drew closer, approaching from the rear, Maker saw the Panoptes lean over and seemingly say something to a man sitting to the left of him. The man turned around, looked directly at Maker, and then motioned him over.

Of course; the Panoptes, with eyes all over its body, had seen them approaching — even from behind. Presumably, Browing had provided it with an image of Maker or some other means to identify him.

The man who had waved them over stood as Maker approached. He was a little taller than average, with a milky complexion and long, blond hair braided in cornrows that extended down his back. He looked over Maker and his fellows, subjecting them to heavy scrutiny, then eyed Maker in a way that suggested he might want to frisk him.

Not gonna happen, Maker thought, returning the man's stare. At that point, two other individuals came to their feet: a short but powerfully-built ursine alien who had been sitting to the right of the Panoptes, and a brawny giant (at least as tall as Fierce) who had been sitting to the left of the man with the blond braids. It didn't take a genius to figure out that these last two were hired muscle.

"It's fine, Croy," the Panoptes said, defusing a situation that undoubtedly had the potential to turn very ugly.

The man with the blond braids, Croy, nodded, then gestured for Maker to take his place sitting next to the Panoptes. Wayne sat down on the other side of Croy, while Erlen took up a position near Maker's knee. The bodyguards resumed their positions as bookends for the group.

"I'm Quinzen," the Panoptes announced, still facing forward towards the action in the pit.

"Pleased to make your acquaintance," Maker said, deliberately sidestepping a reciprocal introduction of himself. "I thought you were a simple merchant."

"I am," Quinzen replied.

"So why the hired guns?"

"Croy's essentially my aide. I rely on him for just about everything. As for Tranton and Graxel," he said, indicating the giant and the ursine, respectively, "Terminus is a place where even the homeless get robbed. Thus, someone of modest means, like myself, is often viewed as a rich target."

Several of Quinzen's eyestalks poked Maker, apparently more by accident than design (although it was difficult to tell). Maker was tempted to slide slightly to his left, but didn't know if it would be considered rude. He contemplated the matter for a second, then decided to stay put.

"You're early," Quinzen said after a moment, almost irritably. "I honestly wasn't expecting you for another hour or two."

"Oh?" Maker said, honestly surprised. "I must have misunderstood about the time."

"That's quite likely," Quinzen noted. "Many of the species here operate on different time frames, and misunderstandings about meeting times are not uncommon. But it's not of great consequence, since I'd planned to be here all this evening."

"Thanks for understanding," Maker said, to which the Panoptes merely nodded.

"How do you like the arena?" Quinzen asked, inclining his head towards where the two animals were fighting. The squid-like creature seemed to have the advantage at the moment, with two of its tentacles wrapped around its opponent's neck and constricting. The warthog-like creature stung it with its tail, but it seemed to have little effect.

Maker shrugged. "It's not really the type of action I go for."

"I understand," Quinzen replied, nodding. "Still, should you choose to bet, you'd be better off placing your money on the jwaedin." The Panoptes gestured towards the warthog combatant. "The poison in its stinger is often slow-acting, but invariably fatal to most life forms."

At that moment, a fight seemed to break out among two patrons sitting in the bleachers almost directly across from where Maker and his party were sitting. A woman with an eyepatch and wielding a pair of sais stood facing a rugged-looking scamp holding a dirk in one hand and a kukri in the other. For a moment, the crowd grew silent as the two stood there almost motionless, and then

172

there was a thunderous outburst from the spectators as the man and woman closed on each other.

Much like the arena, those watching swiftly gathered around the two in a circle, shouting encouragement (although keeping far enough back to avoid getting accidentally skewered by the fighters). The action in the actual arena seemed to be forgotten, and Maker commented on it to Quinzen.

"Yes," Quinzen agreed. "The spectacle of watching civilized beings slaughter each other has much more appeal in these parts than watching non-sentient creatures do it."

As if in confirmation, Maker saw bets being hurriedly placed on the fight between the man and the woman. Back in the true arena, Maker saw Quinzen's prediction come true as the squid-beast, perhaps as a result of its adversary's poison, lay unmoving on the ground as the jwaedin ripped its tentacles off and began eating them.

Across from them, the fight came to an abrupt end as the woman, with blood oozing from a dozen cuts, performed a feint that her opponent fell for. She then danced nimbly inside his guard and slammed one of the sais into his neck. A moment later, the man collapsed to the ground, convulsing.

There was a sigh of disappointment from the crowd, who began fading back to their original positions, with money exchanging hands between most of them.

"There will be a lull now until the next contest," Quinzen said. "Most times beasts are removed immediately after combat, but it's dangerous to disturb a jwaedin in the middle of a meal." He pointed back to the arena, where the victor was still feasting on the remains of his fallen enemy. Now that he wasn't distracted by the animals battling each other, Maker also noticed a door on the arena floor — presumably to let combatants in and out of the ring.

"The jwaedin's trainers starve it in the days before a fight," the Panoptes continued, "to make it more vicious during the fray."

"It seems to be an effective strategy," Maker commented, "judging from the current results."

"Indeed," Quinzen said. He turned his head towards Erlen, who had been silent and almost motionless since the moment Maker had sat down. "What about your pet? Does it fight?"

Maker frowned, involuntarily balling his hand into a fist. Watching two wild animals was bad enough; the thought of Erlen in an arena like that was incomprehensible.

"No," Maker replied, after a silence that had gone on just a little too long. "He's not a creature with that kind of entertainment value."

"Pity," Quinzen said, but something in his tone suggested that he actually found this to be good news.

They sat quietly as people in the crowd milled about, expectedly waiting for the next bout. After a few moments, Maker found himself growing impatient. They had yet to discuss the real topic of conversation — something he was loath to do in public anyway — but they weren't doing anything else either. The complete lack of activity (and discernable interest) on the part of Quinzen seemed unusual, given the circumstances. It was almost as if they were waiting for something — a thought that made Maker somewhat nervous and anxious.

"I realize that we're imposing on you," he finally said to Quinzen, "so if there's some place we could talk, where we can have a short conversation about what brought me to your doorstep, my companions and I will quickly be on our way."

"Of course," Quinzen replied. "My apologies. I forget what a rush you humans are always in, your lifespans being so short and all. I have a private suite on one of the upper floors here that I use to conduct business."

Maker glanced up, noticing not for the first time that, near the ceiling, the interior walls of the building seemed to support some sort of luxury boxes. He'd seen similar upscale seating at numerous entertainment complexes across the galaxy — places where the rich could enjoy spectacles or exhibitions without having to rub elbows with the masses.

Here, the tinted windows of the opulent booths looked down not just on the specific action in the arena, but across the Pit in general. Based on Quinzen's statement, Maker assumed that each luxury box was also connected to an opulent suite of rooms.

A harsh scream sounded behind him, causing Maker to spin around in alarm. The first thing he noticed was that the railing a few feet away from him had given way, and a portion of it now swung out ominously over the arena. The next thing he realized was that Wayne was missing.

Glancing down, Maker saw the young Marine stretched out in a prone position on the arena floor, slowly trying to rise but obviously stunned. Not far away, the jwaedin, its meal interrupted by Wayne's yell, looked around to locate the source of the commotion. Almost immediately, it spied Wayne lying helplessly on the ground. The creature howled, then dropped the tentacle it had been munching on and turned its attention to its new visitor.

Maker barely hesitated. Placing a hand on the top of the rail, he jumped — going up and over the barrier. As he was descending, he cast a concerned eye towards Erlen and was alarmed by what he saw: Quinzen's ursine bodyguard, Graxel, had gathered Erlen up in his arms and was attempting to hold the Niotan. Maker, however, had no time to dwell on the scene; the short glimpse he'd seen was cut off as he fell below the level of the bleachers and a second later he landed on the dirt floor of the arena.

Maker bent his knees on contact to help absorb some of the impact. At the same time, a deafening roar erupted from the crowd. Having two humans face off against a jwaedin was more than they had expected, and Maker could only imagine the bets — and the accompanying odds — now being made.

His sudden appearance (coupled with the unexpected scream from the crowd) startled the jwaedin, causing the beast to momentarily halt its advance on Maker's comrade. However, it quickly recovered. Screeching, it headed towards what appeared to be the weaker of the two adversaries facing it — Wayne, who had just struggled up to his knees.

Maker drew his sidearm and fired, sending three slugs at the jwaedin's chest. While they obviously did some damage — knocking the creature back and making it yelp in frustration — they failed to penetrate its flesh. Clearly, the jwaedin had an armored hide, and Maker found himself regretting the fact that he'd only brought standard projectile rounds with him.

Taking aim at the jwaedin's head, Maker fired again. The round struck one of the beast's six-inch tusks, snapping it off. The creature howled in agony, stamping around in a circle as its paws went up to its face, soothingly gripping the bloody gap in its maw where the tusk had been.

With the jwaedin distracted by its pain, Maker saw an opportunity to take advantage of the situation. He rushed over to Wayne, who was still on his knees but somewhat cognizant of his surroundings.

"On your feet, Marine!" Maker hissed, slipping Wayne's arm over his shoulder and helping him rise groggily to his feet. "Now move!"

As quickly as possible, they staggered over to the door Maker had seen earlier that led into the arena. It was about eight feet in height and made almost entirely of high-grade steel. The only part that wasn't metal was a small glass window in the middle of the door, obviously intended to let those on the other side know when it was safe to open up.

As Maker could have guessed, the door was locked. However, through the window, he could see movement on the other side.

"Open up!" Maker yelled, banging crazily on the door with his fist. "Open the damn door!"

Either those on the other side were too afraid of the jwaedin, too enthralled by what they were seeing, or too callous to be concerned, because the door remained locked. Behind him, Maker sensed movement and heard a low, savage growl. He spun himself and Wayne around; the jwaedin was staring fiercely at them from about ten feet away, but hadn't charged them. Behind it, Maker could see its scorpion-like tail swinging ominously in the air, the malignant stinger almost pulsing with venom.

It was clear what was happening: having been stopped by gunfire the two previous times that it tried to approach Wayne, the jwaedin had changed tactics. Instead, it was poised to let its tail do the dirty work. Moreover, the light body armor that the two Marines currently wore was unlikely to offer much protection.

Maker kept his eye on the thing's tail. After a few seconds, it suddenly ceased its swaying motion and became still. Maker shoved Wayne away and simultaneously dove to the side as, lightning-fast, the tail lashed between them, striking at the spot where they had stood a moment before. Maker went with his momentum, rolling on the ground and coming up on the balls of his feet. Wayne, on the other hand, had fallen to all fours, but — from the look in his eyes — had come to his senses and fully realized the predicament they were in.

The jwaedin growled fiercely, plainly preparing to strike again, although it was impossible to tell who it would aim for. Seeing that Wayne still hadn't fully recovered physically, Maker tried to ease his way over to the younger man.

Unexpectedly, a body landed lithely on the arena floor just a few feet away from Maker. It was Erlen. Maker also noticed something else hit the ground next to the Niotan — a bloody, severed forearm that Maker recognized as being from Qunizen's ursine bodyguard, Graxel. The person who, just moments before, Maker had last seen trying to hold Erlen.

The jwaedin was momentarily taken aback by the appearance of yet another combatant, but it wasn't about to be cowed by sheer numbers. It howled and seemed to fixate on Maker, who at the moment was between Erlen and Wayne. Before it could do anything, however, Erlen leaped at the beast, making an incredibly powerful jump that not only cleared the horizontal distance between it and the jwaedin, but vertically brought it up to the height of the creature's head.

The jwaedin swatted Erlen aside like an annoying insect, sending the Niotan flying into the arena wall with frightening force.

"Erlen!" Maker shouted in concern, his voice causing the jwaedin to direct its attention once again to the two humans. Wayne, finally appearing to be steady, was just getting to his feet when Maker saw the jwaedin's tail pause. Again, he acted instinctively, racing over and shoving Wayne out of the way just as the creature struck.

Something akin to a white-hot lance pierced the upper part of Maker's chest, just below his right clavicle. He looked down and saw the jwaedin's stinger lodged in his pectoral. Blood arced out as the stinger was viciously yanked out by the creature.

Maker dropped to his knees, stunned. He probably would have fallen forward onto his face had not Wayne rushed over and, gripping Maker in a bear hug, begun lifting him to his feet.

From Maker's perspective, the world seemed to stagger and then go into slow motion. The crowd around the rim of the pit moved like they were under water, limbs and bodies struggling against some unseen resistance. Their lips moved and facial expressions changed at a glacial pace, while their screams and shouts stretched into an unending drone. Off to the side, he saw Erlen rising up from the ground like an aged sloth, as if each muscle in his body had to be individually commanded to move.

Maker found himself concentrating fiercely, trying to remember whether there was anything vital in the area where he had been hit. The blood pounded in his ears; he couldn't focus. Wayne was trying to say something to him, but Maker couldn't make out the words.

He tried to remember what Quinzen had said about the effectiveness of the jwaedin's poison. *Slow-acting, my ass*, he thought. Speaking of the beast, he looked over the shoulder of Wayne and saw the creature preparing to strike again.

At that moment, Erlen roared. Later, both Maker and Wayne would say it was the loudest noise they'd ever heard a living creature make. It was a sound of power, so full of rage and fury and so sonorous that it seemingly drowned out not just the crowd around the arena but everything in the Pit.

With Erlen's cry, the world shifted back into normal speed, but Maker almost didn't notice because the crowd had gone completely silent. Then, with a snarl, Erlen went on the attack, charging at the jwaedin; the spectators erupted into shouts once again.

Maker's perspective shifted as — in a reversal of their roles just moments earlier — Wayne now had the job of supporting his commanding officer and urging him towards the arena door. Glancing back, Maker saw Erlen lunge at one of the jwaedin's legs, claws raking across the larger animal's calf. It screeched and went down to one knee, blood squirting from the injured limb.

He turned his attention forward and found that they were at the arena door again; Wayne was banging on it and shouting for someone to open up. To Maker's surprise, there was an audible click and then the door swung open. Maker couldn't make out anything in the darkened interior, but he wasn't about to look a gift horse in the mouth as Wayne hustled him inside. It was then that he got a good look at their savior: Diviana.

She was still dressed like a stripper, but the look on her face said that she was all business.

"Thanks," Wayne began. "We—"

"Don't thank me yet," Diviana replied, cutting him off as she shut the door. She started to say something else, but Maker couldn't catch it. His eyes fluttered and he struggled mentally to stay conscious.

Glancing around, he saw that they were in some type of antechamber. There were several bodies stretched out on the floor, but Maker couldn't tell if they were alive or dead.

A moment later, Maker found himself being shuffled along, with Diviana under one of his arms and Wayne under the other. He realized they were trying to get him out, but there was something they were forgetting…something important. It came to him almost immediately.

"No!" he shouted, pushing his companions away. "Erlen…" He staggered a few steps towards the arena door, and then started to collapse again before Diviana and Wayne caught him once more.

"We don't have time…" he heard Diviana saying.

"I'm not leaving him!" Maker yelled, barely able to keep his eyes open.

"Alright, alright," Wayne said, easing Maker down to a sitting position.

Maker battled to keep his eyes open as Wayne stepped swiftly over to the arena door. Wiping his forehead with the back of his hand, he was surprised to see it come away drenched in sweat.

Fever, he thought. He was going downhill fast.

He was distracted from his own issues, however, when Wayne — at least he *assumed* it was Wayne; his vision was starting to blur — opened the arena door and something bounded inside a second later, heading straight for him. As it got closer, a familiar growl brought a smile to Maker's face. He closed his eyes as Erlen licked his face a couple of times, then did the same thing to his injury.

"Ugh!" Diviana screamed. "You stupid animal!"

Maker thought he heard a sound similar to someone clapping their hands together once, but he was far too tired to open his eyes and figure out what had happened. He felt himself physically starting to topple over backwards, with Diviana still angrily venting about something as he lost consciousness.

Chapter 22

Maker came to with a start, waking from dreamless slumber to find himself in a field clinic — a tent outfitted with various types of medical equipment. It took him a second to realize that it was his squad's mobile hospital, which meant that he was back at camp.

At the moment, he was lying in a hospital bed. His right shoulder felt oddly constricted, and when he reached to touch it he felt bandages, wrapping around from the right side of his chest up over his shoulder. Of course, his people had cleaned and dressed his wound, and the thought of his injury brought to mind his harrowing encounter with the jwaedin.

As Maker struggled to sit up, his head swam and a dull ache in his chest made him reach involuntarily towards his wound. It was at that moment that he realized that he wasn't wearing a shirt. As he swung his feet to the floor, his leg bumped something and he looked down to see Erlen sleeping next to his bed.

"Move," Maker said softly, nudging the Niotan with his foot; without waking, Erlen obliged by rolling towards the end of the bed. With the impediment removed, Maker was about to attempt to stand when the tent flap opened and Fierce entered.

"Easy, easy," Fierce said, stepping over to Maker's side. "You're still weak."

"Everyone's weak compared to an Augman," Maker countered, causing Fierce to laugh. "But I don't have time to debate the subject. How long was I out for?"

"Just an hour or two," Fierce said, then shouted over his shoulder, "He's awake."

As if on cue, Wayne, Snick, and Loyola entered the tent. They greeted him warmly and appeared genuinely happy to see that Maker was somewhat on the mend.

Wayne in particular looked relieved, and it showed when he spoke. "Glad to see you're going to be okay, el-tee," he said.

"Yeah, well, it takes more than a little pinprick to keep a Marine down," Maker replied.

"I was sure you were good as dead," Wayne replied. "You were feverish, unconscious, and non-responsive."

"So what happened? How'd we get back here?"

"Once Erlen was back with us, Diviana and I started dragging you out of the chambers that connected to the arena. Just in time, too, because the jwaedin came through the door just a few seconds later."

"The jwaedin?"

"Yeah. My guess is that it was coming after Erlen, who scratched it up pretty good," Wayne said, glancing at the Niotan's sleeping form. "Apparently I didn't close the door completely after letting him in, and the jwaedin just had to lean on it and it opened up."

"What happened next?"

"We ran," Wayne answered. "As fast as we could with you slowing us down" — he winked, and Maker laughed — "but Diviana knew her way around. She took us through a couple of passageways that the jwaedin was too large to fit in. You could hear it screaming in frustration behind us."

"Diviana — is she alright?"

"She's fine — and as far as I know she's resumed her cover as a stripper."

TERMINUS

"What was she doing down in that chamber in the first place?" Maker asked. He had meant it almost rhetorically, so he was slightly surprised when Wayne actually answered.

"She said she saw us when we first came in," he said. "She sweet-talked one of the animal trainers into letting her watch from their alcove. She told them she liked to be close to the action."

"So she was keeping an eye on us while we met with our contact."

"Yes, and when things went haywire, she popped a gas pill, knocking out the trainers."

Maker nodded, remembering the bodies he had seen in the room that connected to the arena. Apparently they'd been merely unconscious, not dead. "Then she opened the door and let us in," he concluded. "By the way, how'd you end up on the floor of that arena anyway?"

Wayne cast his eyes down, clearly somewhat embarrassed. "The big guy, the human bodyguard. He just kicked the rail, knocking it loose, and shoved me through. I guess I had my guard down."

"It's alright," Maker said, clapping the young man supportively on the shoulder. "We both should have been a little more on our toes."

"Thanks," Wayne said meekly.

"Wait, so it was a setup?" Loyola asked, speaking for the first time since entering.

"Apparently," Maker concluded. "With me stung and slowing everyone down, I'm surprised they didn't send someone in to finish us off."

Wayne laughed. "Are you kidding? As far as anyone was concerned, there were at least two

185

bloodthirsty monsters down there — Erlen and the jwaedin. Nobody in their right mind was going anywhere near those chambers — which were like a maze, if you want to know the truth — especially with the jwaedin still screaming after us.

"Anyway, Diviana said she'd been cozying up to the trainers for days, so she was aware of some little-known points of ingress and egress. She got us out unseen. Then we got you to the cart, I slapped some cryo-film on you, and then hightailed it here while Diviana went back to the Pit. Even then, I wasn't sure you'd make it — Erlen either."

"What??" Maker asked, clearly startled. He instinctively looked to where Erlen was still sleeping peacefully on the floor. "What do you mean?"

"When I first let him in the chamber," Wayne explained, "he ran over and licked you. Not just your face, but your wound, too. Diviana freaked at that point — called him a stupid animal and smacked him on the nose."

Maker thought back, remembering the clapping sound he'd heard just before he passed out.

"She started cursing at him, and would probably still be doing it if the jwaedin hadn't come through the door as we were dragging you out of there and given her something else to think about."

"So how does that lead to Erlen almost not making it?" Maker asked.

"A short time after we started moving through the chambers, he started slowing down and making these weird noises. I didn't understand what the problem was, but Diviana knew right away."

"He'd swallowed some of the poison when he licked the lieutenant's wound," Fierce interjected. Up until now he'd been silently checking the equipment around Maker's bed, obviously trying to assess the condition of his patient.

"Yes," Wayne agreed. "By the time we made it to the cart he was barely on his feet. On the way back, he twitched and convulsed a couple of times — I think he may even have bitten you once, by accident, through the cryo-film."

Maker nodded, taking all this in.

"After you arrived, I had to triage — decide who to treat first — and you were the priority," Fierce said, jumping in. "Fortunately, by the time I had you checked out, Erlen seemed to have recovered."

"And the el-tee?" Snick asked. "What's his condition?"

"That would violate the sacred rule of doctor-patient confidentiality," Fierce replied. "Now, since I only let you all in so you could see that he's okay, I need you guys to leave us alone so I can talk to the lieutenant."

"It's fine," Maker said. "They can stay. I've always treated the people under my command as family, and it's to their benefit to know whether or not I'm fit."

"As long as you're okay with it," Fierce said, and then his shoulders slumped and a frown came over his face. "To be honest, I don't know your condition. I mean, my equipment says you're fine, but I'm not sure if it's properly calibrated because I'm getting some weird readings."

"Weird in what way?" Maker asked.

"For starters, there's no sign of poison in your system," Fierce said. "Not even a trace that there ever was any."

"Maybe the deadliness of jwaedin's venom has been over-exaggerated," Snick suggested.

Fierce shook his head. "Unlikely. It may not cause immediate death, but their poison is invariably fatal to humans."

"Maybe its poison glands were removed, surgically replaced with something else — something less than fatal," Wayne suggested.

Fierce shrugged. "Anything's possible, I guess, but I'm not getting an indication of any kind of toxins in his system."

"Well, as long as I've got a clean bill of health," Maker said, rising to his feet.

"Wait, where do you think you're going?" Fierce asked, putting an objecting palm out towards Maker's chest. "I haven't released you yet."

"I appreciate the concern, Doc, but I'm fine," Maker insisted. "Besides, we've got bigger fish to fry."

"What do you mean?" Loyola asked.

"Wayne and I basically walked into an ambush," Maker replied. "That means our contact is probably in cahoots with the Vacra. We need to find out what he knows."

"Even if that's true, you're in no shape to be going out," Fierce insisted. "You need more time to recover. It's only been a few hours since that thing stung you."

"Exactly," Maker stated with conviction. "They probably think I'm either dead or out of commission — Wayne, too. They won't be expecting anything."

"Then why not send Adames?" Fierce said.

"Send me where?" said a voice from the front of the tent. It was Adames; Maker had been so intent on his conversation with the Augman that he hadn't even noticed the man come in. In fact, he hadn't even given any thought to Adames since he'd awakened.

"Good to see you," Adames said, walking over and shaking Maker's hand with a smile.

"Good to be seen," Maker replied.

"Sorry I wasn't here when you woke up," Adames went on, "but I'm on watch. Still, I heard the story of what happened. When I saw these three" — he pointed his thumb in the direction of Wayne, Snick, and Loyola — "slip inside the tent, I figured you were awake. I can only be away for a few minutes, but I wanted to check up on you. So, what's up? Why are you guys batting my name around?"

"The lieutenant here had a hole punched in his chest a few hours ago," Fierce blurted out, "but he still thinks he's ready to take on the world." The Augman then quickly gave the master sergeant a summary of their conversation up to that point.

"It makes sense," Adames said. "You should stay here and let me go take care of it."

"And I probably would except for one tiny detail," Maker said. "You don't know what these guys look like."

"Well, one's a man-sized bird with eye-worms all over its body," Adames said. "It'll be a stretch, but I can probably pick him out in a crowd."

"And he's the only Panoptes on the planet, right?" Maker said. "So the first one you see is clearly your guy, correct?"

189

Adames frowned, exchanging glances with Fierce, then the rest of their squad.

"You can provide renditions of his human companions," Adames suggested. "Work with the graphic AI in the ship to fashion composite images."

Maker shook his head. "That would take at least an hour, and we need to move *now*."

"I see," Adames muttered, biting his lip. "So it'll just be you and Wayne?"

Maker shook his head in the negative. "No. Wayne's had enough excitement for one day. It'll just be me."

"Now you're really talking crazy," Adames said. "No way you're jumping straight out of a hospital bed and into something like this alone. I'm coming with you."

"You can't. I need you here to take over in case something actually does happen to me. We can't leave the mission leaderless."

Adames chewed on that for a moment, and then said, almost angrily, "Fine, but you're not going by yourself. One of our people needs to go with you."

"I volunteer," Loyola said almost immediately.

Caught slightly by surprise, Maker hesitated for a moment, then answered. "Thanks, but if Adames insists on someone coming with me, I think I'll take Snick."

"Sir," Loyola began, "if this is about me being a woman or my eyes—"

"That's got nothing to do with it," Maker almost snapped. "If you've been doing your usual, then you've been out in the desert all day. We're going to need you fresh if you're going to handle your duties tomorrow."

"But sir—"

"That will be all, Sergeant," Maker almost yelled, cutting her off. She gave him a hard look, then stalked from the tent. A moment later, Fierce — after giving Maker a withering glance — went after her.

There were a few moments of uncomfortable silence, and then Snick excused himself to go get ready, and Wayne went with him.

"That was a little harsh, don't you think?" Adames asked when the two men were alone. "The way you dealt with Loyola?"

"I didn't mean for it to be," Maker said, "but I think her skills would be better utilized here. Plus, we don't have time to be worried about someone's thin skin."

Chapter 23

A short time later, Maker found himself in his tent, putting on a fresh shirt. He had spent a few more minutes talking to Adames in the hospital tent before the master sergeant returned to watch duty. Then, with Fierce failing to return, he had discharged himself and departed (although he left Erlen sleeping by the bed).

Maker had just gotten the shirt on when someone outside his tent called to him.

"Permission to enter?" Wayne asked.

"Granted," Maker replied.

Wayne entered and saluted smartly. Maker returned the gesture, and then announced, "At ease. What can I do for you, Marine?"

Wayne didn't say anything for a moment, obviously unsure of himself. Finally, he just said, "Sir, I'd like to come with you."

"With me?" Maker repeated questioningly.

"Yes. Back to the Pit. With you and Snick."

Maker nodded sagely, but said nothing.

"I know I let you down before," Wayne continued, "but I want to show you that you can depend on me."

"You didn't let me down, Marine," Maker said. "You got me out of there — saved my life."

"But you saved mine first. You jumped over that railing to come after me...pushed me out of the way and got stung by that thing in my place."

"Well, they were probably planning to pitch me over the railing after you; I just saved them the trouble. As to getting stung, it's what I would have done for any fellow Marine. And I think you would, too."

Wayne looked doubtful. "I like to think I would, but in truth I'm not sure. The only thing I know for certain is that you saved my life, and I owe you."

Maker thought for a second. "You know, if you really want to pay me back, there's something else you can do instead of coming along on this suicide run with me and Snick."

"Anything I can do, I will, sir."

"Well, I won't hold you to that. I'll give you the option to decide." Maker hesitated for a moment, appraising Wayne as he'd done once before, and the young Marine knew without question what Maker was about to ask of him.

"You remember that device I showed you before…" Maker began.

Chapter 24

The Pit, still overflowing with rabble of all kinds, was the same sentient cesspool that it had been when Maker was last there.

And why should it be any different? he thought. *I was just here a few hours ago.*

Those hours, however, felt like ages — enough time for him to fight a monster, almost die, and then return angry and vengeful.

He had come back and entered the place with single-minded purpose. Now that he was here, however, he wasn't quite sure what to do. Quinzen wasn't hanging out in the arena (big surprise), where two other beasts were now brawling. He also hadn't given Maker any indication of where his shop was, nor provided any other type of calling card. They could ask around, maybe grease some palms (and hope nobody told Quinzen that strangers were asking about him), but truth be told, Maker really didn't have a solid plan for finding the Panoptes.

Maker stood, unmoving, in the middle of the Pit, trying to figure out what to do. Snick, apparently sensing his commander's mood, stood quietly off to the side. Maker was starting to get into a funk about the entire situation when a soft palm caressed his cheek and a seductive feminine voice whispered in his ear, "Care for some company?"

Irritated, Maker pushed the woman's hand away without even deigning to look at her. "Another time," he said, trying to concentrate on the problem at hand.

"Aw, come on, handsome," the woman said, her hand gently stroking his chest where the bandage was located. "I bet you know how to show a girl a good time."

Out of patience, Maker gripped the woman's wrist and turned to face her. "I said, not—" he began, and then the words froze in his throat.

The woman was Diviana.

"Are you sure?" she said, raising an eyebrow. Scantily clad in a skimpy blue outfit that put all kinds of images in Maker's head, she placed a hand beguilingly on her hip. "I'll make it worth your while."

Maker hesitated momentarily, and then said, "You know what, I think I would like some company."

"Come on, then," Diviana said, taking his hand and leading him away. "We have a private area in the back."

She began leading him towards a narrow hallway near the area where the strippers performed. Glancing back, Maker saw Snick standing as if petrified. He was about to go back and check on the man, then Maker realized the issue. Snick, although he had been informed of Diviana's cover, had not been mentally prepared to see her in the role of stripper.

Maker almost laughed as Snick seemed to recover and began moving after them. Maker motioned for his subordinate to stay put as Diviana pulled him into the darkened passageway, which appeared to have numerous doors up and down its length. She chose a door on the right near the center of the hallway and led Maker inside.

They were in a small room, maybe one hundred square feet in size, the most prominent feature of which was a large bed. (Maker did, however, note a plain wooden chair in one corner and a single door that presumably led to a washroom.)

"Quite a recovery you've made," Diviana said, glancing at the area where his wound was located as she closed the door. "I didn't expect to see you back here so soon — if at all."

"Yeah, well, I'm a Marine," Maker said with pride as he flopped down on the edge of the bed. "Death has better things to do than hold my hand and escort me to the pearly gates. Regardless, thanks for helping me and Wayne out before."

"Does that mean you're ready to admit that my plan to come here on my own had merit?"

"Let's not be hasty. We're not done by a long shot — which is why Snick and I are here."

Maker quickly outlined for Diviana his plan to locate Quinzen and figure out what he knew.

"Well, his location is easy," she said when he finished. "He's up in his luxury box here."

"Are you sure?" Maker asked, trying not to sound excited.

Diviana gave him a scathing look. "Intel's my business. If I say it, you can bank on it."

"Alright, your word is gold," Maker said, getting to his feet. "And now that I know where our little friend is, he and I will have a conversation."

"Oh? And how do you plan on getting to see him?" Diviana asked. "There's only one way up to the luxury area, and that's through a lift that's always guarded. Plus, you need a digi-key to operate it, as well as get into Quinzen's apartments."

"So what are we supposed to do?"

"Well, he's bound to leave sometime, so you could just wait him out," Diviana suggested, at which Maker drew in a breath in preparation to explain all the reasons why they couldn't wait. However, Diviana didn't give him a chance, stating, "Or, you could use this."

She held up a short strip of engraved metal that was kind of knobby at one end. A digi-key. She held it out to Maker.

"How were you able to get this?" Maker asked, taking the key and examining it.

"I was able to get it because men are stupid!" Diviana declared, perhaps slightly miffed that Maker seemed to be questioning her skills again. "You always want to show how special you are, how powerful, how well-connected. Everybody wanted to get close to me because I was the new girl — unsullied, so to speak. I had one of the trainers for the arena showing me around the inner chambers within a day, all the entrances and exits. I have one of the local arms merchants eating out of my hand, and he gives me practically anything I ask for, from gas pellets to explosive rounds. And your friend Quinzen's aide, Croy, gave me the digi-key because he wants to sleep with me in his boss' opulent suite."

"Damn, I had no idea you were this good," Maker said.

"I'm more than good. I'm the best."

"Now who's thinking they're special?" Maker asked with a wink.

Diviana smiled briefly, then turned serious again. "You still need to get access to the lift. The guards aren't even going to let you get close if they don't know who you are. They'll ask you who you're there to see and then call up to verify."

"It's a problem, but one that I'm sure we can work around. Good work, Marine."

Maker began heading towards the door.

"One more thing," Diviana said. "Before you try to board the lift, you need to hire at least two other girls — and Snick needs to hire some as well."

"What?" Maker asked, confused.

"Well, you're not going straight from being alone with me to the luxury suites with a restricted key! The first thing anyone is going to ask later is who-was-that-guy? and then someone's going to say that they saw him with me, and the next thing you know I'm hogtied in some basement getting chopped up with a vibro-blade!"

"Okay, I get it," Maker said defensively. "We need for suspicion to be cast on someone other than just you if things go sideways."

"Yes, so just go out there and hire a couple of more girls before you go upstairs with guns blazing."

"But what am I supposed to do with them?"

Diviana gave him a look of sad sympathy. "Oh, Lieutenant. Do you really need the birds and bees explained to you?"

Maker shook his head, a blasé expression on his face. "Fine," he said. "Whatever I have to do."

"Geez, you men are so single-minded," Diviana countered. "You don't have to do anything like *that*. You could just talk — you'd be surprised at how many men want to do no more than that. Also, what's intimacy for humans isn't universal. Other beings like other things — some of which *Homo sapiens* wouldn't even bat an eye at."

"Okay, you're the expert here," Maker acknowledged, opening the door. "What nubile young damsel should I set my sights on out there?"

"Try the one with the orange feathers. Tickling her species under the arms is supposed to give them exquisite pleasure."

TERMINUS

"But what if she gets pregnant?" Maker asked mockingly as he stepped out of the room. Diviana rolled her eyes and shut the door.

Chapter 25

It took about fifteen minutes for Maker and Snick to comply with Diviana's request concerning other girls. During that time, Maker came up with what he thought was a feasible plan for getting to the lift.

The lift itself was just an anti-grav elevator that sat behind a set of double doors. Guarding the entrance to those doors, however, were four armed guards. They were big, burly fellows, and each had a no-nonsense look about him. Thus, even though the Pit's patrons milled about only a few feet away from the guards, none of the customers moved in such a way that their intentions could be mistaken.

"Alright," Maker said to Snick after watching the guards for a few minutes from a spot against the wall. "You're on."

Snick smiled. "Thank you, sir."

Snick walked over to a group of three men in close vicinity to the four guards. He intentionally bumped into one of the men, and when the fellow turned in his direction, Snick punched him in the face, sending him staggering backwards. The man's companions both came at Snick, who stepped in and — deflecting a punch from the first — delivered a punishing kidney shot. The second man immediately dropped to his knees and began vomiting, causing people nearby to yelp and high-step in an effort to get out of the way.

While his second opponent was on the floor being sick, Snick charged the third man. Going in low, he caught the man around the waist with his shoulder, lifting him off the ground. Snick took a few more steps before releasing his hold, sending his adversary flying into a crowd of onlookers. One of them dropped a drink that he was holding after being nudged, then angrily swung at Snick's last opponent; he missed his target (who ducked) but connected with someone else. Within moments, a full-fledged, old-school bar fight broke out.

Someone landed a punch on Snick, sending him sprawling onto the floor near the elevator guards, one of whom stepped forward.

"Move it," the guard said, nudging Snick with his foot, before grabbing him by the collar and hauling him up.

The minute Snick was on his feet, he gripped the guard's wrist, spun, and then punched the fellow in the solar plexus. The blow sent the guard reeling backwards into the melee. The remaining three guards all rushed forward to engage Snick, who backed his way into the fracas.

With the doors clear, Maker wasted no time. He rushed forward and slipped the digi-key into the appropriate slot and turned it. The few seconds that it took the internal machinery to read the entry code embedded in the key's internal circuitry felt like a lifetime to Maker. It was a struggle to ignore the brouhaha going on behind him, but he resisted the urge to turn around. Finally, the elevator doors opened. Maker removed the key and stepped inside. Glancing out, he saw that all of the Pit seemed to be fighting. He did a quick scan for Snick but didn't see him. Then the elevator doors closed and he started to move up.

TERMINUS

Chapter 26

The trip up in the elevator only took a few seconds. When the lift doors parted they revealed a second set of doors, which — after Maker inserted the digi-key into a conspicuous slot — opened directly into a palatial suite, full of expensive furnishings and fine art.

Maker had his gun in his hand as he exited the lift, treading as softly as possible. The place was well-lit, but he didn't see anyone.

He was currently in what appeared to be the living area, with lots of furniture for lounging around. One wall was made entirely of panes of glass. Stepping over to it, Maker realized that the giant window presented a view of all the action in the Pit below.

A sound from the far end of a nearby hallway drew Maker's attention. Quickly but silently, he dashed down the hallway, passing a few bedrooms, a media room, and something that looked like a torture chamber along the way.

The end of the hallway opened up into a small sitting area, with a set of stairs leading up. Cautiously, he began heading up the stairs. However, he'd advanced no more than three steps when Croy appeared at the top of the stairs.

Something akin to shock spread across Croy's features, and he froze, just staring at Maker. A moment later he blinked, then opened his mouth — presumably to cry out. Maker shot him in the face.

Maker's modified gun didn't make much noise, but Croy's body (sans facial features) did as it collapsed and went tumbling down the stairs. Maker pressed himself flush against the wall, letting the corpse roll past and then rushed up the stairs.

The landing at the top of the stairway opened up into another sitting area and connected to a short, dimly-lit hallway.

"Croy?" inquired a voice that Maker recognized as belonging to Quinzen. "What was that noise?"

The voice had come from the hallway, and Maker scrambled to the side of the entrance to the corridor, pretty confident that he hadn't been seen.

Footsteps sounded in the hallway, coming closer. Maker tightened his grip on his gun, held his breath. When he thought that the Panoptes was almost at the end of the corridor, he stepped in front of the hallway and fired.

There was an agonizing squawk, followed by Quinzen falling to the floor, screeching in pain. Maker grabbed him by the beak and dragged him out onto the landing.

Out of the shadowy hallway, Maker could see the damage that had been done. A whole crop of Quinzen's eyestalks had been blasted away on his right side, where a nasty wound now gushed out violet blood.

It was obviously a painful injury, but clearly not a fatal one — nor was it intended to be. (It would be difficult to get answers from a corpse.)

"Your bodyguards!" Maker hissed. "Where are they?"

"Not...not here," Quinzen weakly replied, his remaining eyestalks flopping around feebly. "Take Graxel...arm...medic."

Maker understood. The ursine Graxel had lost an arm trying to hold Erlen, and his companion had taken him for treatment. Also, he suddenly remembered Quinzen's question about Erlen possibly fighting in the arena. The Panoptes must have taken Maker's negative response to mean that Erlen was docile — a miscalculation that had cost Graxel dearly.

"Jwaedin...poison..." Quinzen mumbled. "You, alive...how?"

"Forget that! Why did you set us up?"

"Money..." Quinzen muttered almost matter-of-factly. "Also, no choice...Vacra...humans..."

Quinzen shuddered involuntarily, almost as if he were having a seizure, and several of his eyestalks were now weeping blood.

Movement at the edge of his peripheral vision caused Maker to turn towards the stairway. There, coming up the stairs in full battle armor, was a Vacra.

Maker almost couldn't believe it. Finally, one of the filth decided to show themselves. (Not Skullcap, but a Vacra nonetheless.) After years of waiting—

Movement near the Vacra's hands cut into Maker's thoughts, and a second later he flung himself to the side as laser fire sliced through the space he'd just vacated. Firing from his prone position on the floor, Maker made several direct — but ineffectual — hits on the insectoid's thorax. His weapon couldn't penetrate its armor.

An odd chirping drew Maker's attention back to Quinzen...except he was no longer lying where Maker had left him. Whether he'd been playing possum or the fear of getting shot again had given him a boost of adrenaline, the Panoptes was now shambling down the hallway he'd come from.

Maker took one last shot at the Vacra and then dashed after Quinzen, who entered a doorway at the end of the hall. The Panoptes slammed the door in Maker's face. Maker didn't have to try the knob to know that it was locked, but did it anyway. Sadly, his prediction was confirmed.

He was about to shoot off the lock when laser-fire came blasting through the door from the inside. Maker dropped to the ground; Quinzen obviously had a weapon in there. Moreover, he heard some kind of mechanical grinding noise coming from the other side of the door.

Glancing back the way he'd come, Maker saw a shadow fall across the hallway entrance. In a moment, he was going to be pinned down. Deciding which was the lesser of two evils, Maker fired indiscriminately through the door, sending splinters of wood flying everywhere. He heard a squawk from inside the room, and then a thud. Without wasting a second, Maker ran forward and dove through the remainder of the door, essentially demolishing it.

He hit the floor inside and rolled, coming up with his gun in his hand. He need not have bothered; Quinzen was lying on the floor with a hole in his chest, obviously dead (although a few of his eyestalks still twitched spasmodically). More interesting was the fact that, at the moment, a metal ladder was slowly descending from the twenty-foot ceiling.

Of course, Quinzen had had a secret escape route. It fit the type of duplicitous personality he'd proved to have at the end.

Laser fire came through the door, reminding Maker that he still had an enemy to deal with. Looking around for what was really the first time, Maker noticed that he appeared to be in Quinzen's private bedroom. In addition to the large window-wall for viewing the action in the Pit, there were also several vidscreens and a large case full of unusual objects — some sort of collection.

Maker gripped the case and manhandled it into position in front of the door. It wasn't much of a barrier, but it would buy him some time.

Turning back to the ladder, Maker found himself mentally hurrying it to finish descending when, with a creak and a groan, it came to a sudden stop with the lowest rung still about eight feet from the floor.

No! No! NO!!! Maker mentally wailed. Obviously, Quinzen hadn't made regular maintenance of his escape route a part of his normal routine. Now Maker was going to pay the price for it.

"Thanks a lot," Maker mumbled, kicking the dead Panoptes for good measure. Then he took a powerful leap, grabbed the bottom of the ladder, and began to pull himself up, hand over hand. After a few seconds, he was able to get a foot on the bottom rung, and it was easy going after that.

At the top of the ladder was a hatch. Maker gripped the handle, twisted, and then pushed up. With a screech of grating metal, the hatch slowly swung open. Maker scrambled out, then slammed the hatch shut before looking around.

He was on a flattened, square-shaped portion of the Pit's domed roof. He did a quick recon, noting that the area where he found himself — while railed — joined the sloped segment of the roof without any way to safely descend. There were other buildings nearby, but much too far away for him to jump to.

TERMINUS

A weird droning noise seemed to permeate through the air, indicating that some type of machinery was in operation. A few moments later it stopped and suddenly the wind began to buffet Maker on all sides. Almost immediately, it came to him what the droning sound had been: a force field. (He should have realized that Quinzen wouldn't have had an undefended point of entry into his residence.) Now that it was gone, the wind whipped wildly across the rooftop, making him squint.

Maker thought furiously. It didn't make any sense. Quinzen wouldn't have an escape route that was essentially a dead end. There had to be a way down from the roof. He went back to scouting the edge of the rooftop, going slowly and more deliberately this time, looking for anything he might have missed before.

There! On the domed portion of the roof just below the railing on the south side of the building was a panel that wasn't flush with its fellows. Maker got down on his hands and knees and reached for it. The panel, attached by some type of hinge, swung open. Inside was a hoverboard.

Maker sent up a silent thanks to the heavens, then pulled the hoverboard out of the hidden slot. It was a little old, but that was somehow fitting since he hadn't ridden one of these things since he was a kid. In fact, as he placed it on the ground and then stepped on it, he realized that he really wouldn't be riding it now; his plan was only to use it to get down from the roof, not do a bunch of adolescent tricks like some juvenile trying to impress a girl.

As he stepped on, his weight activated the board. The foot-frames on it closed in on his boots, locking his feet in place on the panel so he wouldn't fall off. Then the anti-grav cells activated, lifting the board up. Maker wobbled slightly, trying to remember how to keep his balance. Behind him, he heard the hatch being swung open.

Maker bent his knees and did a little hop. The hoverboard, sensing his intentions, rose up and Maker guided it over the railing. He smiled as he floated there alongside the dome, waiting for the Vacra to catch sight of him as it crawled out onto the roof. When it did, Maker flipped it the middle finger on both hands, and then directed the board to descend as the insectoid raised its weapon.

The board descended about four feet and then halted, sputtering. A moment later, it also began shooting sparks. Maker's arms pinwheeled as he struggled to maintain his balance, wondering what was wrong. Then the anti-grav cells cut out.

Maker reached crazily for the roof as he dropped, managing to get a hand on the edge of the flattened portion. It was all that kept him from falling to his death.

Damn you, Quinzen, he thought. Apparently the escape ladder wasn't the only thing that the Panoptes failed to maintain.

Wriggling like a worm on a hook, Maker managed swing around and get a grip on the roof with his free hand. He was just about to start pulling himself up when he heard footsteps approaching. Looking up, he saw the Vacra standing at the railing above him, its weapon pointed at his head.

Maker stared at the Vacra, wondering whether it would be better to fall and die by his own hand rather than give this thing the satisfaction of shooting him. No, letting go would be the equivalent of giving up, and he was determined to fight to the bitter end.

"Go on, then," he said to the Vacra. "Do it."

He kept his eyes on its helmet, determined not to look away as the Vacra seemed to tighten its grip on its weapon. Then half the insectoid's head was sheared away, and it fell over backwards, twitching.

The comm piece in his ear, which Maker had practically forgotten about, crackled with life, and Loyola's voice — laced with static — came through in a flat tone, saying, "You're welcome."

Chapter 27

For one of the few times in his military career, Maker was actually happy that a subordinate had disobeyed one of his direct orders.

"It wasn't really disobedience," Loyola explained when he asked her. "Right after you and Snick left, Adames ordered me to hop on a hovercycle and go after you. Thus, I was actually obeying the orders of the ranking military member on hand."

Happy to be alive, Maker wasn't about to argue with her. As he understood it, both Loyola and Wayne had followed Snick and himself to the Pit. (Apparently Wayne, still feeling that he owed his life to Maker, had insisted on coming when he found out where Loyola was headed.) By Maker's estimate, they had arrived around the time he was sneaking into Quinzen's suite.

"The dampening field in the Pit is weaker the higher you go," Wayne had said when telling the story from his perspective, "so by the time we got here, my tracker had a little bit of a fix on you via your p-comp. We debated on it for a few minutes, then decided to split up. I went inside to see what was going on, while Loyola turned the anti-gravs on her hovercycle to high and floated up outside."

And it was from the seat of a floating hovercycle, while being buffeted by high winds, that Loyola fired the shot that saved his life.

At present, they were all huddled in Quinzen's bedroom (courtesy of the Panoptes' secret hatch): Maker, Loyola, Wayne, Snick, and even Diviana. They sat lounging in several easy chairs around a small table, after having performed a thorough search of the premises.

Maker had tried to show some decency by tossing a sheet over their late host's body, but no one seemed particularly disturbed by its presence. Also, feeling that it was kind of conspicuous on the roof, Maker had also dumped the Vacra's body — stripped of all weapons — back inside, but it sat uncovered (and occasionally twitching) in a corner.

"So," Snick said, summing things up, "Quinzen was in bed with the Vacra."

"Yes," Maker answered. Then he turned to Diviana. "Have you had a chance to take a good look at the Vacra?"

Diviana nodded. "Yes."

"Well, you've been here all night — at least since me and Wayne got here that first time. Did you ever see that thing come in?"

"No," she answered, shaking her head. "I can't swear that I saw everyone who came and went, but we've seen images of the Vacra before and I was on the lookout for them. I mean, they're the reason we're here."

Maker nodded, chewing his lip.

"What are you thinking, el-tee?" Loyola asked.

"If Diviana never saw the Vacra come in, that means it was already in the suite. It was already here when Wayne and I were down there watching the jwaedin in the arena."

"Then how'd you ever slip by it and get in position to kill Croy and Quinzen?" Diviana asked.

Maker shrugged. "Who knows? Maybe it was eating. Maybe it was indisposed. Maybe it needed to don its armor."

"Or maybe it's nocturnal," Wayne said. "Maybe it was sleeping."

211

Maker chewed on that for a moment. "Could be. That might explain why Quinzen didn't seem too happy about us showing up early — and why he wasn't particularly eager to get down to business. Maybe the plan was to invite us up to the suite and let the Vacra blast us as soon as we walked in, but he wasn't sure if his buddy would be ready."

"But what's the point?" Loyola asked. "What's to be gained by killing any of us?"

"I have a theory about that," Maker said, "but I don't think I want to share it just—"

The Vacra shuddered in its armor, the sound causing everyone to look in its direction.

"Maybe that's the corpse you should have covered up," Diviana said. "The way it keeps jerking around keeps me on edge."

"Oh, it's not dead," Maker said. "At least, I don't think so."

"What?" Loyola said, completely surprised. "I blew half its head off!"

"On Old Earth," Maker said, "there's an insect called a roach that can live for days — even weeks — after its head has been cut off. I've come across insectoids that are the same way, and I think the same may be true of the Vacra."

"Then maybe we need to finish the job," Diviana said, pulling out a blade that Maker hadn't seen on her person (and couldn't imagine where she could have had it hidden considering the ensemble she was wearing).

"No need," Maker assured her. "Just because it's alive doesn't mean it's functional. Half the thing's brain is gone; it's a vegetable."

While Maker had been talking, Wayne had pulled out his tracker, the one he had apparently used to locate Maker earlier. He began fiddling with it, pointing it in the direction of the Vacra.

"What are you doing?" Loyola finally asked him.

"Something just occurred to me," Wayne replied. "You know what happens when we're in our armor and get injured?"

"Yes," Snick said. "The armor can assess the injury, administer meds, etc."

"All true," Wayne said, getting up and walking over to the Vacra. "But it also does something else."

"The beacon," Maker said, coming to his feet in alarm and walking towards Wayne. "It sends out a signal on a coded frequency to the soldier's unit, so they'll know where to find him."

At that moment, everyone else seemed to catch on simultaneously. Diviana, Snick, and Loyola all stood up and joined the others over by the Vacra.

"Do you think that the Vacra's armor—" Loyola began.

"Yes," Wayne said. "I'm picking up a signal from it."

Maker closed his eyes in concentration. How long had it been since Loyola had shot the insectoid on the roof...maybe thirty minutes? How long would it be before a bunch of other Vacra showed up?

"There's good news and bad news," Wayne finally said, lowering his tracker. "The bad news you already know — the armor here is sending a signal. What it's saying I don't know, but I'm guessing it's broadcasting distress of some form."

"And the good news?" Snick asked.

"As best I can tell, the dampening field from the Pit is interfering with the signal. My guess is that any friends he has around here may be able to home in on the vicinity, but not his exact location."

"Nice work," Diviana said. "Except for the little fact that we're in the suite of one of their known allies — where this thing may actually have been staying — so I'm assuming that, regardless of what any signal tells them, this is one of the first places his fellow Vacra will look."

They all stared at each other in silence for a moment, contemplating what that meant.

"Alright," Maker said after a few seconds, "let's move out. Snick, get the vehicles ready. Loyola, you're in charge of the weapons we secured from the Vacra. Diviana, you've got two minutes to go through this place for any intel we can use."

As everyone scurried off to carry out their orders, Maker turned to Wayne. "I don't suppose there's any way you could tell us how close any of the Vacra tracking that signal might be."

"No," Wayne said, shaking his head. "I can't tell you how close any trackers might be that are picking the signal up. I can only pinpoint the main hub it's broadcasting to."

"What?!" Maker shouted incredulously.

TERMINUS

Chapter 28

Maker and his squad lay low on the sand several hundred yards away from the gaping mouth of a monstrous desert cave. For the first time since arriving on Terminus, they were decked out in their full battle armor, although they really didn't expect to encounter trouble. After all, their mission was merely to locate the Vacra, not to engage.

It had been several hours since Wayne had casually dropped the bombshell that he could trace where the Vacra armor was broadcasting to. In Maker's mind, that location had to be the base for the insectoids. Thus, upon leaving Quinzen's suite, he had quickly decided that they were going to recon the area in question. They had raced back to camp, donned their gear and headed out.

They'd taken the dropship, landing it a few miles from their ultimate destination. Leaving Fierce with the vessel, Maker and the other five members of his unit had then taken hovercycles to their present location.

It was still somewhat before dawn, and inside his suit Maker struggled to stifle a yawn. At this point he had been up just about an entire day (not counting the time immediately after he was stung by the jwaedin), but the same was true of everyone else. Fierce had issued stim shots for them to take in order to remain alert, but Maker had passed.

Maker activated his comm. "Tinker," he said, remembering to use Wayne's chosen call sign, "are we confirmed on this being the location?"

"Yes, sir," came the response. "The signal is going to that cave."

TERMINUS

Maker stared at the entrance to the cave. The visor on his helmet had automatically switched to night vision based on the ambient light available. Ergo, he could see almost as well as in daytime.

The cave opening was enormous. Although nothing like a battle cruiser was going to be able to fit inside, there were a lot of other spacefaring vessels that could.

As to location, the cave had actually been found along the path where they had been directing their daily drones. Wayne had estimated that they probably would have come across it in another two weeks or so on their own. Whether or not they would have realized there was anyone inside it was another story.

Maker magnified the view through his visor, getting a close-up look at the cavern. Unfortunately, he still couldn't see very far into the interior.

"Switching vision to infrared," Maker announced over the comm, knowing that the others would follow his lead.

The view through his visor suddenly changed, becoming a mixture of odd hues of various colors, like orange and purple. Looking at the area around them, he could see various bugs and small animals scurrying about on the desert floor, their bodies appearing as amalgams of orange and red.

Turning his attention to the cave, Maker could now perceive bodies in motion inside. There were about two dozen of them, all apparently Vacra based on the images he was receiving: six-limbed, segmented bodies with wavering antennae.

"Jackpot," Adames muttered over the comm, echoing Maker's own sentiments. "I guess this one's a wrap."

Maker reluctantly agreed. It seemed like an anticlimactic end to the mission considering everything that had happened thus far. (Not to mention that he'd failed to achieve a personal ambition on this mission, which was to at least set eyes on Skullcap again.)

Oh well, everything can't always be fun and games, he thought. He was about to order them back to the dropship when Wayne called his attention to something.

"Sir, I'm getting an odd visual," the younger Marine said. "Can you look towards the right of the cave, just beyond the entrance?"

Maker did as he was bid, wondering what had caught Wayne's eye. As before, he observed a number of Vacra wandering about the place, including the area in question. He was about to ask Wayne to be more specific, and then he saw it. The image was clear, unmistakable — especially in the presence of so many others that were so radically different in form.

There was a human being in there with the Vacra.

TERMINUS

Chapter 29

It was a relatively easy decision as far as Maker was concerned: there was no way in hell he was going to leave another human being to the Vacra's tender mercies. (As if in confirmation of Maker's assessment, he saw one of the insectoids seemingly speak to the person — who appeared to be a man — and then roughly shove him, knocking him down.) Thus, it was only a few seconds after realizing that there was a person in the insectoids' hideout that he ordered his squad to prepare for assault.

"Our goal is extraction of the person in that cave," he said. "I know it's outside our initial mission parameters, but that was before we knew that they were holding a human being — presumably as a captive."

"What type of ammo?" Adames asked.

Maker spent a moment considering his response. Despite his feelings about the Vacra, he really wasn't a bloodthirsty savage. From what he could see via the infrared, most of those in the cave were only carrying small arms, and none appeared to be wearing battle gear. Thus, his group probably already had the edge in terms of weapons and armor. Assuming they could maintain the advantage of surprise, the outcome of this encounter was unlikely to be in doubt, but there was no need to turn it into wholesale slaughter.

"Non-lethal rounds," Maker said after a few seconds, almost reluctantly. "Engaging in two."

****

In the course of his military career, Maker couldn't recall ever being part of a mission that went one hundred percent according to plan, and this one was no different. Their ad hoc rescue strategy centered on using their hovercycles to get to the cave as quickly as possible, and then surging inside with an impressive and overwhelming display of force, grabbing the hostage, and then leaving.

As with most missions, it looked good on paper so to speak, but execution was an entirely different story. Somewhere between their initial hiding spot and the cave entrance, while on their cycles, the group apparently hit some sort of proximity sensor. (Although Wayne had scanned for and disabled a number of them before their squad initiated the assault, he had clearly missed at least one.) All of a sudden there was frenzied activity in the cave and they could hear what sounded like an alarm as they got closer.

Beyond that, however, it was essentially a textbook operation. The Vacra didn't even have guards posted outside (perhaps to avoid even a chance of being seen — or a display of overconfidence in their hiding spot). Thus, Maker's unit was able to ride right up to the mouth of the cave completely unmolested. They quickly dismounted, leaving their cycles to the side of the cave entrance, and charged the opening.

At that juncture, however, some of the insectoids reached the grotto opening and started shooting. It was the first time Maker had seen one outside of its armor and he couldn't help taking mental notes.

The Vacra's segmented bodies were about six feet tall on average and a deep red in color — probably more like maroon. Their large, compound eyes were creepy — expressionless black ovals that dominated a large portion of their faces. Their hands, ending in three lengthy digits, angrily squeezed the triggers on their weapons.

As anticipated, it was small-arms fire and couldn't penetrate their armor. Nevertheless, they instinctively ducked behind a large outcropping of rock nearby.

Snick, the last to take cover, laughed as a couple of rounds hit him, saying, "That tickles."

"Stay sharp!" Adames snapped over the comm. "You can bet that somewhere inside, someone's grabbing a weapon with more firepower."

"Let's make this quick," Maker said. "On my mark. Go!"

They rushed forward, and the battle was child's play from that point on. The ammo that Maker's group was using, although designed not to penetrate, had devastating impact — typically shattering bone upon contact. (In fact, although designated as non-lethal, a headshot from one of those rounds could indeed kill.) In no time at all, the Vacra at the cave entrance were down.

Inside was a madhouse, with the insectoids insanely scrambling in all directions — some obviously seeking cover, others trying to engage the invaders of their erstwhile home.

Near the back of the cave, not unexpectedly, was an alien ship. Based on the size, it was clearly not a long-range spacefaring vessel, but something more in league with their dropship.

Maker's team fired almost indiscriminately, the ammo routinely knocking their adversaries off their feet and leaving them incapacitated. However, the Marines scrupulously avoided firing too close to the area where the human hostage was.

Weapon at the ready, Maker made his way towards the man, who was crouching near what appeared to be a table. Maker was so focused on his target that he almost overlooked a Vacra who was standing near the man.

This particular insectoid was a little different than its fellows. It was a little bigger, and its coloring was just a shade lighter. Moreover, where the others had a full set of fully-formed middle arms, this one didn't. Instead, one of its middle arms appeared stunted, deformed — perhaps some kind of birth defect.

Almost completely still, it stared at Maker from about ten feet away, the only movement coming from the pinchers around its mouth. After a moment, its head tilted slightly to the side, as if it found Maker somehow interesting. Suddenly, its head snapped back and its antennae began wriggling wildly. It yelled, some sort of mad chittering coming from its mouth, as it charged at Maker.

He fired, hitting the Vacra dead center in the thorax, sending it flying backwards. It hit the ground with jarring force, so hard that — non-lethal or not — Maker thought that it might be dead.

He turned his attention back to their whole reason for being here: the man crouching nearby. Maker took a moment to look the fellow over.

He was dirty and disheveled, with a thick, matted beard and wild, unkempt hair. His clothing, consisting of some type of uniform that seemed oddly familiar to Maker, was practically rags. All in all, it was pretty clear that grooming and hygiene had not been a priority for this fellow in quite some time, and Maker could tell just by looking at him that the guy probably smelled quite ripe.

Maker walked over and reached out a hand, intending to help the fellow up.

"No, no!" the man pleaded, leaning away.

Maker switched on the external audio in his armor. "It's okay," he said, gripping the man by the upper arm and hauling him up. "We're going to get you out of here."

"No, no!" the man said. "You have to leave me!"

He tried to yank himself free of Maker's armored grip but failed. He probably couldn't have done it even if Maker wasn't wearing a battle suit — the fellow was essentially skin and bones.

Frustrated, the man beat ineffectually at Maker with his free hand. Intending to calm him, Maker gave the man a light tap on the side of the head. However, either Maker overestimated the amount of force needed or the man was a lot weaker than he realized, because the blow knocked him out.

"Great," Maker muttered sarcastically, and then slung the man over his shoulder. He was so light that carrying a child would have caused more exertion.

Maker caught movement in the corner of his eye and turned to see the Vacra with the stunted arm staggering away, clearly in pain. He was tempted to shoot it again, but decided against it.

"Hostage retrieved," he said over his comm. "Prepare to move out."

Moments later, they were all at the mouth of the cave, with Maker's companions laying down suppressive fire as he exited. On impulse, he looked back inside. Almost all the Vacra he could see were on the ground, incapacitated in some fashion. As Adames had predicted, a few had gotten their hands on more powerful weapons, but were firing from behind poor cover and didn't have a good angle.

Something resembling a gun turret on top of the alien ship swiveled in their direction, but Maker barely noticed. Instead, his attention was captured by another sight.

Back in the cave, he saw the Vacra he had shot just a few minutes earlier, recognizable by his deformed middle arm. In one of its primary arms, it was holding something Maker recognized — a long, lance-like weapon that Maker had only encountered once before: on a derelict ship in the Beyond.

The Vacra with the maimed arm was Skullcap.

Maker's mind was racing. The deformed arm... Lots of insects can regrow limbs. Skullcap's body had obviously attempted to do so, but the trauma at the wound site must have been too much for the arm to regenerate properly. Thus, he'd ended up with a stunted limb.

"Take him and get out of here," Maker said, handing the man he was carrying over to Snick as he watched Skullcap board the Vacra ship.

"That goes for all of you," Adames said to the others. "Get back to the dropship on the double!"

Not needing to be told twice, the other four members of their unit jumped on their cycles and took off, with Snick also taking their rescued hostage.

Now unencumbered, Maker took a step back towards the interior of the cave just as the gun turret fired. From where Maker stood, the sound of the blast was almost deafening; inside the cave, it must have bordered on painful. In addition, the entire cavern shook from the combination of vibrations from the recoil of the gun turret and the echoing report, causing stalactites to fall from the ceiling.

Simultaneous with the gun turret firing, something swished over Maker's head at high speed, and a moment later there was an explosion in the desert behind him. Glancing back, he saw a deep, smoking crater where an explosive projectile had obviously hit the ground. Off in the distance, he was relieved to see Snick and the others still safely retreating in the direction of the dropship.

"Holy crap!" Adames said, bringing Maker's attention back to the activity in the cavern. "They've literally pulled out the big guns."

The gun turret began swiveling again, the barrel starting to angle down towards where Maker and Adames stood. Even more, there was a high-pitched whining that he couldn't quite place, but immediately identified as an engine coming on line after he saw the alien ship start to rise. On the cavern floor, Vacra seemed to be running pell-mell all over the place.

Maker ground his teeth in frustration. The one Vacra he desperately wanted to go toe-to-toe with was on the alien ship, which had more firepower than his entire squad could handle, let alone just him and Adames. At the same time, this was his best — and maybe *only* — opportunity to have a crack at Skullcap. In the grip of indecisiveness, he stood there, frozen, as the Vacra ship cleared the ground and started to come forward.

"We have to move!" Adames shouted. He pulled a handheld grenade launcher from a holster on his armor. "Move!" he yelled at Maker once again, giving him a shove towards the cycles to get him going. Then Adames raised the grenade launcher and fired at the ceiling right at the cave's entrance.

The grenade exploded on impact with an earsplitting boom, sending tons of rock cascading down, effectively blocking the entrance. There was no way the Vacra were coming after them now; the aliens would be digging themselves out for quite some time to come. Somewhat disappointed, Maker mounted his cycle and left, with Adames flanking him.

TERMINUS

Chapter 30

"What?!" Browing screamed, coming to his feet.

"I said we found the Vacra," Maker announced, repeating what he'd said a few moments earlier. "Then we got into a firefight with them."

"But you had specific orders not to engage!" Browing hissed angrily.

They were in Browing's office at the consulate — Browing sitting behind his desk while Maker and Dr. Chantrey sat in chairs facing him. (Erlen was also present, but lounging in a corner, where he casually licked the wall.) Following their battle with the Vacra, Maker's squad had headed back to their base. After taking a short breather to change out of his armor, Maker had ordered his unit to break camp and be ready to move out asap. Next, he had piled into the hovercart with Erlen and their still-unconscious guest, and then headed to the Diplomat District. Once at the consulate, he had turned the rescued man over to the medical staff and gone to see Browing to make his report.

"From my perspective, the mission parameters changed the second it came to light that they had a hostage," Maker said defensively.

"Where's the man now?" asked Dr. Chantrey, cutting in.

"I left him with your medics," Maker answered. "He appeared to be in pretty bad shape."

"Do we know who he is?" she asked.

"No, he's been unconscious most of the time," said Maker, averting his eyes. "But my impression is that they've been holding him for a while."

226

Browing frowned. "Holding him? For what purpose?"

"I don't know, Browing," Maker said impatiently. "Maybe they'll fill out the survey I left for them and tell us."

Browing's hands gripped the arms of his chair in white-knuckled frustration. "So you've essentially gutted the mission. Knowing their location is useless to us, because they're definitely not going to stay where they are. You should have just reported back the second you found them."

Maker callously replied, "You'd feel differently if you were the one getting a taste of their hospitality. You do have a point, though." He turned to Dr. Chantrey. "Why do *you* think they were holding that guy?"

The doctor was nonplussed. "You're asking me?"

Maker nodded. "You're the behavioral scientist."

"My expertise is *human* behavior," she corrected. "I don't think my skill translates very well for other species. An entomologist would probably do a better job in this instance."

"Speculate then," Maker said.

She seemed to dwell on this for a few seconds before finally speaking.

"Alright, I'll give it a try," she said. "These things seem a lot like ants, which — back on Earth — were known to keep not just other ant species but also other insects, kind of like pets. For instance, some ants kept aphids, feeding on their secretions."

"Kind of like humans with cattle," Browing interjected.

"Exactly," Dr. Chantrey agreed.

"Well, I think this guy was producing more *ex*cretions that *se*cretions, and I doubt even the Vacra were consuming any of that," said Maker. "So the question is, what were they getting from him?"

Before anyone could answer, a musical chime sounded. Browing turned to an expensive comm unit perched on the edge of his desk and hit a button. The image of a lovely young woman, from head to shoulders, appeared above the unit. Maker recognized her as one of Browing's assistants.

"I'm sorry to disturb you, sir," the young woman began, "but they need you in Medical. Something to do with that vagrant who was brought in."

"I'll be right there," Browing said, then pressed a button on the comm. Link disconnected, the young woman's face disappeared.

Browing stood up. "Let's go see what's happening."

TERMINUS

Chapter 31

It only took a few minutes for Browing, Maker, Dr. Chantrey, and Erlen to reach the medical wing of the consulate. Once there, a white-haired man whose nametag identified him as Dr. Gill began to explain the situation, which he described as an emergency.

"We were just giving a routine scan to the man they brought in when we found it," Dr. Gill said.

They were presently in an operating room. The man who Maker's team had rescued lay facedown in a surgical bed, his bare back exposed and with numerous tubes and wires connected to his skeletal frame. Around him, various types of medical equipment and surgical apparatus hummed and droned, indicating that they were in operational mode.

Dr. Gill tapped the screen of a nearby computer, and an image appeared in the air next to him. It appeared to be the internal view of someone's back — presumably the man in the surgical bed.

"It was attached to his spine," Dr. Gill continued, "and if you look closely you can see it right *here*."

He touched his finger to a portion of the image and it expanded in size, revealing the white bone of a vertebral column. Flush with the spine was an odd, oval-shaped device about the size of a fist. On it was a small diode that was slowly flashing red in color.

"At first, we thought it was some sort of spinal aid," Gill said. "Or some kind of artificial or supplemental organ."

"Like an auxiliary heart," Dr. Chantrey suggested.

Dr. Gill nodded. "Precisely. But when we tried additional scans, we didn't see it performing any kind of helpful biological function. And then it seemed to…activate."

A frown surfaced on Browing's face. "What do you mean, 'activate'?"

Gill looked nervous as he answered. "That diode you see was dark before, but after one of our scans it started flashing. Something we did seems to have initiated a sequence in it."

"So what does that mean?" Browing asked, plainly dissatisfied with what he was being told.

"We're not sure," Gill answered honestly. "In fact, about all we can tell is that it's an alien device of some sort, containing some components and chemicals we can identify, and others that are basically unknown to us. In short, we don't know what it is."

"I can tell you what it is," Maker said flatly. "It's a bomb."

Chapter 32

There was complete silence after Maker made his announcement, but the reactions were fairly diverse. Browing appeared angry, Chantrey appeared incredulous, and Dr. Gill just seemed to collapse in on himself. Erlen was the only individual who seemed to take the statement in stride, remaining where he was at Maker's feet, face expressionless.

"Wh-What did you say?" Dr. Gill asked, sounding like he'd been punched in the gut.

"It's a bomb," Maker said again. "And you're going to have to take it out of him."

"Wait a minute," Dr. Chantrey said, shaking her head as if to clear her thoughts. "It's an alien device. How do you know it's a bomb?"

"Because I've seen it before," replied Maker. "The design, at least."

Dr. Chantrey thought for a second, and then the answer came to her. "The derelict ship. The explosive you found on your shuttle."

Maker nodded.

"This is too much," Dr. Gill said, growing increasingly pale. "I need...I need to get some air."

He began walking towards the door but didn't get far as Maker placed a firm hand on his shoulder.

"No," Maker insisted. "What you need to do is take this device out of this man right *now*."

"But you said it was a bomb," Gill stated nervously. "I don't do bombs. I'm a doctor, not a munitions guy. I won't do it."

Maker considered various incentives he might use to convince the doctor to operate, but in the end rejected them. He didn't want to punish the doctor for just being afraid — it was a natural response — and he also didn't know how much time they had. (Glancing at the diode, he saw that it had started to blink faster.) He turned to Browing. "Do you have another doctor on staff?"

"We have three, but they rotate shifts," Browing said. "Gill's on duty at the moment, although he's probably walked his last rounds as far as I'm concerned. I'll try to get one of the others over here, but it may take time."

"Time's a luxury we may not have," Maker said. He seemed to deliberate internally for a moment, and then stated, "I'll do it."

This time, all three of the other people in the room had dubious looks on their faces.

"Do what?" Dr. Chantrey asked.

"The surgery," said Maker, rolling up the sleeves of his shirt.

"What? There's no way!" Gill said, suddenly pompous. "You're not a surgeon. You're not qualified to do this. You'll just end up killing this man."

"You're right. I'm not qualified to do this," Maker admitted. "But in a minute, I will be."

He held out his bare forearm towards Erlen, who took it in his mouth and bit down on it — not hard enough to cause real damage, but with enough force to break the skin. When the Niotan released him, there were two puncture wounds on Maker's forearm where Erlen's fangs had penetrated.

Maker's eyelids fluttered, and Dr. Chantrey noticed him smile slightly as his body seemed to sway momentarily. Without warning, his eyelids snapped open, and she placed a startled hand to her mouth. Maker's eyes had changed color and were now red.

Shocked, Browing involuntarily uttered a curse and then said to Maker, "That animal! It's not the pet — *you* are!!"

Maker ignored him and went to work.

****

The operation was a success, as Maker had known it would be. Browing, Gill, and Dr. Chantrey had watched as he'd begun, and then — realizing their proximity to what was probably a deadly explosive device — they had hightailed it out of there and watched the remainder of the operation on a vid screen in Browing's office.

Gill had tried to offer some advice during the surgery using Browing's comm unit, but Maker found the man irritating and cut the audio off on his end.

In the end, he safely removed the device and handed it off to a bomb unit that Browing had called in while the operation was going on. (They later confirmed that it was indeed an extremely powerful explosive.) Afterwards, Maker found himself hustled off by a security unit to Browing's office after being patted down and having his sidearm confiscated.

"You've been lying to us from the moment we met," Browing said when two security guards escorted Maker in.

Maker, his eyes back to their normal color, raised an eyebrow. "Oh? About what?" He took a seat in a nearby chair, Erlen next to him, while the guards who had escorted him went to go stand by the door.

"Everything!" Browing replied, making an all-encompassing gesture. "Your pet, the derelict ship you encountered, the Vacra… All of it. It's time to come clean."

"Fine," Maker replied. "I've been lying, but not for the reasons you might think. If you really want the truth, I'll tell you — but only on two conditions. First though, this info isn't for public consumption." He nodded towards the guards as he leaned forward and began scratching Erlen's nose.

"No, they stay," Browing declared, crossing his arms.

At that moment, Erlen coughed — a harsh, grating sound — and then spat something into Maker's hand.

"I'm afraid I must insist," Maker said, rising and pointing a small firearm that he now held in his hand at the guards. The two men on the business end of the weapon, which was wet and dripping some sort of liquid, slowly raised their hands.

"You idiots!" Browing yelled. "I told you to search him!"

"We did," one of the men replied. "He was clean except for the sidearm we took from him."

"Speaking of which…" Maker said, snapping the fingers of his free hand and holding his palm open. The guard who had taken his sidearm slowly handed it over. Maker then motioned towards the door and the two men backed out of the room. Maker locked the door.

Browing was still grumbling. "Those two are so fired…"

"Don't be too hard on them," Maker said. "It's not their fault. They really did do a good job of searching me."

"Then how'd you end up with a weapon?" Dr. Chantrey asked.

Maker smiled. "Didn't I tell you? Erlen has two stomachs. One's for digesting food, and the other's sort of a…"

"Smuggler's pouch?" Dr. Chantrey suggested.

Maker shrugged. "That's as good a term as any."

"So anything you need, he can just swallow and regurgitate at will," Browing surmised. "So what will you do now, hold us prisoner?"

"Not at all," Maker said, putting his sidearm back in its holster and placing the smaller weapon in his pocket. "Like I said, I'll tell you everything, but with two conditions."

"Which are?" Dr. Chantrey asked.

"First, if I'm going to spill my guts, then you have to answer all of my questions as well," Maker said.

The doctor and Browing exchanged glances, and a silent conversation seemed to take place between them. After a few seconds, Dr. Chantrey gave a noncommittal shrug.

"Agreed," Browing said. "And your other condition?"

"That you tell no one — *no one* — about what you saw happen between me and Erlen in the operating room."

"Fine," Browing agreed, "but you have to tell us the truth about that…*thing*." He inclined his head towards Erlen.

235

Maker frowned at the term Browing used in reference to Erlen, but merely said, "Agreed."

"Now why don't you start out by telling us the real story of what happened on that derelict four years ago," Dr. Chantrey said.

"The truth really isn't a lot different than what I've already told you," Maker said. "Everything happened exactly as I said up until the point where I had the fight with Skullcap on top of the shuttle. When he had me down and was about to run me through, Erlen saved me."

Dr. Chantrey seemed surprised. "Erlen?"

"Yes. He had a nasty habit of sneaking aboard vessels whenever I had a mission," Maker said, scratching the Niotan's head. "He doesn't like getting left behind."

"Which explains why just about every time we see you, we see him," Browing concluded.

"Anyway, when the Vacra was about to finish me off, Erlen came up out of the shuttle behind him," Maker said. "He tackled Skullcap — knocking the lance from his grip, which I picked up — and then ripped his arm off."

"Wait a minute," Dr. Chantrey said. "I thought you said the Vacra you fought — Skullcap, as you call him — was in armor."

Maker nodded. "He was."

"And Erlen ripped his arm off?" she asked, eyes wide in surprise.

"As you've probably guessed by now, Erlen's a little special," Maker said with a smile. "Anyway, the rest is pretty much exactly as I told you before, except Erlen was with us when we hightailed it back to the *Orpheus Moon*."

Browing frowned. "So what's the big deal? Granted, your little beastie wasn't supposed to be there, but you haven't mentioned anything earth-shattering. Why lie about any of that?"

Maker paused, taking a deep breath. "I lied because the derelict was a sub rosa ship."

TERMINUS

Chapter 33

There were all kinds of rumors about the types of things that existed or took place in the Beyond. There was supposedly a world where magic was as real as science. Legends also told of a gigantic space dragon whose fiery spittle turned into stars. One of Maker's own cousins — a commercial starship captain — claimed to have once encountered a shapeshifting monster out there.

One of the tall tales that may have actually contained a grain of truth concerned a group of brilliant academics and technology specialists who prized knowledge above all else. Convinced that the pursuit of higher learning transcended morality, these demented doctors and rogue scientists allegedly performed forbidden, heinous experiments in all areas of science and medicine. When their activities were uncovered, they purportedly fled to the Beyond, where they still practice their immoral crafts aboard secret vessels known as sub rosa ships.

It was generally accepted that the mad scientists origin story was hogwash. However, there were constant claims over the years, as humanity spread across the stars, that various government organizations adopted the practices mentioned in the tale. It was said that the military in particular continually engaged in and conducted experiments regarding weapons and technology that were forbidden by treaty, diplomacy, or plain decency and morality. These and other similar activities purportedly took place in secret, unmarked vessels — sub rosa ships — situated in the Beyond. It was this type of vessel that Maker was declaring the derelict in his story to have been.

After making his announcement — that he had actually been aboard such a ship — Maker wasn't sure what to expect. Guffaws, perhaps. Maybe even questions about his mental health. What he didn't expect was another silent exchange between Dr. Chantrey and Browing.

Maker frowned, somewhat perplexed by their reaction, and then it dawned on him.

"You knew," he said. "You already knew it was a sub rosa ship."

"Yes," Browing admitted. "It was a ship that certain…special interest groups, shall we say, had long used for classified purposes."

"Mad doctors and secret experiments," Maker said.

"Right, but it was more than just that," Dr. Chantrey said. "It was also a warehouse. Generations of advanced technology and weapons, among other things, were stored there — some of it incredibly dangerous."

"So what happened to it?" asked Maker. "How'd it end up floating dead in space?"

"We're still not sure," Browing said. "As you can imagine, it wasn't a facility that anyone maintained ongoing contact with, although the ship's personnel did provide regular updates. Until the day they stopped doing so, that is."

"Didn't you investigate?" Maker asked.

Browing scoffed. "Yeah, right. We were supposed to launch an official investigation for a ship that's not supposed to exist, conducting illegal experiments, and filled to the rim with banned weapons and tech."

Maker couldn't hide his surprise. "So you just left it sitting out there?"

"No," Dr. Chantrey said, giving him a frank stare. "We didn't."

Her tone and the look on her face seemed to imply something, but Maker couldn't immediately put his finger on what it was. Then the truth hit him like a sledgehammer.

"Me," he said softly, the words tasting bitter in his mouth. "You sent me and my squad."

Maker frowned for a moment, thinking. "That last mission I went on, before we found the derelict. It was a complete farce. The whole point was to get us close enough to pick up the sub rosa ship's distress signal. You *knew* I'd choose to check it out."

"We didn't *know*," the doctor corrected. "But your psych profile suggested it. And just to be clear, I never knew what your last mission was. It wasn't necessary for my analysis, so they never told me."

"You..." Maker said vehemently to Dr. Chantrey, practically spitting the word out. "You were involved back then. It's why you're here now."

"I don't deny it," she said. "Prior to you, we sent two ships — ostensibly on other missions — through that region of the Beyond. The first mission picked up a distress signal so we knew something had happened to the sub rosa ship, but the mission leader declined to investigate. The same thing happened the second time, so we knew that we had to find someone who was unlikely to leave anyone stranded. I was then asked to look at personnel histories, backgrounds, and so on with the specific purpose of finding a soldier who *would* investigate."

"And I fit the bill," Maker concluded.

"Yes," the doctor stated. "I correctly hypothesized what your actions would be then, so they brought me back to give insight into how you'd conduct yourself on *this* mission."

Maker shook his head in disgust. "You people…"

"Okay, stop saying 'we' and 'you' like these were personal choices that the doctor and I made," Browing said acrimoniously. "These were decisions made by people far above the pay grade of anybody in this room, and like you, Dr. Chantrey and I follow the orders we're given."

"You, them," Maker hissed. "You're all in bed together, so as far as I'm concerned you're all the same."

"So what do you think we should have done?" asked Browing, hot with anger. "I've already explained to you that a sanctioned search-and-rescue was out of the question. We couldn't just leave the ship out there floating around. We needed to know what happened — to the ship, its crew, and its cargo. Because sooner or later, somebody was going to find it, and who knows what they'd do with what they discovered on board."

Maker blinked, Browing's words turning his thoughts in a new direction. "Salvage rights."

"Yes," said Browing with a nod. "Any civilian vessel that comes across a derelict or abandoned vessel can lay claim to it and its cargo. Trust me, that far out, the ship was more likely to be found by a band of pirates or criminals, and if you knew half the things that were housed on it, you'd pass out at the thought of them ending up on the black market."

"Also, even though the ship was unmarked, there was always the possibility that it could be traced back to humanity," Dr. Chantrey said. "The layout, design, sleeping quarters, food. They all point towards *Homo sapiens*, not to mention the distress signal itself. If that happened, the political fallout would be devastating."

"So because of salvage issues, among other things, you needed to figure out what happened to your mad scientist lab before anyone came across it," Maker commented. "And the crew of a military vessel doesn't get salvage rights."

"Yes," Browing said. "Kind of a quid pro quo, since on the flip side, military vessels are *protected* from salvage claims."

Maker had a tough time hiding his contempt. "You guys have been playing me from the very start."

"That's the pot calling the kettle black," Browing countered. "You still haven't told us how you knew it was a sub rosa ship, or — more importantly — how you made that nine-point hyperspace jump."

There was silence for a moment, and then Maker let out a long, exhaustion-filled breath. "The head," he said. "The head in the jar. One of the things I was able to make out that it was saying was 'sub rosa.' That also explained why a lot of equipment and stuff I saw on the derelict look unfamiliar to me."

"Wait," Dr. Chantrey said. "I've seen hundreds of hours of vid footage of you talking about what happened, and you've never mentioned unfamiliar equipment before."

"I didn't mention *anything* that might have indicated that I knew it was a sub rosa ship!" Maker snapped. "If I had, I never would have seen daylight again, and instead of being here right now, I'd be strapped down in some windowless room getting my brain sucked dry — if I was lucky!"

242

"So you lied," the doctor said in summation. "Did it ever occur to you that — somewhere in between all the times you talked about what happened — you probably spoke to someone who actually knew something about that ship? That they might have been in a position to help you if you'd only told the truth?"

Maker scoffed at the notion. "Lady, we're talking about a sub rosa ship. Telling the story I did is probably the only thing that kept me from disappearing without a trace or dying in a 'training accident,' because it showed that I knew how to keep my mouth shut. That's what your puppet masters really wanted."

"Assuming all that's true, it doesn't explain you lying about your little pet," Browing said, nodding in Erlen's direction. "Why lie about his role?"

Maker shook his head in frustration. "You weren't paying close enough attention. I said that Erlen saved my life when I was fighting Skullcap on top of the shuttle."

"We got that part," Dr. Chantrey said. "What's so special about that?"

"We were in the landing bay at the time, one with no atmosphere," Maker replied.

His two listeners frowned, but didn't seem to make the proper connection.

"Don't you get it?" Maker went on. "Erlen can survive in the vacuum of space!"

TERMINUS

Chapter 34

His words seemed to have caught them by surprise.

"Huh?" Browing muttered after a moment, obviously befuddled.

"What, did you think he had a space suit?" Maker asked disdainfully. "Erlen doesn't need protection from the temperature change, lack of atmosphere, anything."

There was silence as the other two people absorbed this, casting odd looks at Erlen.

"How's that possible?" Dr. Chantrey said.

Maker shrugged. "I don't know. But what I do know is that, had I told the truth about him, they would have torn him apart to find out what makes him tick. I couldn't have that. I'm responsible for him."

Dr. Chantrey tilted her head, looking at Maker in an odd manner. She knew from his profile that he was incredibly attached to Erlen (as many people were with respect to pets — despite Maker's disagreement that the term applied to the Niotan). However, there was something about that last sentence he'd said… The way he'd spoken, with utter conviction, seemed to imply something more than simple devotion.

"Explain that," she said. "Your being responsible for him."

Maker seemed taken aback, apparently not realizing how much he'd said. He was clearly reluctant to speak about the subject — even more so than he'd been about the sub rosa ship, which was odd.

"He was entrusted to me," Maker finally said, looking down at the Niotan as he spoke. "I swore to take care of him."

"Swore to who?" asked Browing, surprisingly intrigued by the direction the conversation was going.

Maker sighed. "You might recall that during our first meeting I mentioned that there were worlds within the Mezzo — in the *civilized* regions of Gaian Space — that you wouldn't want to be stranded on? Well, years ago, I found myself stranded on a world well out in the Beyond."

Maker's eyes took on a faraway look as memories as fresh as yesterday came unbidden to the forefront of his mind.

"It was an absolute nightmare planet, horrible beyond anything you'd believe," he continued. "I've never come across a world so bred to kill. Insects, birds, plants, animals… Everything, and I mean *everything*, was deadly and dangerous — either infectious, noxious, poisonous, or carnivorous. I've never seen anything like it before or since."

"But you survived," the doctor noted.

Maker laughed derisively. "No, I was *saved*. There was a native population there — primitive, but sentient. We made a deal. They would keep me alive, and in return, I would take Erlen."

"What do you mean, 'take him'?" Browing asked.

"As I understand it, the indigenous population was responsible for him, but could no longer care for him for some reason," Maker said, petting Erlen's head. "In return for their help, I became responsible for his welfare. He was just a babe at the time — practically newborn — but he grew on me. About six months later, I was rescued."

"At which point you smuggled Erlen aboard the rescue ship and brought him back," the doctor concluded.

Maker snickered. "I didn't smuggle anything. I brought him on board in my arms — everyone saw him."

Maker thought back humorously on the incident. His rescuers had initially tried to tell him that, according to protocol, they couldn't bring an unknown and unclassified life form back with them — that Erlen had to stay behind. Maker had made it clear in no uncertain terms that that was never going to happen.

Next, they had told him that the ship's rules dictated that the Niotan needed to be put into quarantine. Maker blatantly stated that the first man who tried to do so would get a broken arm; the next was going out the airlock. After that, no one mentioned anything about Erlen. In fact (probably to save their own hides for not following protocol), his rescuers had failed to note anything about Erlen in their report of Maker's rescue, which is probably how the rumor of his smuggling the Niotan aboard got started.

"The natives of that planet," said Dr. Chantrey, interrupting Maker's walk down memory lane, "where did they get Erlen?"

Maker held open his palms in a hell-if-I-know gesture. "All I could discern is that he came from a planet called Niota."

"So explain what happened in the operating room," Browing almost demanded. "He did something to you in there."

Maker rubbed his eyes with his thumb and middle finger before speaking, trying to think of the best way to say this next part.

"There have been drugs around for ages that can enhance cerebral functions," Maker began. "Give you better memory, a greater attention span, and so on. Erlen basically injected me with a serum that boosted my brain power."

"So," Dr. Chantrey said, taking this in, "his bite can inject you with a stimulant that makes you smarter? He can do that?"

Maker nodded. "Yes, and a whole lot more."

"Like what?" she asked, intrigued.

"Like make acid," Browing chimed in, remembering his fashionable hat that Erlen had destroyed during their first meeting in Maker's cabin.

"He's a living, breathing chemical factory," Maker said. "Almost any element he encounters he can metabolize, synthesize, and reproduce…as well as create its antithesis."

Maker involuntarily rubbed his shoulder where the jwaedin had stung him — the wound Erlen had licked. Wayne had later seen the Niotan bite Maker, presumably injecting an anti-venom. It wouldn't have been the first time that Erlen's unique abilities had saved his life.

"At least now we know why he's always running his tongue all over everything," Dr. Chantrey said.

"That's just for show," Maker commented, then explained about the taste buds in Erlen's footpads.

"Going back to the brain boost that Erlen's bite gives you," Browing said, "how exactly does that turn you into a surgeon?"

"It magnifies my intelligence exponentially, although the effect is only temporary," Maker said. "It lets me remember everything that's ever happened to me, any book I've ever read, everything I've ever seen. And just about anything I've ever seen — or seen another person do — I can imitate."

"What do you mean?" asked Browing.

"I've been in more skirmishes than I can count, and I've seen men suffer all kinds of grievous wounds on the battlefield," Maker responded. "More to the point, I've also seen doctors and field medics operate on them, trying to save their lives."

"And, having seen surgeons in action before," Browing realized, "you can mimic their actions. Perform surgery yourself."

"Only when I get the serum from Erlen," Maker agreed. "And it also helps that I've worked hard on gaining some practical experience."

"The medical module," Dr. Chantrey muttered, remembering the surgical simulator she had seen in Maker's cabin at their first meeting.

"Exactly," Maker said with a nod. "I used it and similar modules to bone up on various subjects, and just about any topic I've read about or experienced, whether in actuality or via simulation, I can actually put into practice. Like physics, medicine—"

"Or hyperspace travel," the doctor concluded. "That's how you did that nine-point jump. Erlen pumped up your IQ."

Maker smiled. "Very good. But he also did something else. When I started plotting the jump, I was attacked, psychically."

"What do you mean?" Dr. Chantrey asked.

"The Vacra had some kind of psychic on their side. I could feel it in my head when I was working on the coordinates. I think maybe that's how they were able to follow us each time we jumped, by reading the mind of the person inputting the data."

"Or they used some of the sub rosa tech to read the instruments," Browing suggested.

Nodding, Maker said, "That's possible. Regardless, Erlen sensed what was happening and somehow helped me shut the psychic out."

"Helped you how?" the doctor asked.

"I don't know exactly, but we were able to block the attack," Maker stated.

"Psychic pets and mind-enhancing drugs," Browing said softly. "I can hardly believe it. So, with all that extra brain power, are you like some uber man now?"

"Hardly," Maker said, laughing. "As I said, the effects of the brain boost are only temporary, and I don't go around juiced all the time — only when I need to."

For some reason, Browing and Dr. Chantrey seemed relieved by that statement.

"Now you know all my secrets," Maker said. "What are you going to do?"

Chapter 35

Thankfully, in the end, they didn't try to take Maker into custody again. Instead, Browing asked him to hang around for a bit while he and Dr. Chantrey discussed what he'd told them — just in case they had further questions. In the meantime, Browing invited Maker to make use of a guest suite in order to wash up.

The room turned out to be very nice, but fairly less luxurious than Maker had imagined guest quarters to be in the consulate. He took a quick shower, contemplating everything he had been through in the past twenty-four hours: the jwaedin, the Vacra, the surgery he'd performed.

He was exhausted, and it was more than obvious. The shower had revitalized him a little, but not enough. These thoughts flitted through his mind as he got dressed. He could always take a stim shot (or better yet, get something from Erlen — who was sleeping in a corner of the room — that would perk him up), but the truth of the matter was that, like the Niotan, he really needed to rest. He cast his eyes towards the suite's large, inviting bed.

Maybe he could lie down for just a few minutes...

****

An unrelenting musical chime woke Maker up, pounding its way into his skull. It took him a moment to realize where he was, and that the chime was the suite's comm unit, located on a nightstand next to the bed. Erlen, already awake, was sitting on the edge of the bed, staring at him.

"No, thanks," Maker said sarcastically to the Niotan. "I'll get it."

He reached over and activated the comm. A moment later, an image of Dr. Chantrey's head appeared.

"Glad to see you're up," she said. "We debated waking you, but decided it was better to let you recuperate."

"You really shouldn't have," Maker said, probably more seriously than he intended once he noticed how long he'd been asleep: nine hours!

Maker leaped off the bed. "I need to get back to my squad asap."

"It's okay," the doctor said. "Browing sent them a message, told them you were conked out and that we'd send you on your way as soon as you woke up."

"How'd you know I was asleep anyway?" Maker asked.

"Room sensors," she said. "We like to keep an eye on some of our more distinguished visitors. Based on your breathing pattern, heart rate, and some other stuff, it was clear that you were catching forty winks."

"Well, I'm done winking," Maker said. "Erlen and I will be out of your hair in two minutes."

"That's fine," she said in understanding, "but before you go there's someone you should see. Can you meet me in the medical wing?"

Maker agreed, then dashed from the room without even disconnecting the comm link. A few minutes later, he was in the medical wing, standing outside the recovery room of the man he'd operated on, talking to Dr. Chantrey and Browing.

"We've been able to find out who he is," Browing was saying. "His name's Solomon Planck. He was the chief scientist on the derelict you found."

"I knew he was related to that ship in some way. Those raggedy clothes we found him in — it was the same uniform we'd seen on the dissected bodies in the derelict's sick bay."

"He's still not in great shape," Dr. Chantrey said, "but he's finally conscious."

"Can I talk to him?" asked Maker.

"Sure," Dr. Chantrey said. "He's actually been asking about you."

Maker, Erlen, Browing, and Dr. Chantrey slipped into the room. Planck, now clean and looking infinitely better, was lying in bed. He turned his heads towards the door as his visitors entered.

Planck smiled and struggled to lift his hand towards Maker.

"You're the one who saved me, I take it," Planck said as Maker shook his hand. "Hard to tell since you were in that armor before, but I recognize your friend." He inclined his head towards Erlen. "His image was on your breastplate."

"Yes," Maker said, his mind flipping back to the scene at the cave. Now he realized what Skullcap had been looking at just before the Vacra charged him — the likeness of Erlen engraved on his armor.

"—ving my life," Planck said, bringing Maker back to the present.

"That's what Marines do," said Maker with a smile. "The insectoids we found you with... can you tell us anything about them?"

Planck's face twisted in an odd way, displaying numerous emotions at once: fear, distrust, hatred, and more.

"The Vacra," he finally said. "Evil, vicious creatures from some world we haven't seen yet."

"Do you know how long you'd been with them?" asked Maker.

"From what your people tell me, it's been about four years, but it feels like it's been ten times longer."

"I understand. Do you remember how you came to be captured by them?"

Planck looked nervous for a moment, his lips suddenly sealed. It took a few seconds for Maker to recognize the problem.

"It's okay," Maker finally said. "We know all about the sub rosa ship you were on."

Planck seemed relieved. "To be honest, I don't know how it happened. Some way, they were able to get on board, secretly, and from there they gained control pretty quickly. After all, we were scientists for the most part, not soldiers."

"How did you survive?"

Planck looked pained, then closed his eyes before replying. "By making myself valuable to them, giving them what they wanted. I helped them incorporate the sub rosa tech into their arsenal."

Tears came out of the corners of Planck's eyes, running down towards his ears due to the position he was lying in.

"It's okay," Maker said supportively. "You didn't have a choice."

"There's always a choice," Planck said in disagreement. "I just chose to live."

"Regardless, don't worry about that now. What more can you tell us about the Vacra?"

"They're a lot like other insectoids. Hive mentality. Focus on the group rather than the individual for the most part. Warmongers, constantly staging raids on other species. A lot like army ants from Earth, if you want to know the truth."

"What about Skullcap?" Maker asked. When Planck gave him a confused look, he quickly added, "Uh, the one with the deformed arm."

"Oh," Planck said, and then his eyes went wide. "Oh! Him!"

He began laughing weakly. After a few moments, he regained his composure.

"I'm sorry," Planck said, smiling. "Skullcap! That's a great name for him."

"But what do you know about him?" asked Maker.

"He's the leader of this particular expedition."

"So, does he have some kind of rank or position?"

"He does, but it's not like human beings. With us, a person may have certain natural attributes, but he usually gains knowledge and a skill set associated with a particular subject, whether it be sports, the military, business, what have you. If he's good at what he does, eventually he may be promoted to a job with more power and responsibility. With the Vacra, it's a little different.

"In insect colonies, everyone typically has their roles established at birth. Queens are born to be queens and nothing else. Drones will always be drones. Soldiers can only be soldiers. There's no change in roles, no promotion, and so on. What you are at birth is what you'll always be."

"What's that have to do with Skullcap?"

"Your friend was born to be a leader. That's his role in the Vacra hierarchy. Do you understand? He's *literally* a natural-born leader."

Maker took a moment to process this before moving on.

"The bomb that was attached to your spine," Maker said. "You knew about it. That's why you didn't want to come with us."

"It was a bomb in my back! Of course I knew about it. It was a method of keeping me under control."

"Why didn't they set it off after we captured you?"

"They didn't need to. The bomb had a proximity sensor and a timer. If I went too far from the ship for too long a time…Boom!"

Maker raised his eyebrows in surprise.

"But the Vacra can be fairly single-minded. After they put it in me, they simply assumed I was under control, so they didn't closely monitor my activities unless they needed me to do something. Thus, over the years, I was able to figure out a lot about the explosive and tried to construct a device to jam the signal should they ever try to activate it. But it was only partly complete, so I didn't think I could leave yet."

"And we dragged you away from there," Maker said.

Planck nodded tiredly. "Yes, but apparently it functioned well enough to buy the time needed to remove the explosive."

The conversation, while helpful, was obviously taking a toll on Planck. He didn't seem to have much more to add about the Vacra, so Maker exchanged a few more pleasantries with him, and then everyone left so the man could get some rest. He'd been through quite an ordeal. (Before they parted ways, however, Planck did pass on that — shortly after Skullcap lost his arm — the Vacra completely destroyed the sub rosa ship.)

Outside his room, Maker turned to Browing and Dr. Chantrey.

"You see now why I wanted to blast the Vacra to bits, and then blast the bits into atoms," Maker said. "Surgically implanting a bomb into another sentient being? This kind of behavior is" — he was tempted to say inhumane, but of course, the Vacra weren't human — "uncivilized. Barbaric. These are monsters we're dealing with."

He waited for some type of response from the doctor or Browing, but neither said anything.

"Well, my squad and I have done our part," Maker declared. "Mission complete. We're leaving this rock. Call us if you decide you're serious about dealing with the Vacra."

With that, Maker turned and left, followed by Erlen.

Chapter 36

Maker was happy to see that nearly everything was packed up and loaded into the dropship by the time he returned to camp. About the only thing left were a couple of sleeping tents — his own and that of the two women, who were in the process of taking theirs down.

"Glad you made it back, el-tee," said Diviana. "I was afraid you might have gone back by the Pit for one last hurrah with Talla."

"Talla?" Maker repeated with a frown.

"The one with the orange feathers," Diviana said. "She swore she'd never been tickled like that in her life."

She gave him a wink and started to laugh as Maker felt the blood rushing to his cheeks. Diviana was about to say something else when she suddenly gasped and turned, looking out towards the desert.

Maker, sensing her change in attitude, followed her gaze. He saw nothing but featureless dunes.

"What is it?" he asked. "What's wrong?"

"There's someone out there," she replied.

Maker looked again. He didn't see anything. "Are you sure?" he asked.

Diviana's reply was unequivocal. "Yes."

"She's right," Loyola chimed in. She moved over next to Diviana, staring in the same direction and pointing. "I see them, too. A lot of them, closing fast. Vacra."

Maker tapped his comm. "We've got inbound! Fierce, get the dropship ready to take off! Everyone else, prepare for assault with heavy weapons!"

There were acknowledgments from everyone, and then Wayne spoke.

"Sir, I'm not picking up anything on the visual," he said.

"They've got some kind of stealth suits," Maker said, flashing back to what he'd seen on the derelict. "But Diviana can feel them and Loyola, somehow, can see them."

"Their suits are only hiding them across the visible light spectrum," Loyola stated. "They're perfectly clear on other wavelen—"

Loyola yelped in pain and put a hand to her forehead, and across the comm Maker heard similar cries from the rest of his squad. In his own head, he felt an enormous pressure, like a migraine suddenly building up.

"Diviana!" he yelled. "They've got a psychic! Get a mind shield around everyone! Now!"

Diviana gave a curt nod and Maker ducked into his tent. A second later, he was running towards the dunes with an odd weapon — something like a rifle, but with a larger-than-normal barrel.

"Wait!" Diviana cried out. "I can't shield you if you go too far!"

"Forget about me! Focus on the others!" Maker replied as he ran, Erlen at his heels. "Loyola, how far out are they?"

"About a hundred yards in the direction you're facing," she said.

After about fifty feet, Maker came to a stop. He adjusted the controls on the weapon, then raised it and fired.

There was a puff of smoke from the weapon as a large projectile went flying from it. A moment later there was a massive explosion about thirty feet directly above the area where Loyola had indicated the Vacra were. A large mass of dark, viscous fluid splattered all over the entire area.

Maker smiled, hustling back towards where the rest of his squad (minus Fierce) were gathered next to Diviana and Loyola.

"What was that?" Adames asked.

"Large-scale paint bomb," responded Maker. "Typically used in target practice and war games, but today… Well, take a look."

They all glanced in the direction he'd come from. Oddly enough, the desert seemed to have come alive. A large portion of the area Maker had fired over was covered in dark paint, and — almost completely covered by the dark liquid — a number of figures seemed to be wriggling.

From their vantage point, it looked to Maker's group like some kid had dumped ink on a pile of ants. Dressed in their battle armor, the Vacra could now be seen and — thankfully — engaged.

"Fire at will!" Maker said.

His squad spread out, putting distance between themselves, and for a minute it was a turkey shoot. They didn't make the mistake that the Vacra had at the cave, trying to take down armored combatants with small-arms fire. Instead, they relied on the heavy weapons that Maker had called for at the onset of the attack — high-intensity lasers and such. Thus, they were able to target and take down the Vacra at will, who were not only visible but seemed to be so covered with paint that they couldn't see well enough to pinpoint Maker's group. Even Wayne's little robot Jerry got in on the action, zipping forward and firing little bolts of electricity at their enemies.

TERMINUS

Maker kept his eyes peeled for Skullcap. Unfortunately, none of the Vacra in the assault party appeared to be him.

Suddenly, Diviana stopped firing and turned around, so fast and aggressively that it shocked Loyola and Snick, who were to either side of her.

"To the rear!" Diviana shouted, and then started firing.

Less than concerned about the paint-covered Vacra before them, Maker and the others turned around. He couldn't see anything, at first, but then he noticed a mass of footprints appearing of their own accord in the sand about a hundred feet away. Another group of Vacra had been approaching them from behind.

Maker hit the ground, rolling over as weapons-fire ripped into the sand around him.

Stupid, stupid, stupid! He'd fallen for one of the oldest plays in the book. He'd not only gotten wrapped up in the distraction that the first party of Vacra were obviously meant to be, but he'd cockily thought that they'd win this fight without even breaking a sweat.

Skullcap hadn't been with the first party of Vacra. That meant...

An explosion suddenly went off in front of the second wave of Vacra, sending body parts flying as battle suits were blown apart and thrusting a huge cloud of sand into the air. Maker recognized the report of the weapon that had fired: Adames' grenade gun. It had bought them a little time, but would be useless as the Vacra closed in, as likely to harm friend as foe.

He thought about another paint bomb, but he'd only loaded one projectile into the paint gun, and he wasn't about to waste time running into his tent for another.

He glanced in the direction of the Vacra. His eyes went wide with surprise at the sight before him. He could see them! (Or rather, as the sand from the grenade explosion fell around them, he could make out their charging forms.)

Maker wasn't foolish enough to let his group get pinned down between two sets of armored foes when they weren't in their battle gear — even if one band of enemies was covered in paint.

"Everyone to the ship!" Maker screamed, getting to his feet.

No one had to be told twice. Everyone in Maker's crew was on their feet and charging towards the dropship as soon as the words were out of his mouth, firing as they ran.

Maker was about halfway to the dropship when he was blindsided and tackled by a brick wall. All of the air went out of his body in a giant whoosh as Maker hit the ground. His training took over and, despite the pain, he rolled and came up with his gun drawn. No one was there. Or more accurately, there was no one there he could see.

But Maker didn't have to see who it was. He knew.

Skullcap.

Maker fired his weapon, randomly shooting wherever he thought his adversary might be. After a few seconds, something rapped his gun hand painfully and he dropped his weapon. As he stood there nursing his injured hand, the air shimmered just a few feet in front of him, seemed to glow for a second, and then the light faded. Standing in front of him, holding his lance (which is probably what he had used to knock Maker's weapon away), was Skullcap.

He still wore the same armor for the most part. The odd skull was still melded to the helmet, and the others were still around his neck. About the only difference Maker could see was that the armor had been refitted to accommodate the stunted arm he now sported.

Skullcap motioned with the lance, making a come-hither gesture that Maker recognized as a challenge.

"Alright," Maker said, pulling the vibro-blade that he'd taken from Kepler from a sheath on his hip. "Let's get it on."

Suddenly, Skullcap twirled the lance over his head and they began.

It wasn't really a fair competition, to say the least. Skullcap had a height advantage, a reach advantage (thanks to the lance), and he was armored. However, Maker was pretty sure that the concept of "fair fight" would be considered an oxymoron under present circumstances.

That said, Maker did a more than adequate job of defending himself. Being unarmored, he was faster, more nimble than his opponent, able to step out of the way of a blow or run in for a cut almost at will. The problem, of course, was that Maker's blade couldn't penetrate Skullcap's armor. Even worse, the longer the fight went on, the more tired Maker would get. And as he got tired, he would start to slow down. And if he got too slow, he wouldn't be able to avoid his adversary's lance.

After about a minute, Maker knew that he needed a way to end the fight, and end it quick. By now his squad was probably already on board the dropship. He considered running to join them, but had no doubt that Skullcap would cut him down from behind.

Maker watched Skullcap closely, looking for an opening. It took a wild swing by his opponent with the lance for Maker to see it, but when he did, he wasted no time.

Skullcap's deformed arm was obviously an oddity among the Vacra, and whoever had modified his armor to account for it had done a poor job. Beneath the arm was a small space where the armor did not fit perfectly.

Seeing this, Maker stepped in, lifted the arm (which appeared feeble and lacked strength) and jabbed the vibro-blade into the gap he'd seen.

Skullcap screamed. His body jerked reflexively, and Maker went flying through the air.

All the wind went out of his lungs as Maker hit the ground. He lay there for a moment, then tried to rise but only managed to prop himself up on his elbows. Taking stock of his surroundings, he was surprised to see that he had landed not too far from the ship. Glancing back to where he'd been tossed from, he saw Skullcap gingerly pull the vibro-blade from his side, then let the bloodstained weapon drop to the ground. With menacing stride, he advanced on Maker, swinging the lance so ferociously that it whistled through the air.

Realizing that the fun and games were over, Maker tried to move, but found himself too exhausted. A second later, Skullcap stood before him. The insectoid pulled the lance back, preparing to run Maker through.

Suddenly, the Vacra convulsed. Maker watched, fascinated, as little arcs of electricity danced across Skullcap's armor. Without warning, the insectoid dropped to his knees, and Maker saw what had saved him: Jerry.

TERMINUS

The little robot had sent a bolt of electricity through the Vacra.

Unexpectedly, Skullcap swung behind him with the lance. It struck Jerry with tremendous force, sending the robot tumbling backwards along the sand, pieces of his metal frame flying loose.

Skullcap stood up and turned his attention back to Maker, who began scuttling backwards along the ground like some mad crab. It did little good; there was no way he could scramble faster than Skullcap could walk. Still, he was nearly to the ship when Skullcap swung.

Maker rolled right, the lance missing him by inches and digging into the sand. Skullcap yanked it out of the ground and swung again. Maker rolled left, the wind from the lance rustling his hair as it bit into the ground right next to his head. Maker didn't know if Skullcap was toying with him or had genuinely missed, but there was only one way the game was going to end. Skullcap pulled the lance from the ground and raised it up again.

At that moment, a giant shadow fell across Maker, and he heard a noise like a thunderclap sound directly in front of him. Maker blinked, not quite believing what he was seeing.

Standing over him, one leg to either side of Maker's waist, was Fierce. His hands were joined together over his head, palm-to-palm, and between them was Skullcap's lance.

It was blatantly obvious what had happened. As Skullcap had swung the killing blow, the Augman had stepped in and caught the lance mid-strike. Now, the Vacra pulled in vain, trying to free it from Fierce's grip.

However, the Augman's genetically enhanced strength was too great.

Without warning, Fierce changed his grip, grabbing the lance in one powerful fist. Then he yanked on it, hard, snatching it out of Skullcap's hand. The Vacra was thrown off-balance but didn't fall.

Fierce stepped forward and began twirling the lance in his hand; Skullcap stepped back defensively. Fierce took another step forward and the Vacra matched him, taking an additional step back. And so they continued, with Skullcap retreating to avoid the weapon in the Augman's hand and Fierce advancing, but twirling the lance far faster and more elaborately than Skullcap had done. It spun in his right hand, like a pinwheel, then he passed it to his left, behind his back, over his head…

Skullcap pulled a firearm from near his abdomen, but he had barely gotten it clear of the holster before Fierce smacked it with the lance, sending it flying. And all the while, the lance never seemed to stop twirling.

"El-tee!" someone screamed from behind Maker. He looked back and saw Adames and Loyola at the doorway of the ship, firing from inside.

"Get in!" Adames yelled.

Maker had been so engrossed in the interplay between Skullcap and Fierce that he had practically forgotten that he was still lying on the ground in a very vulnerable position, and enemy combatants were still around.

He scrambled to his feet and dashed inside, hardly daring to believe his good fortune. When he glanced back out, he saw Fierce running back to the ship, still holding the lance in one hand and some familiar items in the other.

"Lieutenant," Fierce said, extending his hand as he stepped aboard, "I believe these belong to you."

Maker held out his hand and Fierce placed his sidearm and vibro-blade in it.

"Thanks," Maker mumbled as he put the weapons away. "That was incredible. I've never seen anything like what you did out there."

"Well, just because Augmen don't like to fight doesn't mean we're useless in battle," Fierce said.

"I'll try to keep that in mind," replied Maker. "What happened to Skullcap?"

"Tripped over his own feet and fell," Fierce said. "Then he hit some button on his suit and vanished."

Maker ground his teeth in frustration at the thought of Skullcap getting away. Of course, it's not like Fierce would have killed the insectoid, but still…

"Who's at the controls?" Adames suddenly shouted, interrupting Maker's thoughts.

"Me!" yelled Diviana.

"Let's roll!" Adames cried out.

"Incoming!" Loyola suddenly screamed. Maker glanced out the still-open door and saw a Vacra aiming something that looked like a shoulder-mounted cannon with a barrel six inches in diameter at them. There was a boom as the Vacra fired, and Maker saw an exhaust trail as the projectile wound its way straight towards the dropship doorway.

Faster than Maker would have believed possible, Fierce stepped outside the vessel, putting himself directly in the path of the oncoming projectile, which appeared to be a small missile about the length of a man's hand. In his mind's eye, Maker saw what the next few seconds would bring: the approaching missile would strike Fierce, blowing him to bits. The concussive force would batter the dropship, and probably everyone in it. They'd all end up dying out here in the middle of an alien desert.

To Maker's great surprise, none of that happened. When the missile got close, Fierce — with a speed and agility no normal human could match — actually reached out and grabbed the damn thing in his fist. Still in motion, he spun in a circle and then flicked his wrist upward, letting the projectile's jets take it into the sky. Moments later there was a dull boom as the missile exploded above them and Fierce jumped back inside.

Diviana wasn't waiting around to give the Vacra another shot. Loyola and Adames were still in the process of closing the dropship door when she put the ship in motion, zipping up and forward as fast as the ship would go.

Everyone breathed a sigh of relief as they left the camp — and the Vacra — behind. There were a few smiles exchanged. And then everyone began excitedly talking all at once.

Maker smiled to himself. It was like this after almost every battle — the euphoria of coming through a deadly skirmish alive.

"Lieutenant!" Diviana shouted, getting Maker's attention.

He worked his way to the cockpit, where Diviana was flying and Wayne was sitting in the co-pilot's seat.

"You rang?" Maker asked.

"I need a destination," Diviana said.

"Mission's over for us. We can head back to the *Mantis*, I guess, see if we can get authorization for Captain Henry to take us home."

"No can do, sir," said Wayne. "You were probably too busy to notice, but the dropship took on some damage back there. Thankfully, somebody had the foresight to add some extra plating in key areas."

Wayne winked at him, and Maker remembered requesting the younger Marine's help with bulking up the dropship's offensive and defensive capabilities.

"It would have been nice to have some guns on this puppy, too," Maker said.

"Not enough time or people to do both, so I made a command decision and went with the idea that we'd be better served if the ship was able to take a punch."

Maker nodded in understanding. "The best offense is a good defense."

"Exactly," Wayne agreed. "She's still good enough to zip around the planet in at the moment — just not spaceworthy. Not until we make some repairs."

"Alright," Maker said. He turned towards Diviana. "Let's head to the consulate. They have their own ships there and should have anything we need to fix this old girl up."

"Yes, sir," said Diviana.

Maker was making his way back to where he'd been sitting when he noticed that Wayne had left the cockpit, following him.

"Excuse me, sir," Wayne whispered to him, "but that device you asked for? It's ready."

He handed Maker a small metal square with a flip-up top. Maker opened it; inside was a button — a trigger — that was clearly intended to activate something. Maker closed the top again.

"That was fast," he said to Wayne, who nodded. "You must have started working on this the minute you left my tent."

"Actually, I started working on it as soon as you asked me about it — back on the *Mantis*."

Maker's eyebrows went up in surprise, but he said nothing.

"I know I said I wasn't interested at first, but I love to tinker and, well, nobody had ever asked me to make anything like that before."

"So you started working on it," Maker concluded.

"Just for fun," Wayne insisted. "I mean, I thought it would be a challenge to work on for a while — until I got my next real assignment. I never intended to finish it."

"But then you changed your mind about it," Maker said.

"Actually, after that thing with the jwaedin, I changed my mind about *you*," Wayne corrected. "So when you asked me about it again, I was happy to do it."

"Thanks," Maker said. "This is just what we needed."

"No problem," Wayne said. A moment later, he nervously added, "Just, uh, be careful with that, sir. Please."

"I will," Maker assured him. "And as things stand now, I doubt I'll ever have to use it."

"I'll keep my fingers crossed on that," Wayne said, then headed back to the cockpit.

Maker sat and took a moment to look around at his crew. They'd all made it through a tougher-than-advertised mission in essentially one piece. It had been a

269

long time since he'd felt success on this level. The way his last mission had ended, with just him and Erlen—

A sudden feeling of dread came over Maker, like some otherworldly spirit had wrapped its icy fingers around his heart. He fought to keep panic out of his voice as he stood up.

"*Where's Erlen??!!*" he screamed.

TERMINUS

Chapter 37

The dropship came in fast, approaching the consulate at a speed that was more suited to an out-of-control vessel than one under the command of a seasoned pilot. Maker, having replaced Diviana in the pilot's seat, would have gone even faster had the ship been capable of it.

As they neared their destination, Maker saw a sleek craft leave the consulate roof, taking off for space.

"Browing..." Maker muttered in anger, recognizing the man's ship. He gripped the controls of the dropship so tightly that his knuckles turned a bloodless white.

Immediately upon noting Erlen's absence, they had doubled back to the campsite. It had been about twenty minutes since the battle, but the camp was deserted. The surviving Vacra had fled, taking their fallen comrades with them. Erlen was nowhere to be found. (They had, however, made a quick stop to retrieve what they could find of Wayne's little robot, Jerry.)

Everything had pointed to the Vacra having the Niotan. Maker had briefly considered going back to the Vacra cave, but every cell in his brain told him that place would be deserted. Moreover, he couldn't shake the feeling that time was of the essence.

The insectoids had come into their camp and taken the Niotan hostage. How had the Vacra even found them? And immediately upon asking himself that question, he knew the answer. A minute later, they were heading towards the consulate as fast as possible.

Now that they had arrived, Maker set the ship down almost carelessly in his haste, rattling the teeth of his passengers and frightening the maintenance personnel on the roof.

"Wayne," he called out, "how long will it take for those repairs?"

"I can probably get it done in a couple of hours," came the reply.

"You've got fifteen minutes," Maker told him. "Everybody else, give him a hand."

The rest of his squad filed out. A moment later, Maker heard Adames arguing with some of the consulate personnel about prioritized use of equipment, requisitioning supplies, proper authorization, and a bunch of other related matters.

He turned his attention to the comm panel, opening a channel to Browing's ship. To his surprise, the man answered. He appeared on the dropship's comm screen, Dr. Chantrey next to him, as always.

"Lieutenant Maker," Browing said with a smile. "Always a pleasure. What can I do for you?"

Maker's brain bubbled over with questions that he wanted to ask, but in the end he settled on just one.

"Why?" Maker asked.

"Can you be a little more specific?" Browing asked. "Why what?"

"The Vacra," Maker answered. "It was you who told them where to find us, right?"

For a second it looked as though he might deny it, but then Browing sighed and said, "We've been dealing straight with each other recently, so let's keep all the cards on the table. Yes, it was me who told them where you were located."

"I knew it," Maker muttered. "You were the only one I told where our new camp was — you and the good doctor."

Browing glanced at Dr. Chantrey, who looked upset. "Don't blame her. I'm the one who did it."

"Again, why?"

"It was a trade-off, Maker. The Vacra wanted your little pet, so they approached us with a deal: everything they pulled off the sub rosa ship in exchange for Erlen."

"How do you know they even have it? That ship could have been raided long before the Vacra ever got there and set that trap for my team."

"As a goodwill gesture, they gave us some of the stuff from the ship, *gratis*. It was the real deal."

"Doesn't that strike you as odd, that they'd give an entire ship's worth of irreplaceable — probably invaluable — cargo for Erlen?"

Browing shrugged. "Back on Old Earth, some guys once traded an entire island for a bunch of beads and trinkets. We can't figure out foreign cultures within the human race on many occasions. Don't even try when it comes to alien species. Sometimes they just want what they want."

"But didn't it even occur to you to ask?"

"Sure. The translation wasn't perfect, but it appears that Erlen is like an ancient enemy of their race or something. They've actually been looking for him for years — at least since your little run-in on the derelict ship, and, based on how you say you got him, perhaps even before. Getting their hands on him is like getting crowned king of the universe for them."

Maker shook his head in nigh-disbelief. "So why go through this entire charade? Why pretend like you needed us to find them and all that jazz? Why not just hand Erlen over to them gift-wrapped right at the start?"

"Trust me, it was considered. If they'd had their way, the Vacra would have shown up at Ginsberg where you'd buried yourself the past few years, taken your pet, and blasted anyone who got in their way."

Maker started to feel odd vibrations permeating through the ship. (Presumably the repairs were under way.) He ignored them, focusing instead on getting answers.

"Fortunately for you," Browing went on, "we can't have alien ships entering Gaian Space and attacking our worlds at their leisure. Sets a bad precedent."

"Still, you could have sent in a contingent of Marines, given them orders to take Erlen and shoot me dead if necessary."

"Two problems with that. First, the Vacra were insistent that Erlen be delivered unharmed. Any kind of assault ran the risk of him getting hurt or killed."

"And the second issue with a raid on *Casa de Maker*?"

"Kroner. For whatever reason, he's got your back. He's really not a player, but has enough connections and knows where enough of the bodies are buried to cause problems."

"So you came up with a plan to have me deliver Erlen to them myself. A fake mission to a world in the Beyond, where people get killed all the time."

"Yes, although again you're talking like these were plans I personally came up with. I'm just a guy following orders."

274

"So why have us jerking around in the desert for days on end? Why all this clandestine crap with fake allies and contacts and so on?"

Maker reflected briefly on the ambush that had been arranged by Quinzen, whose plan he now figured had been to let the Vacra in his suite kill Wayne and Maker, and then take Erlen captive.

"Again, Kroner," Browing answered. "If you'd arrived here and gotten your ticket punched the first day, he would have been suspicious. However, a couple of days is just enough time to get in trouble around here — especially hanging out in places like the Pit."

"So this has been nothing but one gigantic setup — the long con."

"That's an apt way to put it," Browing said with a nod. "For the record, though, even though the bigwigs felt your death would be an acceptable casualty, I'm personally glad you made it."

"Thanks," Maker said sarcastically. "That really means a lot to me."

"No problem. Now, if you'll excuse me, we've got to board the *Mantis* now and then rendezvous with the Vacra for the full exchange."

"Browing, you're making a mistake. The Vacra can't be trusted."

"That may be, but again, I'm just a guy following orders."

TERMINUS

Chapter 38

Maker didn't know what kind of job Wayne and the others did on the ship, but after fifteen minutes they were all back aboard and ready to go. Again, Maker pushed the dropship — and his squad — to the physical limit, rising as fast as he could go.

The minute they cleared the atmosphere, he was on the comm to the *Mantis*, requesting permission to come aboard.

"I'm sorry, Lieutenant," said the comm officer he spoke to. "We're in the countdown stage of our jump. Opening the bay doors would jeopardize that."

"But we're already here!" Maker insisted as the dropship closed on the *Mantis*. "It will only take a couple of minutes at most!"

"I'm sorry, but the captain has given strict orders," the officer said. "No one else is allowed to board at this time."

"But we're right outside!" Maker almost screamed. "Just open the damn bay!"

"That's not going to happen, Maker," said Browing, taking over the comm. "I'm sorry, but you're too late. We go to hyperspace in thirty seconds."

Browing disconnected.

Maker sat in the pilot's seat, thinking at a furious pace. If ever he needed a brain boost, now was the time. He needed a plan.

"El-tee," Adames said after about ten seconds, causing Maker to turn towards him. "It's over. We need to be moving."

Adames appeared deeply concerned, and rightfully so. The area that a jump engine would shift into hyperspace was known as the jump field, and it typically didn't extend beyond a spaceship's exterior. However, most experts agreed that anything that got too close when a jump drive activated ran a real risk of being torn apart, with a portion of it being dragged into hyperspace and the rest left behind.

"Gant," said Adames when Maker failed to respond, "we gotta go."

"No," Maker said, coming to a decision. "Everyone, make sure you're strapped in tight."

Maker turned back to the controls, guiding the dropship forward until they were almost flush with the hull of the *Mantis*.

All of a sudden everyone pitched forward in their seats as the dropship came to a sudden halt.

"What the hell was that?" asked Diviana. "Did we ram them?"

"Not quite," Maker said over his shoulder. "I activated the magnetic clamps."

Six pairs of eyes suddenly bulged in surprise, staring at Maker.

"We're attached to the hull of the *Mantis*," he stated.

"Oh my G—" Loyola began, just as the *Mantis* leaped into hyperspace.

TERMINUS

Chapter 39

Captain Henry was on the bridge of the *Mantis*, nervously drumming his fingers. His ship had just come out of hyperspace in some unknown region of the cosmos even farther out than that open sewer of a world known as Terminus. (Scans revealed that they were in a solar system with three planets, none of which contained any life.) Now they were supposed to hang out here for who knew how long until that popinjay Browing had some super-secret meeting or other.

He looked around his bridge. In addition to the usual complement of officers, he also had Browing present, Dr. Chantrey, and — sitting in a hoverchair because he was allegedly too weak to walk — some guy who looked like he'd done hard time in the worst penal colony in the galaxy.

"Captain," one of the officers on duty said. "I've got an airlock opening on the starboard bow."

"What?" Henry was more than a little perturbed. "Where was the opening sequence initiated?"

"Outside the ship," came the answer.

"What does that mean?" asked Dr. Chantrey, who was a little intrigued by what she was hearing.

"It means we've been boarded," answered the captain. He turned to one of his officers. "Get a security team down there on the double."

"Yes, sir," the officer replied and then departed.

A few minutes later, Maker — stripped down to a pair of exercise shorts — was escorted onto the bridge by four armed men.

Neither Browing nor Dr. Chantrey could hide their surprise.

"I don't believe it…" Browing muttered.

"What's this?" Captain Henry asked.

"Sir," said one of the men guarding Maker, "we found seven people who had boarded from the compromised airlock. This one insisted on seeing you."

"Why's he half-naked?" the captain asked.

"They were wearing armor when we found them," the guard replied. "We didn't think we should bring him onto the bridge suited up like that, so we had him strip and leave it by the airlock."

"You didn't have to bring him to the bridge at all," Henry countered.

"Captain," Maker said, stepping forward, "I know my being here is against protocol—"

"Protocol?!" Henry exclaimed. "It merits a court-martial!"

"Fine then, convene a court-martial if you want, but right now you need to listen to me," Maker said. "You're about to be attacked."

"No," Browing said, "you're not. We're here to conduct a peaceful interchange, and there is no indication that anything untoward is going to happen."

"Captain, you're a seasoned officer," Maker said. "From one military man to another, I'm telling you that an attack is imminent. You have to trust me."

"Trust you?" Henry said to Maker. "I don't even know how you got here!"

"Easy," Maker said. "We magnetically attached our dropship to your hull before you jumped."

There were a few harsh intakes of breath as people realized what he'd done.

"I see now that the stories about you are right," Browing said. "You really are a maniac and a madman, only that's an understatement."

"I'll take that as a compliment," Maker said with a smile. Mentally, however, he had to admit that there was a certain amount of truth to Browing's comment. Hitching a ride when the *Mantis* jumped had been a terrible gamble – one that could easily have cost the lives of the Marines under his command.

"Wait just a minute," the captain said. "Are you telling me that there's another vessel attached to the outside of my ship?"

"No sir," Maker answered. "There was, but we detached it before we came inside. It's moving away as we speak."

"Thank heaven for small favors," Browing said sarcastically.

Before Maker could retort, one of the bridge officers spoke.

"Sir, I've got a large ship that just dropped out of hyperspace heading our way."

"That's them!" Maker yelled. "You need to go to high alert!"

"I don't need to do any—" Henry began, only to have his words cut off as the ship suddenly shook violently and klaxons began sounding.

"What the hell was that?" the captain asked.

"Sir, we're under attack. We've got a breach of the outer hull along three decks."

"Get our shields up!" Captain Henry shouted.

"Shields activated, sir," said one of the other officers, just as the ship shook again.

"What the…?" the captain began. "I thought you said those shields were up!"

"Shields *are* up," said the officer in question. "But they're ineffective. The enemy weapon is somehow managing to penetrate them."

The sub rosa tech, Maker thought. The Vacra were using it to blast through the shields on the *Mantis*.

"We're just sitting ducks here," the captain said. "Why aren't we returning fire?"

"The weapons can't get a lock on the target," someone said. "It's like it's not there as far as the instruments are concerned."

"Happy now?" Maker said to Browing. "All your machinations are going to end up with us getting blown to bits in space."

"Me?" Browing said with incredulity. "This is probably your fault. They probably saw your ship out there and recognized it from your attack on their hideout. You've ruined a great deal!"

"You never had a deal, you idiot!" Maker responded, as the ship convulsed again from another attack by the Vacra ship. "You want to know why they were willing to give you some of that tech, maybe even promise you the rest of it? Because they had *him*!"

Maker pointed at Planck, who was sitting in a hoverchair nearby — the man Captain Henry had thought was in bad shape.

"He was the lead scientist and he knew everything that was going on aboard that ship. Anything the Vacra gave to you, he could probably duplicate. But now we have their ace in the hole. Remember that bomb on his spine? They'd rather have him dead than lose him."

281

As if to confirm this statement, the ship got hit again by the Vacra.

"Shield integrity is failing," someone said.

"Enough of this," Maker muttered. He pulled the little square Wayne had given him from a pocket, flipped it open, and firmly pressed the button inside.

For a moment, nothing seemed to happen. Then, a few seconds later, lights on board the ship began flashing and a number of computer screens on the bridge began shooting sparks.

"What in the world...?" Dr. Chantrey began.

"Shields are down!" someone yelled.

"So are weapons!" another officer said.

"And the engines!" said a third.

"What the hell was that they hit us with?" the captain said.

"Instruments are reading it as a solar electromagnetic pulse," was the reply. "It knocked out the shields, weapons, and a few other systems, but we still have some online, like scanners."

"A solar EMP?" Captain Henry said, confused. "We aren't anywhere near the sun in this system."

"The source wasn't the sun, sir," said one of the officers. "It originated from a small vessel — dropship configuration — that is now drifting between our position and the alien ship that attacked us."

"A dropship..." Browing mumbled, then looked at Maker, as did Dr. Chantrey and Captain Henry.

"What did you do?" Browing said to Maker.

"I stopped the Vacra from attacking," Maker replied.

"How?" asked Dr. Chantrey.

"Easy," Maker said. "With a nova bomb."

Chapter 40

Browing tried to laugh, but couldn't.

"Yeah, right," he scoffed in disbelief. "A nova bomb."

"Yes," Maker said. There was silence for a few moments as everyone weighed his statement.

Maker didn't blame them for being skeptical. Nova bombs were banned weapons, explosives that detonated with the force of a sun. One of them could destroy a solar system.

"Are you really trying to say that your dropship is carrying a nova bomb?" Browing asked.

"No," he retorted. "I'm saying the dropship *is* a nova bomb."

"How is that possible?" Dr. Chantrey asked.

Maker simply smiled. Frankly speaking, it hadn't been particularly difficult. Adames had managed to obtain most of the supplies needed (although he surely didn't know what they were for) and had actually done a lot of the work in the form of Maker's "upgrades." After that, it was just a matter of incorporating everything into the ship's structure. (There's no law that says a bomb has to adhere to a certain shape.) Plus, building it into the ship made it easier to hide the weapon from prying eyes. Finally, Wayne had built the trigger mechanism for him, which he had just pressed moments earlier. (Again, Maker felt a debt of gratitude to the young Marine. Even had Maker chosen to have Erlen give him a constant brain boost, he still wouldn't have had time to do everything himself.)

283

"Fine, if that's truly a nova bomb," Dr. Chantrey continued, "how much time do we have until it detonates?"

"Nova bombs are really built to take out entire fleets," said Maker. "They first send out an EMP, which is designed to disable the shields of any ships in the vicinity. Then, when the EMP reaches the end of its outward trajectory, the bomb explodes, destroying the now-unprotected ships."

"That still doesn't answer my question," the doctor said. "How long?"

Maker shrugged. "A large fleet can extend the breadth of a solar system. The bomb doesn't explode until the EMP has a chance to reach all of a fleet's ships. At a guess, I'd say we have twenty minutes, while the pulse is radiating outward from its point of origin."

"But it can't be a nova bomb," Browing insisted. "A nova bomb is initiated by a unique chemical reaction, and the specific elements required for it are kept in secure vaults in secret locations and their exact tally — how much is on hand — is known at all times. Where would he get…"

Browing's voice faded as the truth dawned on him.

"Erlen," Dr. Chantrey said. "He can duplicate any chemical."

"Or a reasonable facsimile," Maker added. "And if you're wondering if I really know how to build a nova bomb, I'm happy to remind you that I had the pleasure of seeing one dismantled once, during that bogus mission I was sent on. Building my own just required me to reverse that process. Plus, the scientist who took it apart had all kinds of plans and schematics to make sure he did it right, and I got a chance to look at them all."

"So all you'd need was a brain boost from Erlen to remember how to do it," the doctor summed up.

"Holy crap!" Browing screamed in frustration. "You've killed us all with this homemade weapon of yours."

"No, I've *saved* you, because right now that weapon is the only thing standing between you and oblivion," Maker corrected. "The Vacra's shields are down, along with their engines, just like us. If they've got weapons available, they're probably terrified to fire them because if our ship explodes it might trigger the nova bomb."

"So, that really is a nova bomb out there?" asked Captain Henry, who had been trying to follow the conversation (but really couldn't because he didn't know half of what they were talking about).

"Yes, sir," Maker answered.

"Do you realize the position you've put us in?" asked the captain.

"I realize it's a bit of a footrace to see who can get their ship back in working order first, but I didn't have much choice. They've got my friend on their ship, and now's the best time for a rescue, while they've got their hands full trying to—"

Captain Henry held up his hand. "Hold on, you've got a friend on that ship?"

"It's just a *pet*," Browing interjected. "One that made the trip to Terminus with him."

Maker frowned but said nothing.

"Alright, even if I were willing to help you — and I'm not," Henry insisted, "what you've done in simply building that bomb is a major crime, let alone activating it."

The captain turned to the men who had escorted Maker in. "Guards, take him away. And this time keep him off my bridge."

"I'll personally see to it, sir," said a voice Maker recognized but had practically forgotten about.

Kepler.

Maker had been so intent on warning Captain Henry about the Vacra that he hadn't even noticed the man, who was apparently part of the bridge crew.

"Thank you," the captain said.

Kepler and the guards moved to flank Maker, but found their way blocked by Planck, who had unobtrusively floated over next to Maker while everyone was talking. Quickly, he said something to Maker too softly for anyone else to hear. Maker nodded to Planck, and then allowed himself to be escorted from the bridge.

Henry spent the next few minutes cracking the whip on his people, reminding them that they had roughly twenty minutes to get the *Mantis* back on her feet. They were in a tough situation thanks to that nut Lieutenant Maker, but he wasn't about to give up.

"Sir," said one of the officers near the captain, "I've got another air lock opening."

"Is it from the outside again?"

"No, sir. It's from the inside this time."

Henry frowned, a sudden distasteful thought occurring to him.

"Check on the security team who just escorted the lieutenant off my bridge," Henry said.

One of his officers answered with "No response," a few seconds later.

"Have the closest security guard check the route they took with the lieutenant," Henry said, now worried. The answer came back moments later.

"The security team is down, sir," was the response.

"All of them?" Henry asked.

"Yes, sir. All."

Henry closed his eyes and massaged his temples, feeling a massive headache coming on. Assuming they survived, this was going to go into the captain's log as the worst day ever.

TERMINUS

Chapter 41

Wearing his jetpack and a waist pack around his midriff, Maker rocketed across the space separating the *Mantis* from the Vacra ship. He had wasted valuable time dealing with the guards (including that douche Kepler) and then having to don his armor again.

He was a little miffed at having to activate the nova bomb; that was supposed to be a last resort. (To be honest, he hadn't even been sure the trigger would work – it wasn't the kind of thing you could test out – even though Wayne had built it exactly in line with the specs Maker had provided.) However, it was pretty clear that the Vacra would have blasted through their shields and destroyed them while everyone on the bridge of the *Mantis* debated the situation. Besides, it was actually a pretty weak EMP; twenty minutes should be plenty of time to get the relevant systems (specifically, the jump drive) back up and running. The real question was whether he'd make it back in time.

As he closed in on the Vacra vessel, passing the dropship en route, Maker reflected back on what Planck had whispered to him on the bridge. In essence, Planck had told him that — if Erlen was indeed on the Vacra ship — he'd most likely be in the insectoid version of the brig, located at the port bow. Maker headed there.

Off to one side, Maker noticed a gun turret, which seemed dead (courtesy of the EMP). Nevertheless, he prudently skirted the weapon, taking a path that would make it impossible for the gun to get a firing resolution on him if it did happen to be active. A few moments later he arrived at an area that — as best he could determine from the alien design — was his destination.

TERMINUS

Maker turned his body, angling so that his feet would hit the hull of the ship, and then slowed his momentum with the jets. Still, he struck a little harder than he intended, and he imagined the sound of his landing echoing inside the ship.

His magnetic boots locked onto the hull, stabilizing him. Having safely arrived, he unzipped the waist pack and reached inside. A moment later, he pulled out a long coil of what appeared to be wire with a bunch of small black squares attached.

Maker scanned the hull, looking for an ideal location for what he needed to do. The outside of the ship was mostly sleek and smooth, with an occasional man-sized block of metal sticking out. Finally he shrugged, thinking that one spot was as good as another. Kneeling, he laid the wire down in a circle about two feet in diameter. The undersides of the small black squares, magnetic in nature, stuck to the metal hull. Satisfied, Maker grabbed the end of the wire that ran through the squares and pulled hard. The wire whipped smoothly out of the squares, which began blinking red.

Maker jumped, breaking contact with the ship, and then hit his jets, moving towards a square hunk of metal that stuck out of the hull. He zipped behind it and then hunkered down, waiting.

The little black squares were shaped charges. They were designed to blow inwards, but he wasn't taking any chances. The last thing he needed was for the explosives to misfire and send a bunch of shrapnel his way.

Fortunately, the charges worked as intended, blasting a hole inward into the ship. A second later, however, all manner of items from the interior of the vessel began flying out of the hole like shot from a gun.

Maker realized that it was the pressure equalizing between the interior of the alien craft and outer space.

Even the Vacra themselves weren't spared, as at least half a dozen of them came blasting out of the hole, limbs flailing. (Several seemingly empty Vacra battle suits flew out as well.) Dying in space would not be an easy way to go, but — bearing in mind the insectoids' treatment of Planck and the fact that they'd kidnapped Erlen — it was hard to feel sorry for them.

When it seemed that nothing else was going to come out, Maker headed to the hole and went inside. The interior was filled with floating debris, much of it alien to Maker in terms of appearance and function.

He did see one thing he recognized: a suit of Vacra battle armor. It seemed to be wedged into a corner between something like a desk and what was apparently a bed. The sight of it put him on edge, making him suddenly wonder how he'd managed to get this far without the Vacra trying to engage him. Surely they had seen him coming.

As he thought about the situation, Maker realized that there was something wrong about the armor. He went over to inspect it, and got an unexpected surprise.

There was a Vacra inside it, apparently alive.

Instinctively, Maker drew his weapon. The Vacra, however, never moved. Maker frowned, trying to make sense of the situation. Maybe the Vacra in the armor was stunned in some way.

He didn't have time to try to figure the mystery out. He needed to find Erlen.

He went to the door of the room he was in, intending to head out and search this region of the ship. If Planck were to be believed, Erlen would be somewhere close by. Maker began fiddling around the door, looking for the manual controls since the automatic functions were not working. He had been in a number of insectoid compounds before, so he had an idea of what he was looking for, and after a few seconds he found the crank handle. Shortly thereafter, he got the door open and left.

****

The murky interior of the ship had an atmosphere and gravity, but beyond that only seemed capable of supporting dim, flashing lights every few feet. Still, it only took him about five minutes to find Erlen, whom he located about three levels down from where he'd entered. Along the way, he'd encountered numerous other Vacra, all immobile in their battle armor. It wasn't until he found the third one that he realized what was going on, and as the realization hit him, he had laughed.

The EMP! It didn't just affect ship systems (which explained the flashing low-wattage bulbs), it affected battle armor, too. The Vacra — at least a great majority of them — had been in their battle gear when their ship was firing on the *Mantis*. Now, with their armor lacking power, they were immobile and helpless.

Not for the first time, Maker was grateful for the investment he'd made in customizing his own armor, which was not only spaceworthy but also shielded against things like EMPs. He probably had the only suit of working armor between the two ships.

After that, he'd practically run through the Vacra vessel, heedless of caution, looking for Erlen. He only came across a few unarmored Vacra during that time, all of whom he shot and killed. The others he left unmolested in their armor. Shooting them while they were like this would just be…criminal. Erlen, however, took a different view of the matter.

When Maker finally came across the Niotan, he was in a large chamber that looked like some kind of operating room or lab. In Maker's eyes, it was a scene of carnage. The room was filled with the torn-apart bodies of Vacra — most of whom were still in their armor.

From all appearances, the Vacra had barely been able to hold and subdue Erlen while their armor was functional. Once those shut down, the insectoids were severely outclassed.

Maker activated his suit's external audio. "Let's go." He turned and left the room, with Erlen following.

They hustled back double-time, with Maker's intent being to exit via the same hole that he'd entered. By his estimate, they still had close to ten minutes to get back to the *Mantis*.

They were in a large area stocked with numerous Vacra in armor, just about to enter the final passageway leading to the first room Maker had entered, when a shadow came through it from the other side. Maker knew instinctively who it was.

He took a few steps back as Skullcap, recognizable by his deformed arm, exited the hallway. Unsurprisingly, he wasn't wearing any kind of protective gear. However, what he lacked in armor he made up for in armaments: he was holding a gun that looked capable of punching a hole in a tank.

With virtually no hesitation, Skullcap fired in Maker's direction. Although there wasn't much distance between him and his adversary, Maker reacted quickly, reaching for a nearby, immobilized Vacra and yanking it in front of him. A metallic shell struck the Vacra that Maker was using as a shield, the force of it lifting both human and insectoid off their feet and slamming them into the far wall.

Maker, stunned, wondered how he was even alive. At the range the Vacra had fired and the power of the weapon, it should have drilled a hole through both him and his living shield.

He had no time to dwell on it, however, choosing to focus his efforts on diving aside as Skullcap fired at him again. The projectile — about the size of Maker's hand — hit the wall, embedding itself roughly halfway through. An odd hissing sound began around the edges of the lodged shell, and Maker knew that it had penetrated the hull.

Now he knew why the shell hadn't killed him. Skullcap wasn't firing at full power, nor was he shooting any kind of explosive round. The room they were in had an exterior wall. If the Vacra got too crazy with the weapon he was holding, he could blast a hole in the ship and get himself sucked into space.

At the moment, however, Skullcap had his hands full trying to keep Erlen back. The Vacra was using the long barrel of his weapon to ward off the Niotan. As a clear indication of how nervous he must have been, Skullcap fired twice at Erlen from point blank range and still missed.

As Maker observed this, the lights flickered wildly, then came fully on. In addition, the armor of the Vacra in the room began to flash, coming to life.

The Vacra systems were coming back online. Skullcap had probably just been stalling them.

Maker reached into his waist sack and pulled three black cubes out. Freed of the string they had been on, they were already flashing, indicating activation. Maker smacked them on the wall next to the embedded shell, where they stuck.

"Erlen!" he shouted, as he grabbed the insectoid he'd used to block Skullcap's shot. "Fire in the hole!"

He looked back to see the Niotan heading towards him. Then the black squares exploded.

There was a sound like a typhoon, and all the air suddenly began rushing from the room as if sucked out by a vacuum cleaner. Everything not nailed down was soon flying out the ship — including a number of armored Vacra.

Maker had released his living shield, letting it get sucked into space as he grabbed a nearby column that ran from the floor to the ceiling of the room they were in.

Skullcap, having let go of his weapon, had his arms around a similar column and was hanging on for dear life. Erlen had found purchase by digging his powerful claws into the floor.

"Erlen!" Maker screamed. "Let go!"

Maker knew Erlen trusted him completely, but the Niotan seemed to hesitate momentarily. Then it retracted its claws and practically went bounding out through the hole. Maker said a quick prayer, then let go of the column and, after banging against one side of the ragged hole made by the explosion, was sucked out into the void as well.

TERMINUS

Chapter 42

Upon being blown out of the ship, tumbling end over end, Maker immediately activated his jets. He was thus able to stop his wild flight and bring himself under control. Upon doing so, he noticed a red light flashing in a corner of his visor.

"Warning," said a seductive female voice. "Oxygen leak detec—"

Maker turned the voice off so he could think. According to the gauge, he was losing oxygen — fast. When he'd banged against the side of the hole he must have damaged his suit (or at least the air tank).

He immediately began scanning the area for Erlen, almost in a panic. Apparently more crap than he realized had gotten suctioned from the alien vessel, and it was difficult to visually sort through it all. (One thing he took particular note of, however, was the dropship, which had moved a lot closer to the Vacra ship.)

He hadn't been exceptionally worried at first because he knew from experience that Erlen could survive the vacuum of space. What he didn't know, however, was for how long, and his own oxygen problems were exacerbating the issue. After what seemed like a lifetime (but was in truth only a few seconds), he spied the Niotan spinning away from him at an angle. He turned the jets on full and went roaring after him.

Maker didn't really slow down; he just kind of went in, hooked the Niotan on his shoulder, and then arced towards the *Mantis*. He risked a single glance back and didn't like what he saw. The Vacra ship was lighting up, regaining power. They'd recovered from the EMP. Even worse, he saw the gun turrets begin to move.

A second later, little flashes of light danced around them, which Maker recognized as weapons fire. Thankfully, they made a pretty small target — especially considering that the guns were used to engaging spacecraft of some sort. He checked his gauge and saw that he was down to about fifty percent oxygen.

Maker did his best to forget about the shots, zigzagging slightly to throw off any potential targeting the Vacra might try to do. His main focus, however, was on the *Mantis*. She needed to come alive in the next few minutes if they were to have any hope of surviving.

As if on cue, lights on the *Mantis* began to come on, indicating that some — if not all — of the ship's power was back to normal.

"Woo-hoo!" Maker screamed giddily. "We're going to make it!"

An odd glistening appeared around the *Mantis*, then disappeared. It had only been there for a nanosecond, but it left a bad taste in Maker's mouth.

"Oh no," he whispered, realizing what had happened.

He changed the view in his visor, switching over to a different wavelength of light, and then he saw it. The *Mantis'* shields had activated, creating a globe of soft, white light around the ship. Maker and Erlen wouldn't be able to get through it, and if they could get through, they'd probably be stranded if the ship went to hyperspace. (Which it would definitely do to get away from the nova bomb.)

Maker opened a channel on his comm and began frantically hailing the *Mantis*. There was no answer. Trying to stay calm, his mind raced through the possibilities. The comm was typically only used to cover short distances, so maybe he was out of range. Maybe it had gotten damaged somehow when he was on board the Vacra ship. Maybe his armor wasn't completely shielded from the EMP.

Maybe, maybe, maybe…

There were simply too many possibilities, and even if he knew what the problem was with the comm, he didn't have time to fix it. No, he needed to focus on finding another solution. Unfortunately, as he and Erlen headed towards the shield (and his oxygen hit twenty-five percent), he couldn't think of a single, solitary thing to save them.

As luck would have it, he didn't have to. The Vacra came up with the solution.

Maker was scanning the shield around the *Mantis*, looking for any kind of weak spot that they might be able to penetrate. It took him more than a little by surprise when a bright beam of red light whizzed by him and struck the shield — and then continued through it and hit the *Mantis*, rocking the ship.

Of course! The Vacra weapon they had used when he was on the bridge! They were firing it again. More to the point, Maker could see where it had punched a hole in the shield — a hole that now appeared to be closing, as the shield was self-repairing to a certain extent.

Red lights started flashing on the interior of Maker's armor.

"Warning," said the female voice. "Oxygen depleted."

Maker tried to discontinue the lights and voice a second time but couldn't. Apparently this was a safety feature that couldn't be overridden when something critical — like running completely out of oxygen — occurred.

He blasted ahead, oblivious of everything around him except the hole in the shield. He was only a hundred yards away when the voice in the suit interrupted its warning about the lack of oxygen to tell him of another threat.

"Warning," the voice said. "Massive heat wave and shock wave detected."

The nova bomb. It had exploded. And unlike the detonation of a conventional bomb in space, the force of the explosion wasn't dissipating.

Maker felt his eyelids fluttering. The lack of oxygen was going to cause him to pass out soon. Then he'd die of asphyxiation. Erlen, however, might still live.

He fought to stay conscious, to stay on course. The hole in the shield was getting smaller — even now they might not be able to squeeze through. And they had the nova explosion at their back.

They were almost at the breach in the ship's shield when Maker simply couldn't keep his eyes open any more.

Chapter 43

Maker woke up in a hospital bed, only this time it wasn't in some field medic tent. He was in an actual sick bay aboard a ship. He sat up, stretched, and for a second contemplated getting out of bed, but then decided against it. Resting had been underrated in his book of late; it was about time he played catch-up.

He was still lying there, thinking of everything that had happened, when Fierce came in half an hour later.

"You're awake," the Augman noted. "How are you feeling?"

"You tell me," Maker said.

Fierce smiled. "I'd say you're doing great for a guy who almost got asphyxiated, roasted, and pulverized. That said…"

"What?" Maker asked after the Augman didn't say anything else.

"Remember back on Terminus, after the jwaedin stung you? I scanned you and got some odd results, so I thought the equipment down there was faulty. But I'm getting the same readings up here."

"Speaking of here," Maker said, "where are we?"

"We're still on the *Mantis*."

"How long have I been out?"

"Roughly two days — and stop trying to change the subject."

"Okay then, Doc. Just tell me — what's wrong with me?"

"That's just it. There's *nothing* wrong with you."

Maker frowned. "And that's a problem?"

"Not if you're a gene-job, like yours truly. But you're not."

"No, I'm just an ordinary human."

Fierce shook his head. "Human, maybe. But far from ordinary."

"If you say so."

"Well, your body says so. For instance, you've got the cleanest bloodwork I've ever seen. No waste products, no toxins, nothing. That just doesn't happen in nature."

"That's just from being in the Marines. It purifies you."

Fierce laughed. "I get it; you don't want to talk about it. That's fine. Just be grateful that I'm your doctor and insisted on being the one to treat you while you were out. Who knows what Captain Henry's people would have done if they'd found out."

"So where's the rest of the crew?" Maker asked, sitting up. "I should go check on them."

Fierce gave him an odd look. "You don't know, do you?"

"Know what?" Maker asked in surprise.

"There are two guards posted outside your door. You're under arrest, pending charges of treason."

****

Since he couldn't leave, Maker's crew eventually came to see him after Fierce gave the okay, all of them piling into his hospital room at the same time, including Erlen.

Adames was the first one in and actually gave him a hug as the others crowded around his bed. "Gant, you've got to be the craziest SOB in the Marines! I've never heard of anybody making a hyperspace jump outside a ship — *any* ship — before!"

"What?" asked Maker, confused.

"You don't know?" asked Loyola.

Maker was completely lost. "Know what?"

"You barely made it through the shield in time," Diviana said. "In fact, we thought we'd left you and Erlen until we dropped out of hyperspace and there you both were, floating next to us."

"Yeah," said Wayne. "Normally you'd expect anything outside the ship to get left behind, but something — either the EMP or the Vacra weapon — completely distorted the jump field. The end result seems to be that anything within the ship's shields got dragged along for the ride when we went into hyperspace."

"Well, I don't recommend it as the ideal way to travel," Maker said.

"We're just glad you're okay," said Loyola with a smile.

Maker frowned, a new thought occurring to him. "What about you guys? Are you all okay?"

"We're fine, sir," Snick said. "The doc here checked us out shortly after we made the jump."

"No," Maker said, shaking his head. "I meant, in terms of everything that's happened. Has anyone told you what the Corps is going to do to you?"

There were several sidelong glances, and a couple of eyes turned down to the ground.

"Nothing," Adames finally said. "They're not going to do anything to the rest of us. Browing has basically pushed the story up the chain that — like him — we were just loyal soldiers following orders. Anything you did, you did on your own."

"Perfect," Maker announced, "and that's exactly what I want all of you to say if asked."

"But—" Diviana began.

"No 'buts,'" Maker said. "My military career is definitely done after this and I'll probably spend the rest of my life in prison. There's no reason any of you should have to suffer through that. All I ask is that someone look after Erlen."

They all turned to look at the Niotan, who had climbed onto the bed and placed his head in Maker's lap.

"I'll do it," Wayne said.

"We'll all do it," Fierce corrected. "But I don't think he's going to let you go anywhere without him — even prison."

Everyone had a hearty chuckle at that.

"So, tell us what happened," Diviana said. When Maker seemed a little perplexed, she added, "After you got taken to the bridge."

Maker nodded, having practically forgotten that no one knew the complete story but him. He told it in rather succinct fashion, painting with a broad brush and leaving out many of the minute details. Even so, when he finished, they all just stared at him.

"That's incredible," Wayne said, clearly in awe.

"Probably more lucky than anything else," Maker said. "Lucky the EMP took out their armor, lucky they were *in* their armor at the time, lucky their psychic didn't seem to focus on me—"

"Oh," Diviana interjected in surprise. "You don't know."

"Know what?" asked Maker.

"Back during our skirmish at the camp," she said. "I was mentally able to pinpoint their psychic among the Vacra. He stopped being a problem before we even left."

Maker nodded, once more impressed by Diviana's skill set. All of them, in fact. Every member of his team had made outstanding contributions and proven their value. It had been a long time since Maker had felt it, but in that moment he was once again more than proud to be a Marine.

"Great job, everyone," he said. "No matter what happens to me, personally, we all went above and beyond here. We saved lives, and got rid of the Vacra to boot."

There were smiles all around until he got to that last statement, at which point he felt the demeanor of the room change.

"What is it?" Maker asked.

Adames sighed. "Shortly before we jumped, the *Mantis* detected a small craft leaving the Vacra ship — like a personal transport. It headed in the opposite direction, then jumped just as the nova bomb exploded."

Maker's hands balled into a fist. "Skullcap," he said, staring off into space.

"You don't know that," Adames said. "It could have been any of them."

"No, it was him," Maker countered.

"How do you know?" asked Wayne.

"Because he's like me — a survivor."

TERMINUS

Chapter 44

The court-martial was a very simple affair. It occurred in Captain Henry's meeting room roughly a week after Maker regained consciousness. In addition to Maker himself (who was seated at a table that had been brought in), those present included Browning and Captain Henry, who was serving triple duty as a material witness, witness to the proceedings, and senior officer on board the *Mantis*.

It was his first time being in a room with Browning since Terminus. A week earlier, Maker probably would have throttled the man, but over the past few days his outlook had turned rather stoic. What was done was done; beating Browning to within an inch of his life wouldn't solve any of Maker's problems (although it might provide some level of entertainment and satisfaction). At some point, he had just decided that Browning wasn't worth the effort.

On a vid screen was a three-person tribunal that would decide Maker's fate. The panel consisted of Admiral Wong of the Navy (who sat in the middle, presiding), General Pallo of the Star Forces, and General Kroner.

They had already taken statements from everyone else, so it was just a matter of getting Maker's version of events. He told his story with little fanfare or embellishment (except when speaking of the loyalty and devotion of his squad), starting from the day Kroner, Dr. Chantrey, and Browning had showed up on Ginsberg. The only thing he left out were certain vital facts relating to or regarding Erlen.

"So, as I understand it," Admiral Wong said in summation, "you were recruited only to *locate* the Vacra, whom you found — and subsequently engaged, despite orders to the contrary."

"Only because we felt another person's life was at stake," Maker added, trying not to twitch in his seat.

Admiral Wong continued as if Maker hadn't said a word. "You then went on to have yet a second skirmish with them."

"On that occasion, *they* attacked *us*," Maker clarified.

"Son, we're just summing up the events," General Pallo said. "No need to be defensive. If it helps, we don't think anything you did merits adverse action — up until the point of the nova bomb, that is."

"Speaking of which," Admiral Wong said, "I don't think we need to detail the list of laws and treaties you broke by constructing that thing — we would be here for days. In short, we know what you did. We just haven't been given an adequate explanation of why."

The three general officers looked at Maker expectantly. He lowered his eyes for a moment.

"You already know about the sub rosa ship, right?" Maker asked. "And the deal that was made with the Vacra?"

"Yes," General Kroner responded.

"And those officials involved, both military and civilian, will be punished to the full extent of the law," Admiral Wong added.

Yeah, right, Maker thought, struggling to keep the skepticism from showing in his face.

"That ship," said Maker. "It had been out there for decades, serving as a platform for all kinds of illicit

305

experiments and tests. That meant that the Vacra had access to generations of sub rosa tech and hardware. Conventional weapons weren't going to cut it. We needed to fight fire with fire."

"And when you activated it, did you realize you were putting Captain Henry, his ship, and his crew in danger?" General Pallo asked.

Maker cast an apologetic glance at Captain Henry, whose face was unreadable, before responding.

"I admit that it was a calculated risk," he stated. "But I knew that the captain and his crew were highly competent, and they'd have enough time to get the *Mantis* back in working order. Moreover, stopping a hostile alien species who had possession of advanced weaponry seemed to be a higher priority."

"Higher than the lives of everyone around you?" Wong asked. "Your squad? Captain Henry and his crew?"

"I was less concerned about individual lives," Maker said, "than I was about the welfare of the human race."

Browing raised an eyebrow and one corner of his mouth turned up slightly in an odd half-grin, as if he thought Maker was laying it on a little thick.

On the vid, the three general officers were whispering among themselves. After a moment, Kroner looked up and said, "We're going to take a short recess. We'll reconvene in an hour."

Captain Henry and Maker came to their feet, saluting as the vid screen went dark. Captain Henry then left without a word. A moment later, Browing departed as well, leaving Maker in the room by himself.

Maker sat back down, reflecting on how the court-martial was going thus far. It was pretty clear that the tribunal was presently deciding his fate, and would render their decision when the trial resumed. Maker didn't harbor any delusions about the outcome. He'd known that what he was doing was both criminal and dangerous, but had done it anyway. Now it was time to face the consequences of his actions.

He briefly debated stepping out and saying goodbye one more time to his squad. After all, he would probably be remanded into custody immediately following the tribunal's ruling. However, he'd already said his goodbyes to everyone; no need to go through that tearjerker process again.

Unexpectedly, the door to the room opened and Dr. Chantrey stepped in. Maker was more than a little surprised. He had seen little of her since his rescue, and when their paths *had* crossed, she hadn't seemed interested in speaking to him.

"I'm still angry with you," she said, taking a seat at the table across from him. "You could have gotten us all killed."

"So everyone keeps telling me," Maker said. "But the military is about to make sure that I never get a chance to do anything like that again."

"So it's looking bad?"

"It sure isn't looking good. But I'm sure you didn't come in here to chat about the life sentence I'm about to get."

"Straight to the point as always," she said with a smile. "Okay, I have a question — something in the way of professional curiosity."

"Okay," Maker said. "Shoot."

"My expertise is basically human nature, figuring out what people will do in certain situations. And occasionally, finding the right man for any particular job."

"Okay, I got that. So what's your question?"

"You handpicked your squad for this mission. They weren't the people I would have selected, but they all ended up being perfectly suited for the task. So my question is, how did you know who you'd need for this assignment?"

Maker shrugged. "I didn't know who I'd need besides Adames and Diviana — or rather, someone like her."

"A psychic."

"Yeah, although her intel background was an unexpected bonus. I'd known a guy from Wayne's homeworld, and he was the smartest, most inventive man I ever met. I needed someone with his kind of creativity."

"And who better than someone with the same background."

Maker nodded. "As to the others, Loyola was a prodigious marksman, and Fierce was a package deal with her. Snick was just an extremely competent combatant, but it was a skill set that I felt would balance us out."

"Well, they probably worked out at least as well, and maybe a lot better, than the team I chose for you — the one you rejected when you were first offered this mission."

"Hmmm...I thought Browing put that team together."

"No, that was my doing. Now that you mention Browing, however, you shouldn't be too hard on him. He kept his word and didn't say anything about Erlen being 'special.' Neither did I."

"Thanks," Maker said, speaking more sincerely than he'd imagined himself capable of.

She seemed to be on the verge of saying more, but at that moment the door opened. Maker stood as Captain Henry came into the room, followed by Browing.

"They're ready," Henry said. He then gave Dr. Chantrey a hard stare, which indicated that she should leave. Although clearly not intimidated, she took the hint and departed, following which the room's occupants all sat down. A few minutes later, the vid screen came to life.

The tribunal sat stone-faced for a moment, as if for dramatic effect, and then Wong — after ordering Maker to stand — began speaking.

"Lieutenant Arrogant Maker," Wong stated, "you stand accused of various crimes which we shall waive specifying at this time, mostly because you admit to the activities you participated in. The law is pointedly clear about what should happen in this instance. Crimes require punishment.

"However, not every facet of the law can be examined in a black-and-white context. Sometimes the law we try to enforce is actually injustice, and occasionally an unlawful decision is actually the right course of action.

"Once, as a young officer, I was commanding a ship in battle that got cut off from the rest of the fleet. We were completely surrounded by the enemy with no way to escape. I requested that the fleet fire on our position — there were so many enemy ships around us that it would be impossible to miss. Our ship took a lot of damage and many of my crew died, but our willingness to sacrifice ourselves allowed the fleet to have a decisive victory."

Wong paused for a moment, plainly reliving what was probably a bittersweet memory.

"In your instance," Wong said, finally continuing, "you faced a similar situation and took steps to ensure that our side obtained victory. Rather than illegal, we prefer to call your methods unorthodox, and therefore acquit you of the charges."

Maker was stunned. This was so far from the outcome he envisioned that he couldn't speak.

"Moreover," said Kroner, "since the Vacra are still on the loose — and possibly still in possession of sub rosa tech — we view your mission as currently incomplete."

"I-I-I'm sorry," Maker stammered. "Are you saying that you want me to go after them?"

"That's exactly what we're saying," Kroner stated. "We're placing the *Mantis* at your disposal" — he looked at Captain Henry, who gave a curt nod of acknowledgment — "and Browing will be working with you, too."

"Browing?" Maker mumbled, the man's name tasting bitter in his mouth. "Wasn't he in on that entire trading scheme with the Vacra?"

"He was just following orders, much like the members of your own unit," Pallo replied. "Surely if we aren't going to convict *them*, you wouldn't expect us to do so with *him*."

Browing stood up, extending his hand to Maker, saying, "It will be great to work together."

Maker stared at the man's hand like it was an asp covered in feces. He'd rather get stung by the jwaedin again than work with Browing. However, doing so would mean that he could continue his hunt for the Vacra —

310

specifically, Skullcap — which was far more important to him.

With that in mind, Maker swallowed his pride and shook Browing's hand. (He made a mental note, however, to kill the man at the first opportunity if Browing even looked like he was thinking of betraying him again.)

"Well, don't just stand there like a babe lost in the woods," Kroner said. "You've got your orders, Marine. Dismissed!"

Maker saluted, and then almost skipped out of the room, eager to give his squad the good news.

THE END

TERMINUS

Thank you for purchasing this book! If you enjoyed it, please feel free to leave a review on the site from which it was purchased.

Also, if you would like to be notified when I release new books, please subscribe to my mailing list via the following link: http://eepurl.com/C5a45

Finally, for those who may be interested, I have included my blog, Facebook, and Twitter info:

Blog: http://kevinhardman.blogspot.com/

Facebook: www.facebook.com/kevin.hardman.967

Twitter: @kevindhardman

Made in the USA
Coppell, TX
23 January 2023

11568969R00187